A MOST UNWELCOME CONNECTION

DAVID LLOYD

ISBN: 9798554953682

Cover design by: Frances Cooley

Printed in the United Kingdom

For Gail, who made me do it.

Chapter 1.

The start to the day had been less than satisfactory. To my dismay, we were out of muesli, and when I pointed this out to Penny in what I considered to be a perfectly reasonable manner, there were, unfortunately, tears. She has not been the same since Jessica left to go to University, and I put this uncharacteristic loss of equilibrium down to the natural distress a mother must feel at the sudden absence of a child. On a personal level, I must confess to a feeling of relief at Jessica's departure. Of course I will miss her, but the opportunity to have relatively unfettered access to the family bathroom will go some way to counteracting any sense of loss I may experience.

It was therefore with mixed feelings that I set out on my walk to the train station to catch the 7.44 from Beckenham Junction to Victoria. After the contretemps over the cereal situation, there had been a certain amount of tension at the breakfast table. I sensibly declined to mention that the toast was slightly overdone, as I felt that this may have led to a further emotional outburst from Penny, something which I am always keen to avoid. But there was still a certain tension in the air, and as I left I knew that a strategic purchase of a bouquet of flowers on my way home would go some way to resolving things.

There was the usual unregulated scrum at the station, as people gathered on the platform in the vain hope that the approaching train would stop in a position which would give them priority access to the doors and the seats inside, thus avoiding the unpleasantness of standing for the thirty minute journey. Although I would always choose to be seated, given the opportunity, I find the prospect of pushing and shoving through the crowd most distasteful, and invariably find that I stand for the journey, pressed uncomfortably closely to a fellow commuter while gazing fixedly into the middle distance and avoiding all possible eye contact. On this occasion however, I was fortunate enough to be close to a door as the train stopped, and it was with some alacrity that I took possession of the nearest vacant seat.

As the train pulled away from the station, I became aware of a young lady in the advanced stages of pregnancy standing next to me. I am aware that modern women do not necessarily expect – or even welcome – the old-fashioned courtesies that were drummed into me as a young child, but in this instance, I felt it was only proper to offer her my seat, and rose to do so. Unfortunately, before I could even open my mouth and suggest she avail herself of the vacant position, a young man in his mid-twenties who was also standing in the aisle took it upon himself to slide into the empty seat.

As Penny will testify, I am not a man given to excessive displays of emotion. Indeed, I find the current vogue for wearing one's heart on one's sleeve, mawkish and over-sentimental. However, I cannot abide bad manners, and therefore felt obliged to point out to the young man the error of his ways.

'Excuse me,' I remarked. 'But I was standing so this young lady may sit down.' Unfortunately, he did not hear me, wearing as he was a pair of the headphones affected by most young people these days, and I was therefore obliged to tap him lightly on the shoulder. He stared up at me and removed the offending ear-pieces.

'What is it mate?'

I must confess that the current vogue for over-familiarity leaves me somewhat cold. I recently had occasion to make a telephone call to arrange some car insurance, and was surprised when the young man on the other end of the line persisted in referring to me as 'buddy,' and even on one occasion, 'fellah.' Whatever happened to 'Sir,' or possibly, once cordial relationships have been established, 'Mr. Cavendish'? However, I digress. Back on the train, I returned the young man's stare with what I hoped was an icy civility, and repeated my statement:

'I was standing in order that this young lady could sit down.'

I indicated the woman, who looked away, somewhat embarrassed, as did the rest of the carriage. I could feel my cheeks beginning to flush, as I realised that I was about to commit one of the cardinal behavioural sins in a crowded train carriage, and 'make a scene.' The young man stared back at me blankly.

'Why?'

To me, this response totally exemplifies the current decline in standards in this country. As a young man of his age, I would not have hesitated to offer my seat to a lady. His reply was ample demonstration of the depths to which we have now sunk when it comes to the common courtesies that used to form the agreed rules of a civilised society. Mindful though I was of creating further upset to an already embarrassed railway carriage, I felt obliged to continue my remonstrations with the young upstart.

'I would have thought it obvious,' I continued. 'Any gentleman worth his salt would offer this lady his seat, as I am sure you will, now that I have made you aware of the situation.'

The young man stared back at me insolently.

'The thing is mate, I'm disabled.'

As you can imagine, this stopped me in my tracks. I certainly had no desire to turf him from his seat should his need be equal to – or even greater – than that of the young lady. In many ways I may have been better to have mumbled an apology, struggled my way through the crowd into the next carriage, and forgotten the whole ghastly business. But something about the smile that played around the corner of the young man's lips led me to suspect that he may not have been telling the whole truth.

'Indeed?' I retorted. 'You look in robust health to me. Perhaps you would be so kind as to inform me of the nature of your disability?'

The cocky smile disappeared briefly. He had clearly not been expecting such a retort.

'That's not the sort of thing you ask, is it?"

'Why on earth not?"

He thought for a while, then played his trump card.

'It's a violation of my human rights.'

Now don't get me wrong. I am all for the freedoms that we enjoy as part of living in a democracy, but this modern infatuation with the rights of the individual is a particular bugbear of mine, particularly when, as in this case, these so-called 'rights' are used as a catch-all excuse for not observing some of the necessary mores of a decent society. Fired up with righteous enthusiasm, I persevered.

'I am simply trying to ascertain as to whether or not any physical impairment from which you suffer puts you in greater need of a seat than this young lady. She has rights too.'

That put the young chap in his place. There was a certain frisson in the carriage as everyone waited for his response, while simultaneously pretending to read their morning newspaper or listen to their portable electronic device. Now it was the turn of the young woman to intervene.

'Please,' she said. 'I'm alright standing, honest.'

Resisting the urge to point out her incorrect grammar – even I could see that this was neither the time nor the place - I sought to reassure her.

'That is most selfless of you. But I feel that there is an important principle at stake here, and I feel obliged to once again ask this young man why he feels that his 'right' to this seat is greater than yours?'

The earlier unpleasantness with Penny had somehow disturbed my normal phlegmatic equilibrium and I had a full head of steam up now. The young man was obviously discomfited by my steely persistence, but unfortunately was in no hurry to surrender his seat.

'I get stressed, you know what I mean.'

'No, I'm afraid I do not know what you mean,' I replied, bridling at his use of this meaningless idiom. 'Perhaps you would be good enough to elucidate?'

'Do what?'

'Explain the nature of the stress from which you suffer, and why it renders you incapable of standing for a relatively short train journey?'

His eyes flickered from side to side, looking for some support from the rest of the carriage. Everybody looked away.

'I can only take your silence on this matter to suggest that this 'stress' is at best a fabrication, and certainly not sufficient cause for you to occupy a comfortable seat while this heavily pregnant young lady is forced to stand. Please be so kind as to let her have this seat.'

I could see I had him cornered. The inexorable force of my logic and reasoning had overcome his complete lack of moral scruples. With a shrug, he was about to stand, when the young woman herself intervened.

'You cheeky bastard.'

I think I am worldly wise enough to appreciate that the use of profane language amongst the young has sadly reached epidemic levels, but I am afraid that I am still sufficiently old-fashioned to find the use of such epithets by a woman even more unsavoury. However, I let it pass.

'Madam, I believe that I have resolved the situation in your favour. There is no need for you to enter into an argument with this gentleman.'

She glared at me angrily.

'Not him, you.'

I was temporarily at a loss to understand why she was directing her ire in my direction. Unfortunately, I was about to appreciate the true nature of the enormous faux pas of which I had just been unwittingly guilty.

'I'm not pregnant!'

I looked dumbfoundedly at her swollen belly, struggling to escape from an inappropriately tight blouse.

'I just like a few pints that's all. And a pizza. And I'm big-boned.'

I was suddenly aware of the whole carriage staring at me. The young man seemed to find this revelation uncommonly funny, and I could see that several of my fellow passengers were also having difficulty containing their amusement. Suddenly a voice rang out from half way down the crowded carriage.

'Well if you don't want it, I do.'

I saw a woman pushing her way down the aisle. She was red faced and perspiring, and as she got closer, I could see without any doubt whatsoever that she was clearly in the advanced stages of pregnancy. She fixed the young man with a gimlet stare and cradled her bulging stomach.

'Twins. Now give us that seat, you cheeky twat.'

The whole carriage was focused on the young man now, to see how he would react. Sensing that the crowd was against him, he reluctantly stood, and the pregnant woman eased herself gratefully into the vacant seat.

'Thankyou. It's good to know that there are still some gentlemen around,' she said, flashing me a grateful smile.

All eyes were back on me now. If there is one thing that unnerves me more than being at the centre of an embarrassing scene, it is unwarranted praise from someone for simply behaving in what I consider to be a perfectly reasonable manner. Just as I wished for a hole to somehow open up in the floor of the carriage and deposit me onto the tracks, a more easily achievable solution presented itself as the train pulled into Crystal Palace station.

'I do believe this is my stop,' I mumbled apologetically - and untruthfully - and thrust my way through the crowded carriage in order to escape from the hideously embarrassing predicament in which I had somehow landed myself.

Thanks to the unfortunate incident on the 7.44, and my resultant unscheduled stop at Crystal Palace, it was some half an hour later than usual that I eventually arrived at Victoria Station. Even then I cast anxious glances around the concourse as I headed towards the exit, in case any of my fellow travellers were lying in wait, ready to point an accusatory finger at a man who had signally failed to notice the difference between a well-developed pregnancy and a woman with an over-fondness for continental lager and junk food.

I glanced up at the station clock and quickened my step as I realised that I would not arrive at the shop before opening time. I knew that my assistant Miranda would certainly be there to unlock the premises, and that there was little likelihood of much trade so early in the day, but as sole proprietor I felt an obligation to my staff and my customers to set a good example and arrive on time. My father had always impressed upon me his preference for arriving half an hour early for an appointment rather than even thirty seconds late, and I must confess that this was a character trait which I had willingly embraced in both my personal and working life.

It may have been my diverted gaze towards the station clock, or indeed my continuing preoccupation with my idiotic behaviour on the train, but for whatever reason I failed to see the woman until she was almost upon me. I caught a fleeting glimpse of a pleasantly pretty face, framed by short dark hair, before she had thrown herself into my arms, embracing me fervently.

'Darling!' she cried. 'It's so good to see you.'

Her face was buried in my neck. I felt the smoothness of her skin against mine, as I breathed in a not-unpleasant aroma of perfume. Recovering from the shock, I attempted to extricate myself.

'Madam, forgive me, but I ….'

I was unable to complete the sentence before she had removed her head from the region of my neck in order to kiss me fully on the lips.

Now Penny and I are no strangers to kissing and canoodling, although I must confess that in recent years our mutual displays of affection have been largely restricted to pecks on the cheek and the occasional hand-holding during our Sunday morning constitutional in Kelsey Park. But I was totally unprepared for the force and passion of this woman's kiss, made all the more unexpected by the strong certainty that I had never seen her before in my life. I felt it was time to explain, although my attempts were somewhat hampered by the fact that her lips were clamped firmly over mine.

'Madam,' I spluttered. 'I really do …'

But this time my protestations were cut short as she proceeded to bite me on the tongue. Not sufficiently to draw blood, but certainly enough to stop me in my tracks.

'Don't say anything,' she mumbled.

With that she thrust her tongue deep inside my mouth and clamped onto me so hard I could scarcely breath. I then became aware that it wasn't just her tongue that she had inserted into my oral cavity, but a small capsule which she appeared to have secreted somewhere inside her mouth. Once more, I attempted to splutter in protest, but she breathed urgently at me again.

'Swallow it.'

I was certainly not minded to do any such thing, and was about to tell her this when she suddenly grabbed my testicles with her free hand and squeezed. I felt a heady rush of intimacy, danger and pain the like of which I had never experienced before. She squeezed slightly harder.

'I promise it won't harm you. But please, swallow.'

She squeezed again. I swallowed.

'Good boy.'

She glanced over her shoulder. I followed her gaze and could see two men weaving their way through the crowd towards us. One of them was short and squat, with a menacing air about him. I noticed a tuft of hair sprouting from the top of his knotted tie in a rather unsavoury fashion. His comrade was taller and lean, with a swarthy looking complexion and a nose which looked as if it had been broken on more than one occasion, sitting as it did at a right angle to the rest of his face. They were both dressed in smart suits and were scanning the crowd carefully, as if looking for someone.

'Kiss me again,' she said. 'And don't stop till I say so.'

Once again, her lips clamped onto mine. I must confess, that shocked though I was by her sudden onslaught, I was finding the whole thing rather pleasant, save for the dull ache in my nether regions. The two men passed a few yards away, offering us scant regard as they did, and disappeared through the rush hour melee towards the underground station.

She watched them go and suddenly disengaged herself.

'Thanks for that – you're a pretty good kisser for an old guy.'

I detected an accent which I took to be American, and which went some way to explaining the remarkable and random nature of our brief interaction. But before I could respond, she had darted away through the crowd, in the opposite direction to the two men, and I was left in the crowded concourse with a sore tongue, aching testicles and in a state of total incomprehension as to what exactly had just occurred.

Chapter 2.

Cavendish and Daughter sits in a small alleyway which runs between Shaftesbury Avenue and St Martin's Lane. I had purchased the leasehold some thirty five years previously, courtesy of an unexpected legacy following the death of my Uncle Bernard. A confirmed bachelor with no children of his own, and no other living relatives save for my mother (his sister) and father, he had generously bestowed a large portion of his modest estate to me. With the proceeds I was able to leave the bank where I was at that time unhappily employed and fulfil what had always been a dream of mine, and open up my own shop, specialising in the sale of rare and collectable scripts, photographs, playbills and other theatrical memorabilia.

I was, at that time, unmarried, and was able to eke out a comfortable living from the shop, while still residing with my parents in Beckenham. The business has provided me with a modest but regular income over the intervening period, and with retirement not too many years away, will offer me a substantial nest egg once I sell up.

The area has changed substantially since the early 1980s, but the shop has remained much the same, save for the addition of 'And Daughter' following Jessica's birth some 18 years ago. The change of nomenclature was undertaken in a flush of parental pride, in the hope that Jessica would one day take over the business. Sadly, she has not shown any interest in the history of theatre, the career of Sir Herbert Beerbohm Tree or the fundamentals of self- employment, and has instead recently embarked on a degree course in Marine Biology at the University of Plymouth.

As you may imagine, it was in a state of some perturbation that I finally arrived at the shop, some fifteen minutes after the normal opening time. As predicted, Miranda had already opened for business, and was more than a little surprised at my late arrival. Understandably I was in no mood for conversation, and disappeared into the small office at the back of the premises, leaving her to deal with any passing trade.

As I sifted through the morning post, my mind was inexorably drawn towards the bizarre events at Victoria Station. Who was the strange and rather attractive woman? Why had she kissed me with such passion? Who were the two sinister looking men in suits? What was the small capsule which she had forced me to swallow? She had told me it would do me no harm, but the whole sequence of events had been so strange, I could not rely on that actually being the case. Maybe it was dissolving in my stomach at that very moment, spreading who knows what form of poison through my body? I briefly considered presenting myself at the hospital, but having briefly explored the nature of the story I would have to tell them at the reception desk, I resolved instead to leave well alone, until such time as I actually began to experience any physical discomfort.

Fortunately, I did not have time to dwell on these potentially unpleasant outcomes, diverted as I was by the arrival of a delivery of several boxes of assorted theatrical programmes which had been offered to me by another collector. I was soon lost in the pleasantly diverting world of late nineteenth and early twentieth century British theatre as I sifted through the collection. Much of it was familiar to me, but I was pleased to see some ephemera from long lost and much-lamented theatres such as St James' and The Gaiety.

So engrossed was I by the variety of my day's reading, that I was taken quite by surprise when Miranda tapped quietly on the office door to tell me that it was five o'clock and that she was making her way home. I bade her a cordial farewell, with an apology for having locked myself away all day. I still had one unopened box to peruse, and resolved to keep the shop open for another half an hour while I did so. I returned to the office, wondering what hidden gems I might yet discover. Some twenty minutes passed, during which I was delighted to uncover a programme from the very first production of The Importance of being Earnest in 1895, which made for most diverting reading. It was therefore with some annoyance that I heard the shop bell ring, indicating that someone had come in through the main door.

I passed quickly through to the shop, and was astonished to be confronted by the woman who had accosted me at Victoria Station. I was even more astonished as she put up the 'Closed' sign on the shop door, locked it, and pulled down the blind.

'Hi,' she said. 'We meet again. Nice place you've got here.'

I was so surprised to see her, that I found myself temporarily lost for words.

'I hope you don't mind me shutting up shop, but I thought it would be good if we had a little chat. Any chance of a cup of your English tea?'

'Of course,' I stuttered, aware that this was a question that could only have one possible answer. 'Would you care to come through to the office?'

****

'May I ask how you knew where to find me?' I enquired some minutes later as I handed over a steaming cup of tea.

'You gave me this,' she replied, producing one of my business cards and laying it on the desk in front of her.

'Colin Cavendish. Nice name. Very British.'

I was somewhat confused, and clearly this showed in my face, as she felt the need to explain further.

'Well, when I say you gave it to me, I took it. Along with this.'

To my astonishment she produced my wallet, in which I always kept my business cards.

'You didn't notice it was missing?'

'Indeed not. I have had no occasion to leave the premises all day.'

'I didn't touch the money, or your bank cards.'

I checked to ensure that this was correct. Nothing seemed to be missing. I determined to find out more about this curious woman.

'Now that you know my name, may I enquire as to yours?'

'It's Anna. Sorry about the wallet, but I needed to know where to find you.'

'May I ask why?'

'You've got something that belongs to me, and I need it back.'

There was something about this woman's brashness which I found rather annoying – and deeply unnerving.

'I can assure you madam, that I have nothing of yours in my possession. However, I feel that you do owe me some explanation for your actions earlier today. And unless you can come up with a satisfactory explanation, I must seriously consider reporting you to the Police for theft and common assault.'

She looked at me quizzically.

'When did I assault you?'

'You forced yourself upon me, bit my tongue and made a most unwelcome connection with my private parts. I now also learn that this appears to have been a ruse to rob me.'

To my astonishment she burst out laughing.

'*A most unwelcome connection.* You're funny.'

Evidently, she could see that I did not regard this as a laughing matter.

'Look, I'm sorry about your private parts,' she continued. Unfortunately I felt that the sincerity of her apology was somewhat diminished by the fact that she was clearly struggling not to burst out laughing again.

'The thing is, a couple of men were after me, and I needed to take refuge in your face for a while. They were looking for a woman on her own, not a kissing couple. Yours was the first friendly face I saw. I was in a bit of trouble.'

'What sort of trouble?'

She paused for a while, as if considering an appropriate response, and I was able to take a closer look at her. I confess to being at something of a loss where women are concerned – my interaction with the young lady on the morning train is testament to that fact. However, I was able to perceive that – to my eyes at least – she was of a reasonably attractive demeanour. She had brown eyes, a fine set of slightly too-white teeth and an excellent complexion. My best estimate was that she was somewhere between thirty and forty years old. It would also be remiss of me not to mention that she had a fine shapely figure which fitted rather well into the plain black dress she was wearing.

She suddenly spoke, breaking my rather pleasant reverie. 'Like what you see?'

I flushed with embarrassment, unaware that my internal musings had been so easy for her to read.

'Forgive me madam, if I have caused any offence.'

She smiled.

'OK, Mr. Cavendish . I'm going to level with you. You seem like the honest type, and I guess I do owe you an explanation.'

I could only agree. Indeed, the events of that morning had been amongst the most remarkable I had ever experienced, and I felt that it would be very helpful to put them into some form of context.

'The thing is,' she continued. 'I suppose you could call me some kind of spy.'

My heart quickened. The world of international espionage was some distance removed from the one which I customarily inhabited.

'CIA?' I enquired. 'You are, unless I am very much mistaken, American.'

She smiled: 'Nothing so grand. I am American, but I live in London. Married a Brit. We run a pretty successful fashion company. My husband designs the clothes, I run the business. There's a big buyers fair coming up where all the major high street stores come and look at our new products. A few days ago, we had a break in at our offices. Someone got in and photographed our entire line. We had a pretty good idea who it was – our closest competitors, trying to pass our ideas off as their own and put us out of business.'

'I had no idea such things went on in the world of haute couture.'

'It's dog eat dog, believe me. Anyway, to cut a long story short, this morning I returned the favour. Snuck into their office and downloaded all the evidence I needed to prove that's what they'd done. I just need to get that to the authorities, and my business is saved.'

I was both fascinated and repelled by this lurid tale of duplicity and espionage, and felt compelled to question her further.

'And what is preventing you from so doing? And – especially considering that you are a married woman – whatever compelled you to launch your assault on me this morning?'

'Stop calling it an assault. To be honest, I kind of enjoyed it, and I think you did too.'

'Madam, I must inform you that I am also married. And that I take my marriage vows considerably more seriously than you appear to. What on earth possessed you to kiss me so passionately?'

'Their HQ is just around the corner from the station. As I was leaving, I was spotted by two of their security guys, and they came chasing after me. I'd had the foresight to download the evidence onto a mini flash drive and put it into a small capsule. If they caught me, I was going to swallow it. Then I had a brainwave. I made you swallow it instead.'

I must have looked even more astonished than I felt. She continued:

'Congratulations Mr Cavendish. You have my company's next line in fashion right inside you. Not to mention all the evidence I need to put my closest rivals out of business forever. Sometime tomorrow, nature will take its course and I'll be on my way.'

I have, if truth be told, led a fairly unremarkable life. Born in Beckenham some sixty years ago, I was the only child of Roger and Marjorie Cavendish. My father worked for an Insurance company in the City, and my mother, in keeping with most women of her generation and social class, stayed at home to keep house and to look after me.

Despite having no brothers or sisters, I must confess that I was not particularly close to either of my parents. My father was preoccupied with his job, and took a very early train to London, sometimes – when I was very young - not returning until I was asleep. He would spend weekends tending his garden – a pastime which never particularly interested me. Although our relationship was perfectly cordial – indeed, I can never remember my father raising his voice to me in admonition – it was also a fairly distant one.

My mother was similarly reserved. She took great pains to inculcate in me proper manners and a keen sense of right and wrong – character traits which I believe have stood me in great stead in later life. However, she was not a warm or emotional person, so my formative years with my parents were largely spent in agreeable silence. It was no wonder that I sought refuge in the world of literature, forming as I soon did a strong attachment to the English classics: Austen, Dickens, Scott and particularly the works of William Shakespeare. Although never a performer, I also became an avid theatregoer. It was this keen interest which ultimately led to my current employment, via an unsatisfactory and unhappy spell working at the bank, until being saved by the previously mentioned largesse of Uncle Bernard.

I feel it necessary at this point to give you these minor details from my early life in order to explain how ill-prepared I now found myself to deal with this unexpected turn of events. Far from being a one-off, as I had originally hoped, it now seemed as if the morning's adventures were to have unexpected, and potentially distasteful ramifications of an extremely delicate nature. I felt it only right to seek some form of clarification on this matter.

'Madam,' I began.

'Please call me Anna.'

'You will forgive me if I do not, given the nature of the conversation which must ensue. Am I correct in thinking that you expect me to salvage this capsule, once it has passed through my digestive tract, and then return it to you?'

'Yeah. Should take about thirty to forty hours, so sometime tomorrow seems about right. I'm guessing you're a pretty regular sort of guy.'

I could not believe that I was having this conversation about my most intimate bodily functions, but found myself agreeing with her.

'First thing in the morning, with another visit after lunch.'

'That's perfect,' she replied, with a smile which I found totally out of keeping, given the delicacy of the subject which we were discussing. 'Looks like it's back to your place then.'

I was becoming aware that events were moving rapidly in a direction which I was finding increasingly uncomfortable. I am, by my own admission, a very private man, with a well-organised and repetitive routine which serves Penny and I very well. The prospect of my arriving home with a rather forthright, and dare I say, attractive member of the opposite sex – and an American to boot – was not one which I felt that Penny would welcome.

'I am sorry madam, but that is entirely out of the question. I understand the importance of this capsule to you, but it will simply not be possible for you to visit me at my home.'

'Why not?'

I was rather taken aback by the brazen effrontery of her question and felt it was about time to respond with equal bluntness.

'Because you would not be welcome, either by myself, or my good lady wife.'

I could see her about to speak again, but I ploughed on regardless.

'However, if you would care to return to these premises at the end of tomorrow's working day, I am sure that by that time I will have had occasion to recover your property, and I will return it to you then.'

She looked at me quizzically.

'How can I trust you? The contents of your stomach are worth thousands in the right hands. Or maybe I shouldn't have told you that.'

I bridled at the suggestion that I would break my word, or indeed try to profit from the sale of items of fashion which, if recent trends were anything to go by, would almost certainly be gaudy, poorly made, and specifically designed to flaunt as much bare flesh as possible.

'Madam,' I replied, icily. 'My word is my bond. The sooner I can be rid of this most unwelcome burden, and return it to you, the sooner we can say our farewells and put this whole ghastly business behind us. Should we say tomorrow at 5 o'clock?'

She looked at me with that half-amused smile of hers playing around her lips. There was something rather disquieting about the frankness of her expression as she looked me in the eyes. Despite my natural modesty, I determined not to look away, and resolutely held her gaze.

'You're a pretty cool customer, Colin,' she replied, after what seemed an eternity but was in fact no more than a few seconds. 'I'll see you tomorrow at five.'

With that she turned and headed abruptly for the exit. Not forgetting my manners, I rushed to open the door for her. As she passed close to me, I caught another whiff of her perfume – something far more complex and beguiling than the lavender *eau de toilette* that Penny wears. Unexpectedly, she pecked me fondly on the cheek.

'You're a nice guy Colin.' She said. 'I'm really sorry you got caught up in all this. I'll see you tomorrow.'

She stepped through the half open door, as my hand went instinctively to my cheek, where she had kissed me. But my foolish reverie was shattered as she suddenly turned, pushed me back inside the shop and slammed the door shut, sliding home the bolt as she did.

'Shit!' she exclaimed. My distaste at her use of this vulgarity was soon forgotten, as for the first time in our brief association I saw a look akin to fear cross her face.

'My dear lady,' I exclaimed. 'Whatever is the matter?'

My eyes followed hers and it was only then, through the window of the shop, that I saw the two men in suits who had been searching for her at Victoria Station that morning – the tall, broken-nosed man and his hirsute companion. They were heading towards us with an intense purpose that immediately filled me with some foreboding.

'Is there another exit?' she enquired.

'Yes. In the office. Behind the curtain.'

'Then let's get out of here. Now!'

I am not sure if it was the look of real fear that I saw on her face, or the natural indignation of an Englishman being threatened in his own castle, so to speak, that spurred me on, but I felt that the time had come to act.

'Madam!' I said, but she was barely listening, so intent did she seem on making good her escape. 'Anna!' I continued, temporarily excusing myself for this over personal form of address, on account of the fact that she had failed to provide me with her surname.

'This is London!' I continued. 'Not some seedy back street in Chicago or New York. Notwithstanding the importance of your clothing collection, I will not be terrorised in my own shop by security guards. They have no power of arrest, and if they persist in this harassment, a simple telephone call to the police will have officers here within minutes.'

'Colin, I don't think you understand ....'

'I understand only too perfectly. You may wait in the back office if you wish, but I intend to give these two fellows a piece of my ......'

I was cut short by a loud noise as one of the two men took hold of the shop's door handle and rattled it violently. I was outraged by this violation of my property and pulled up the blind so as to remonstrate with the thuggish upstart. I was more than a little surprised to find myself staring through the glass and down the barrel of a pistol, held by the hirsute man, which was pointing straight at me.

The man gestured to the door handle with a menacing wave of his weapon. I noticed with some interest that it appeared to have a silencer fitted to it. It seemed as if I had no choice, and my hand instinctively reached for the bolt on the inside of the door. From behind me came Anna's voice. She was deadly calm now.

'Colin. If you open the door, we will both be dead within minutes. If you want to see your wife again, then I suggest we get out of here, right now.'

With that she grabbed my hand and half dragged me towards the office. I was aware of a foot being applied to my front door, and as we headed through to the rear of the building, a faint popping sound, followed instantaneously by the shattering of glass and the thud of what I could only assume was a bullet burying itself into the door frame some inches from my head.

We half ran, half fell into the office. I had the presence of mind to slam the door behind me and turn the key, as Anna pulled back the curtain to reveal the door which led into a small alley which ran down the back of my shop and the adjoining premises.

'Help me,' she cried, as she started to drag my desk in front of the connecting door to further hinder the pursuit. Between us we had the desk in place, and not a moment too soon, as we heard the front door bursting open.

We headed quickly to the rear exit. I automatically stopped and motioned her to pass through first.

'After you.'

Anna looked at me incredulously. 'There are two men trying to kill us. This is not a good time for your stupid English manners. Now run!'

We fled, turning down the alleyway to the terrifying sound of yet more bullets as they ricocheted off the wall behind us. She grabbed my hand and we ran out of the quiet alleyway, losing ourselves in the hustle and bustle of a busy rush hour in London's West End.

Chapter 3.

I was not in any sense a sporty child, apart from displaying an unexpected prowess at pistol shooting – an extra-curricular school activity offered by a rather fearsome ex-paratrooper PE teacher. Team games, and their associated forced camaraderie and veiled insults which passed as 'banter' were never my cup of tea. However, I have always kept myself fit, in the form of long walks and regular visits to my local swimming pool. Even at my age, I have yet to succumb to the aches and pains which increasingly seem to affect my peers.

Even so, it was with some relief that Anna and I finally came to a halt in the gardens on Victoria Embankment, in the shadow of Charing Cross Station. I sank onto a convenient bench, glad of the opportunity to catch my breath and allow my fast-beating heart to return to something close to its normal rate. I noticed that she was still looking anxiously around, as if expecting the two men to suddenly emerge from the bushes.

'We've lost them for now,' she said. 'But we can't stay here too long.'

'London is a city of several million souls,' I replied. 'It would be a remarkable coincidence if those two men were to stumble upon us here.'

I looked around at the well-populated gardens: young people sunning themselves in the last vestiges of late-September evening sunshine, children playing happily, an old woman walking her dog, waiting hopefully with a small plastic bag in order for the animal to do its business. I briefly wondered if Anna regarded me in similar fashion.

'And even if they did,' I continued: 'What harm could they do to us in full view of all these people?'

'Tweedledum and Tweedledee? Quite a lot,' she replied, ominously. 'You saw how they were back at the shop. These are desperate men. And they're not alone.'

I was taken aback by this unexpected revelation.

'You mean there are more of them?'

'That's exactly what I mean. And they have ways of locating people – just like they managed to find me at your shop. Wait there. I need to make a call.'

With that she retreated out of earshot, producing her mobile phone as she did.

You will no doubt have already formed an opinion of me. Conservative. Old-fashioned. A man living outside of his natural time, somewhat lost in an ever-changing world. You would not be the first person to make these observations. My daughter Jessica has a particularly blunt way of expressing herself regarding what she sees as major deficiencies. My natural reserve and sense of decency has also occasionally led to a certain naivety in the ways of the world at large, and a natural inclination to take what people say at face value. However, even I was now coming to the conclusion that the two men who had been pursuing us – not to mention any associates of theirs – were most certainly not security guards for a fashion house.

Anna returned from making her call.

'We need to get going,' she continued. 'Have you got your breath back?'

'I am going nowhere,' I replied defiantly. 'Not until you have given me a full and truthful explanation as to exactly what is going on.'

'We don't have time,' she replied, with more than a flicker of annoyance. 'Those men are trying to kill us, remember?'

'Indeed they are. And, if I may make so bold, I hardly feel that this is the normal course of action for those working in the clothing trade. Why do those men have designs on our lives? I can only assume that it is in relation to the item which you forced me to swallow earlier today. I must also assume that the contents of this capsule hold a far greater significance than that which you have previously relayed to me.'

It may well have been the strain of the circumstances in which we found ourselves, and the inevitable stress which had been engendered by our fugitive status, but I sensed that Anna's mild amusement at what she no doubt saw as my old-fashioned way of communicating, had been replaced by something more akin to exasperation.

'*Than that which you have previously relayed to me?*' she repeated. 'Why the fuck can't you speak proper English?'

I was certainly not in the mood to be lectured in the correct use of the English language, and by an American to boot, particularly one who chose to express herself in such a profane manner.

'I think you will find my use of the English language is exemplary, although I will confess that I am somewhat prone to circumlocution.'

'There you go again. Circum what?'

I found myself bridling at this infernal woman's transatlantic ignorance.

'As you seem to be struggling to understand the finer points of the language, allow me to re-posit my question in a form which you are more likely to understand. What the hell is going on?'

This seemed to get through to her. Maybe it was the simplicity of the question, allied to the use of a mild profanity. Maybe it was the fact that the adrenaline surging through my body had made me more forthright than usual. However, it seemed as if I had finally caught her attention.

'Colin, you're absolutely right. I do owe you a proper explanation.'

Finally, I seemed to be getting somewhere. I decided on another simple question in order to further my line of enquiry. 'May I be so bold as to suggest that the contents of my stomach are not in any way connected to the fashion industry?'

She nodded.

'As I suspected. And might I also hypothesise that the two gentlemen intent on recovering it are not store detectives from some clothing shop?'

She looked at me with what I assumed to be a new-found respect.

'You're good Colin. Really good. I can see I'm going to have to level with you.'

She looked over my shoulder towards the river. I was suddenly aware of a speedboat making its way towards us at a high rate of knots. A look of relief flickered across Anna's face. For a brief moment her composed and efficient mask dropped, and she looked almost vulnerable. Despite the extreme nature of the situation in which we found ourselves, I once again found myself drawn towards this infuriating and yet undeniably attractive young woman.

'But first we have to get out of here,' she continued. 'I have a friend in that boat. He'll take us somewhere safe. Then I'll tell you everything.'

I looked around me. Everything seemed so normal. I was but a few minutes walk from Charing Cross Station, from where I could easily secure a connection to Beckenham Junction, where I could buy some flowers for Penny to apologise for the morning's muesli-related unpleasantness. Indeed, an extra large bunch would be in order, as I would be significantly late for our evening meal. It was a Saturday, so Shepherd's pie would be the order of the day. I would almost certainly find it in the oven. Perhaps a half bottle of red wine from the supermarket might go some way to easing myself back into my wife's good books.

'Can't I just go home?' I asked, simply.

'I'm afraid not Colin,' Anna replied, with what seemed like genuine sadness. 'I'm sorry I got you tangled up in this mess, and I promise that once I've got the capsule back, you can go wherever you like. But until then, you need to stick close to me.'

I suddenly realised the full implications of what she was saying. In all our married life – some twenty years or so, Penny and I had never spent a night apart. Anna must have seen the look of horror that was writ large on my face.

'Look, I know it's tough, but believe me, this is serious. When we get to our safe place I'll explain everything. Then you'll understand why. But if you go home now, they'll find you, and kill you.'

I was suddenly aware of Penny, home alone, mashing potato as we spoke.

'My wife. Will she be safe?'

'Not if you go home. The best way you can protect her is by staying away until we've got this sorted out.'

Penny and I have never been an outwardly affectionate couple, but I hold her in high esteem and with a very fond regard. I would certainly never do anything that would put her in any sort of jeopardy. I looked at Anna and shrugged: 'It seems as if I have no choice.'

She took me by the hand and led me across the gardens, looking around anxiously as we crossed the busy road, weaving our way between the slow-moving vehicles. The rush hour was coming to an end, but London is always busy with traffic, particularly along the Embankment.

A gangway led down to a pier, where the speedboat had pulled up. It was of a sleek, white design, with black flashes down its side. The driver – a dark haired chap with large hands and a heavy five o'clock shadow - nodded an acknowledgment to Anna as we clambered aboard. He looked me up and down with some curiosity.

'Let's go,' said Anna. The driver gunned the engine, turned away from the jetty underneath the Golden Jubilee Bridge and sped at high speed towards the City of London.

Such was the noise of the engine, that any attempts to engage Anna or her mysteriously mute friend in general conversation proved fruitless. Shouting to be heard above the throaty roar of the powerful and foul-smelling motor, she indicated that she would explain all when we reached our destination. Unfortunately, it was not immediately apparent to me what our destination would be. We sped on past St Paul's and Tower Bridge, the Cutty Sark at Greenwich and the monstrous carbuncle that is the Millennium Dome (I do understand that it has changed its name, but I must confess to being ignorant as to its current nomenclature).

Still we travelled: through the Thames barrier, the wastelands of Woolwich and the ill-favoured and foul-smelling Sewage treatment works at Beckton. At last we pulled ashore at a rickety jetty on a muddy beach somewhere beyond Dagenham and Barking. Geography had been a favourite subject of mine at school, however I must confess to being totally unfamiliar with this particular part of London.

By now, it was dark, and an early autumnal chill pervaded the evening as a light mist drifted off the Thames. Tethering the boat to the mooring, the driver – who had remained tight-lipped for the entire journey – led us to a sleek, black saloon car which was parked nearby. It occurred to me that this was the sort of vehicle which one associates with funerals, and I was soon proved correct, as after a few minutes we pulled into an enclosed back yard alongside a similar vehicle and a large black hearse. A sign above the door proclaimed our destination: 'Loveday and Sullivan – Undertakers.'

Our driver unlocked the door and ushered both Anna and I inside. We were in a large workshop at the rear of the premises. Rather unnervingly, an open coffin sat in the middle of the room. I shivered at the unusual nature of my surroundings.

'Don't worry,' said Anna, as if reading my mind. 'There are no occupants here at the moment. We have the place to ourselves.'

She motioned to our driver: 'Why don't you make us some tea? I'm sure Colin could use a cuppa.'

He left the room. I glanced at my watch. It was half past eight.

'Penny will be worried,' I said. 'May I at least telephone her?'

'Sure,' said Anna, who I must confess seemed a lot more relaxed now that we had reached the sanctuary of the Undertakers. 'But first I guess you'd like to know what's really going on?'

It seemed as if I was finally to be offered an explanation for the day's extraordinary events. She perched herself on the edge of a trestle table.

'Why don't you take a seat?' she asked.

With no obvious seating in the workshop I perched myself rather uncomfortably on the edge of the open coffin.

'I suppose it didn't take a genius to work out that my fashion story was a load of crap.'

She saw the look of distaste on my face and corrected herself:

'Forgive me. A load of nonsense, if you'd rather. But I needed to come up with something quick, and that's the best I could do. I thought that if I gave you a story that kind of made sense, then you wouldn't need to get involved. I only needed to spin it out for a day, until nature took its course. Once they tracked me to your shop, everything changed. I'm paid to get involved in dangerous games like this. You're not.'

'You are some sort of espionage operative then?'

She nodded.

'I have to tell you Colin, you have walked into something pretty big here. What I'm about to tell you is the truth, but it may not be all of the truth, if that makes any sense. I'm going to brief you on a need-to-know basis.'

There was a pregnant pause in the room as she considered her next words. Behind me I heard the sound of a kettle boiling.

'Your first guess was spot on. I work for the CIA. For some time now, we've been hearing rumours of the existence of certain information which would be of great interest to us.

'What information?'

She smiled back briefly: 'You don't need to know, so I'm not going to tell you. Word recently reached us that the owner of this information was in London, looking to sell to the highest bidder. I was sent over to make a deal with him. Which I did. That information is stored on a flash drive which is currently passing through your GI tract. The thing is, other people are after it too. Bad people.'

I swallowed hard, hoping maybe that this simple action might hasten the egress of my most unwelcome burden.

'Clearly, the bad guys want it too. They know that the minute I can plug that drive into a laptop and send it to Washington, they're in a whole heap of trouble. And they'll stop at nothing to get it back.'

My throat was dry. I realised that I hadn't eaten or drunk anything for quite some time. Absurdly, I thought of the shepherds pie slowly incinerating in the oven, and wondered what must be going through Penny's mind right now. I hoped she hadn't telephoned Jessica. The poor girl had only just settled in at Plymouth after some initial home-sickness, and would certainly not benefit from unnecessary concern over my well-being. The door opened behind me as the driver returned, and I found myself looking forward to the restorative power of a good cup of tea.

'May I ask who these so called 'bad guys' are,' I asked.

Anna looked at me. Any hint of a smile had gone from her now. I could see that she was being deadly serious.

'Believe me, there's a list. The Chinese MSS. Mossad. Your MI6. In fact, every major intelligence service in the world would like to get their hands on what's in your guts right now. But these particular bad guys are the SVR.'

'SVR?'

'The Russian secret service. Formerly the KGB. The information on that drive was kind of theirs in the first place. And they'll stop at nothing to recover it. If they catch you, they won't hang around waiting for nature to take its course. They'll cut you open, right down the middle, and keep searching until they've found what they are looking for. They tend not to bother with anaesthetic either.'

I felt my sphincter tightening at the very thought of this. I had set out for work this morning following a minor contretemps over breakfast cereal, and now it seemed as if I was in danger of being eviscerated by Russian espionage agents, who themselves were at the head of a queue of people who would stop at nothing to rearrange my internal organs. Anna smiled at me reassuringly.

'Don't worry Colin,' she continued. 'Tomorrow, we'll get our property back. But in the meantime, we need to do whatever is necessary to keep it safe.'

I sensed movement behind me and half turned. As I did, I felt a sharp pain in my left arm. I looked down to see that far from bringing me a cup of tea, the driver had plunged a large hypodermic needle through my jacket, deep into my skin. The room span as I felt my senses slipping away from me. I tried to stand. I needed to run from this place. Find a telephone: call Penny, call Jessica, call the Police. But as I stood, my legs buckled underneath me. I suddenly felt very tired, and the last thing I remember was falling backwards into the open coffin.

Chapter 4.

I came to gradually. My head throbbed abominably and my lips were dry and cracked. It was stiflingly hot. I had no idea how long I had been asleep, but I was sure that it was morning and that I needed to be getting myself ready for work. I reached out for Penny, expecting to find her lying next to me, but instead my hand touched bare wood. I opened my eyes, but found myself in pitch darkness. As I accustomed myself to the stygian gloom, I could see two tiny crepuscular shafts of light shining down above me. They illuminated things sufficiently for me to see my immediate surroundings. I was still in the coffin, and the lid was closed.

I have never been one to panic. Experience has taught me that the vicissitudes of life sometimes present themselves in a random and unregulated fashion, and a steady constancy is the best way to avoid being swept away on an unnecessary tide of emotion. I have always been adept at steering a steady middle line through what The Bard would describe as the slings and arrows of outrageous fortune, but I must confess that this particular set of circumstances found me as close as I had ever been to screaming aloud in terror.

The pinpricks of daylight were what stopped me from doing just this. I reasoned that at least I was above ground. Gingerly I pressed against the lid of the coffin, but it wouldn't budge. Just as I was wondering what to do next, I heard the muffled sound of a door opening, and two voices deep in conversation. The first was that of a man, and alarmingly he spoke in what sounded very much to me like Russian.

I had no idea what he'd said, but I froze in terror. What had happened? Had the SVR somehow gained control of the coffin while I had been unconscious? And if so, what had happened to Anna? I soon found out, as the next voice I heard was hers.

'Speak in English. You know my Russian's a bit rusty.'

'You've been away too long,' said the man, in a heavily accented voice. 'Should I check on him?'

'Leave it. He'll soon let us know when he wakes up. He's gotta be bursting for a pee at the very least.'

She was right. I was suddenly aware that my bladder was rather full. And I was exceptionally thirsty. But something stopped me knocking on the lid, or calling out. Anna spoke Russian and it appeared she had spent some time in that country. It occurred to me that she may well not be in the CIA after all. Even in my half-awake and befuddled state I knew that it would be far better for me to keep my powder dry, so to speak. If I kept my counsel, I may well glean some vital information as to exactly who these people were, and why they had abducted me in this bizarre fashion.

'It's not his pee I'm bothered about,' continued the man. 'And another thing – I'm not going to be the one to go hunting for that drive when it finally comes through.'

'Don't worry,' replied Anna. 'He's too much of a gentleman to let us do that.'

'We need to get it done. Everybody is going to be looking for us now. Only a matter of time before they track us down.'

'No-one knows about this place.'

'No-one? What about Aaron?'

'Why should he?'

'Because he knows everything! He's one scary dude, and since he's gone rogue ...'

'Don't worry about Aaron. He's MI6's problem now. They know how to deal with traitors. Hopefully they'll find him before he finds us.'

'Hopefully?'

'You worry too much. Colin's going to hand the drive over, nice and easy.'

'How do you know.'

'Because if he doesn't, I'll tell him we'll kill his wife. That should do it.'

I froze. Kill Penny? Why on earth would they want to do that? She had done them no harm. Neither had I, for that matter. I would most certainly hand over the wretched thing, just as soon as nature took its course. Then I'd be done with the whole business, and Penny and I could get on with our lives. I might even close the shop and retire early. This whole awful affair had reminded me that although our lives may lack excitement, I couldn't imagine mine without my dear wife. Maybe it was time to spend more time at home.

The man grunted with pleasure at the prospect of killing Penny, then spoke the words that chilled me to the bone.

'Then we kill him, right?'

There was a long silence. I imagined Anna mulling over his threat, and felt sure that she would veto this barbaric suggestion.

'I'd rather we didn't.'

'Why not? You were going to kill Platonov if he didn't hand over the information.'

'But he did hand it over. Besides, Colin's harmless.'

I was relieved that she seemed to be sticking up for me. The man continued:

'You're sure he doesn't know what's really on that drive.'

'How could he? But maybe I should tell him. Then he'd really crap himself and do us a big favour.'

The man laughed long and loud at this. I heard muffled steps as he moved towards the coffin.

'I'm going to check if he's awake yet. That stuff has to wear off soon.'

I heard the sound of what must have been a large ratchet screwdriver as the man worked on the screws holding the lid in place. I had to think fast. If they knew I was awake, then they would soon guess that I had heard their conversation. It was clear to me that the minute they had got what they wanted from me, I was of no further use to them. At that point I would most likely be returned to the coffin, but almost certainly in the inanimate state for which it had been designed. Instinct told me that my best option was to lie low and say nothing.

I closed my eyes, and despite the fearful pounding of my heart, attempted to look as relaxed and asleep as possible. The coffin lid was lifted off, and I was immediately aware of the scent of Anna's perfume as she looked down at me. Her hand stroked my cheek affectionately. She suddenly slapped my face firmly with her open palm, and it was all I could do not to open my eyes or flinch at the blow.

'Still sleeping like a baby.' She said, as she stroked my stinging cheek. 'Poor Colin. You don't deserve this. Any of it. Come on Sergei – let's get a cappuccino. Then we'll wake him.'

I heard the lid being lifted back on, and a screw being inserted into the first fixing hole. It seems as if I was to be entombed once again, with no hope of escape. I may as well let them know I had heard everything and bow to the inevitable. But before I could open my mouth to call out, Anna spoke again, and gave me the first glimmer of hope I had experienced for quite some time.

'Don't bother with that. We won't be long.'

The man – Sergei - grunted in assent, and I heard receding footsteps, followed by the opening and closing of the door. All was silent. I waited a few moments, to be sure that they had left, and carefully lifted the lid. Through the crack I could see that the room was indeed empty. Cautiously, so as not to send it crashing to the floor, and with some difficulty, as it was very heavy, I slid the lid aside and clambered out of the coffin.

I looked around me, taking in my surroundings. I was in what looked like a disused office. A dusty desk sat in the corner, alongside a battered filing cabinet. It seemed as if the office had not been used for quite some time. Last year's calendar hung from the wall, showing the days of the month, next to a pneumatic and scantily clad young lady in a yellow bikini. The month heading said 'Luglio,' and the bottom of the calendar was covered in adverts that seemed to be in a language which I took to be Italian. I was at a loss to understand why this nondescript office should have an Italian calendar hanging on its wall. Where on earth was I? I crossed cautiously to the window and looked out.

The office was in a small shack, perched on a hillside, with a winding track running down towards a road which snaked through the middle of a deep valley. On the other side of the valley stood huge grey cliffs, studded with vertiginous seams of what appeared to be white rock. An enormous digger was in the process of moving huge square blocks of the rock into a capacious earth moving machine. Another similar machine emerged from a narrow tunnel dug into the side of the mountain and moved slowly upwards, before disappearing into another tunnel.

To my astonishment, I knew exactly where I was. Some months previously I had sat down with Penny and watched a most enjoyable documentary programme about this very place. Having been injected with some powerful sleeping agent somewhere in the East End of London, I appeared to have been transported – presumably in the coffin - to one of the famous marble quarries in the mountains above the Italian coastal City of Carrara. I looked at my watch. It was just after nine o'clock – presumably in the morning. I must have slept for a whole twelve hours.

A battered van with an Italian number plate sat outside the office. Presumably this had been the vehicle which had transported me to this isolated spot. At the bottom of the track, some fifty yards away was a small roadside café. As I looked down, I could see Anna seated at a table with the man I took to be Sergei - the voice I had heard from inside the coffin. Exactly why they had brought me here could wait for another time. The only thing I knew was that I needed to find some way of escaping, and fast.

A holdall sat on the desk. I quickly opened it, to reveal a jumbled assortment of clothes, presumably belonging to Sergei. At the bottom of the bag, hidden in a pair of rolled up socks was a wad of euro notes. I quickly stuffed them into my pocket. I consider myself to be a man of honour, and up to this point at least, had never knowingly committed an illegal act in my life. But I was alone in a strange country. I spoke no Italian. A mysterious American woman and a homicidal Russian were about to kill me. Somewhere out there I could only assume that the tall swarthy man, his squat companion and the rest of the world's intelligence agencies were also on my trail. I needed every possible advantage if I was to get out of this alive, and money would certainly help.

I looked again out of the window. To my dismay I could see Anna and Sergei draining their cups. The menacing Russian tossed some coins onto the table and they started to walk up the winding track towards the shack. If I was going to make good my escape, it was now or never. The track disappeared beneath the lee of the protruding rock, meaning the shack would be hidden from their view for a minute or so. I had no time to lose.

I replaced the lid carefully on the coffin. If they waited a while before opening it, I could buy precious minutes in which to make my escape. I squinted through the crack in the partly open door, and the minute that Anna and Sergei disappeared from view, I slipped out of the door, closing it carefully behind me. Creeping round behind the van so that they would not see me as they passed, I took refuge from the hot Mediterranean sun.

I was uncertain as to my next move but instinct told me that I would be better served by heading down the mountain rather than up. Should I make for the small roadside café and beg sanctuary there? They would certainly have a telephone in order to alert the authorities to my plight. But I quickly realised this would be futile. At best I would only have a few minutes start on my pursuers. The café owner could well be part of their conspiracy. I reasoned that my best bet would be to put as much distance as possible between myself, Anna and Sergei. I would head for the nearby town, find the nearest police station, pray that somebody there spoke English and demand to be locked safely in a cell pending the arrival of the British Consul. Anna had mentioned that MI6 were also interested in the contents of the capsule. As a loyal subject of The Crown, I would ensure that it was handed over to an official representative of the British Government.

Anna and Sergei crested the hill and headed towards the shack. Now was my opportunity. Looking down the hillside, I could see that if I took the straight line down to the road, rather than following the winding path, I would remain hidden from view for a little longer. Carefully I started to edge my way down the steep slope. The surface was hard and rocky, and dotted with small pebbles which I was anxious not to disturb. The noise from the ensuing rock fall would alert Anna and Sergei, and my flight for freedom would be cruelly curtailed even before it had begun.

I was half way down the slope before they must have discovered that the coffin was empty. I heard a shouted oath in Russian, the door of the shack burst open and Sergei emerged, soon followed by a frantic looking Anna. By now I had emerged from the lee of the overhanging rock and I was in plain view. The time for caution had gone, and I launched myself headlong down the slope.

I have no idea how I survived my headlong tumble down that rocky Italian mountainside. Within seconds I had lost my footing and found myself rolling head over heels amidst a small avalanche of tiny pebbles. I was dimly aware of a much larger rock passing inches in front of my nose. Instinctively I used my hands to try and stop my fall, but to no avail. Eventually I came to rest at the foot of the slope. My hands were lacerated and bleeding. My trousers had been torn at the knee. Gingerly I tried to stand. Remarkably, I did not seem to have broken any bones.

I looked back up the slope to see Sergei running at some speed down the track. I was temporarily relieved to see that he did not appear to be carrying any sort of weapon. Behind him Anna was climbing into the driving seat of the van and starting up the engine. I looked around frantically. A small motor scooter sat outside the café, presumably the property of the owner or another customer. The keys were in the ignition, and for the second time in a few minutes, I realised that my best, indeed only chance of escape must needs involve another act of larceny.

Fortunately, I was not a complete novice when it came to riding a two-wheeled vehicle. Back in my twenties, before I could afford a car, I had owned a small moped which served to get me to the bank and back. Although it had been many years since I had ridden one, this was certainly not the time to wonder whether I still could. I straddled the machine, turned the ignition, engaged first gear and headed for the road, determining to head downhill at the first possible opportunity. I glanced over my shoulder. The van had pulled up alongside Sergei, and he was climbing in next to Anna.

I reached the road, but to my horror, my plans to head downhill were immediately foiled. A large blue arrow pointed to the right and up the mountain. This was clearly a one-way system: hardly surprisingly given the narrow tunnels, which were scarcely wide enough to accommodate the large lorries which transported the marble. I turned and accelerated up hill.

I use the word 'accelerate' advisedly. The engine on my scooter was not the most powerful, and as I took another quick look over my shoulder, it was with some alarm that I could see the van getting ever closer. If I continued in my current course of action, they would be upon me in no time.

There is a certain state of mind involved in being British: the belief that in no circumstances whatsoever should one ever consider making a scene in public, a recognition that the queue is a vital and fundamental bastion of a civilised society, and that under no circumstance should one ever disobey the rules of the road which are there for the common good. In our increasingly diverse society, these traditional ways of doing things seem to have fallen by the wayside, and I often look back with a fond nostalgia to the moral certitudes of the 1950s and early 1960s.

However, at this moment, even I had to admit that a rigid observance of the Italian highway code – should such an unlikely thing even exist – would only lead me to my death. And so, with a skidding turn worthy of a seasoned motor cycle rider, I pivoted around my left foot and proceeded with some speed back down the road, passing the startled Anna and Sergei as I did so. I heard a screech of brakes behind me as the van executed a clumsy three-point turn in the narrow road. I looked behind me to see them hot in pursuit, but was pleased to note that I had significantly widened the gap between us with my unexpected and law-breaking manoeuvre.

As I looked down the road, I could see that if I continued on my present course I was about to indulge in yet another illegal act, which was potentially far more dangerous than the others. The tunnel loomed up in front of me, with two large no entry signs positioned on either side. By this stage, I was less concerned about flouting another traffic regulation. My only hope was that I would not encounter a vehicle coming in the opposite direction.

I entered the tunnel, and was immediately plunged into darkness as I struggled to find the headlamp switch for the scooter, hoping as I did that Anna would give up the pursuit, rather than run the risk of coming face to face with another vehicle. Unsurprisingly, such hopes proved immediately groundless as I found myself illuminated in the bright glare of the van's headlights as it pursued me into the tunnel. Despite the extra momentum afforded by the downhill gradient and the extra yards I had gained by my unexpected change in direction, I could sense my pursuers getting closer and closer.

I rounded a bend and my spirits were briefly lifted as I saw daylight at the end of the tunnel. Once I escaped from its confines, I hoped that there might be a narrow track down which the van could not pursue me, thus allowing me to make good my escape. But no sooner were my hopes raised than they were dashed again, as I saw a large lorry heading towards the tunnel entrance. Even from a distance I could see that once it entered the tunnel, there would be insufficient room for me to pass on either side of it. Unless I could escape before it entered, I was trapped.

With the van getting ever closer behind me, turning back was not an option. Aware that I was not even wearing a crash helmet – not that it would have done me much good in a headlong collision with a lorry weighing several tons - I coaxed every last ounce of speed from the scooter's engine and headed straight for the lorry.

The next few moments passed in a blur. One second I was yards from the exit to the tunnel, just as the lorry was about to enter. Surely I was about to lose my race for survival? I saw a glimpse of the lorry driver's startled face, as he suddenly saw me heading towards him, but it was too late for him to stop. I veered to the left and somehow passed through the narrowest of gaps at the mouth of the tunnel, my right knee brushing the lorry, while my left scraped against the tunnel wall. Then suddenly, there was no wall there anymore. I was back out in the hot sun, with open road ahead of me.

Behind me I heard the blare of the lorry's horn and the squealing of brakes, followed by an enormous explosion as lorry and van met each other head-on. I skidded to a halt and turned just in time to see a ball of fire and smoke emerged from the tunnel entrance.

My first thought was to head back and see if I could render assistance, such had been the force of the impact and the ferocity of the explosion. But I was immediately reminded of the peril in which I still found myself, and realised that my original plan of escape must remain my priority. I prayed that the lorry driver had survived the terrible impact. Whatever had happened to Anna and Sergei, they would be in no state to pursue me. I felt quite certain that neither of them could have survived the terrible collision. Indeed, given their stated desire to kill both me and my wife, I must confess that at that point I was not too bothered at the prospect of their demise.

I set off down the hill, anxious to put as much distance between me and the scene of the accident as possible. But I had barely travelled a mile or so before I was overtaken by an increasingly urgent realisation. Unsurprisingly, given the length of my incarceration in the coffin, not to mention the terrifying ordeal to which I had just been subjected, I found myself in urgent need of a visit to the lavatory.

Chapter 5.

I will spare you the exact detail of the ensuing ten minutes or so, which were spent behind a roadside bush.

Suffice to say, following my most necessary and welcome ablutions, I found myself looking down at a small metallic capsule the size of a small peanut which had finally passed through my body, and which I had been able to cleanse thoroughly in a nearby stream. I unscrewed it carefully to reveal, as Anna had promised, what I presumed to be a tiny computer flash drive. Who knew what it contained? One thing was certain. A large number of ruthless people seemed intent on possessing it, and would stop at nothing to take it from me.

Unsurprisingly, there was no clue on the device to show its contents. But as a patriotic Englishman, there was only one obvious course of action. I must get it to the British authorities and arrange my safe repatriation. The need to do this as soon as possible was emphasised by the sudden sound of approaching sirens. I ducked down behind the bush as an ambulance and a police car headed up the hill towards the tunnels. I needed to keep the drive as safe as possible, and with a sinking feeling realised there was only one thing I could do. Placing the drive carefully back in the capsule, I screwed it tight, ensured that it was properly clean, and with an air of resignation, popped it into my mouth and swallowed.

I am not a well-travelled man, preferring to take my holidays in England, rather than jetting off to foreign climes. As Jessica grew up, we used to take our annual family holiday in the same small cottage on the Roseland peninsula in Cornwall. Days would be spent pottering on the beach and walking the Cornish countryside, evenings reading and doing jigsaw puzzles. I was always perfectly contented with our well-established arrangements, but as Jessica entered her teenage years it became apparent that she was hoping for something more exotic.

Four years ago, at Penny's behest, I reluctantly agreed to a trip to the Normandy coast of France, which I found intolerable. I was not well-suited to the hot sun, the peculiar diet or the excitable tendencies of the French. Since then, Penny and Jessica have taken annual holidays abroad in Barcelona, Venice and this year, Berlin, while I have remained at home with my books and unrestricted access to my own bathroom. We have all found the arrangement highly satisfactory. Now that Jessica has left home, she may not choose to holiday with either of us in future. I may well need to discuss with Penny the possibility of revisiting our old haunts on the Roseland.

It was therefore with some trepidation that I rode into the nearby town. Realising that I was in possession of a stolen motor vehicle, I reasoned that it would be in my best interests to divest myself of the scooter as soon as possible. I left it leaning up against a wall, promising myself that once all this was over, I would seek out the owner and make appropriate recompense.

My first thought was that I was both hungry and very thirsty. Summoning up my courage, I entered a small bakery shop where with some difficulty, thanks to the language barrier, I was able to negotiate the of purchase some exotic looking bread and a bottle of water. I was also aware that the lady serving behind the counter, a jovial well-rounded woman with a friendly smile and a small moustache, was looking at me somewhat askance. As I left the shop I caught a glimpse of myself and could see why. My jacket was tattered and creased, my trousers were torn at the knee and I was covered from head to foot by a thin layer of white dust from my headlong tumble down the mountainside at the quarry.

Having made short work of my provisions, and tidied myself up as best as I was able, I eventually found a local man who spoke some English. He was able to point me in the direction of the local *Stazione Carabinieri* . It was some ten minutes walk away, and I set off purposefully, secure in the knowledge that my terrible ordeal would soon be over. I could surrender myself to the Italian authorities, telephone Penny to reassure her that all was well, and await the arrival of someone from the British embassy. Notwithstanding the ferocity of the explosion in the tunnel, I still expected Anna or Sergei to suddenly appear at any moment, and it was with some relief that I arrived at the street which led to the Police Station, a large white stone building situated in the centre of the town.

I was about to cross the busy street and throw myself at the mercy of the Italian Police, when I was suddenly aware of a familiar looking figure coming out of the building. To my horror, I recognised him as Tweedledee, the swarthy looking SVR man who had pointed a pistol at me outside my shop only yesterday. He was accompanied by a uniformed Policeman. The two of them shook hands and the man headed off down the street.

A feeling of terror coursed through my body. There was no sanctuary for me here. The Italian Police were clearly in league with the Russian Secret Service. It seemed as if the whole world was out to get me. I made my way as quickly as possible away from the Police Station. I needed time to think, and work out what on earth I was going to do next.

I made my way to a park at the edge of the town. The sun was higher in the sky now, and I was glad to take refuge in the shade of some trees. The park was deserted, and once I got over my overwhelming conviction that the town would soon be plastered with 'wanted' posters bearing my name, I was able to take stock of my current situation and consider my next course of action.

Having disposed of Anna and Sergei, the realisation that the SVR – if that is indeed who they were – had apparently followed me to Italy, brought home to me the peril with which I was currently faced. Whatever was in the capsule, it was clearly of major significance. What had Anna said, back at the premises of Loveday and Sullivan?

'Every major intelligence service in the world would like to get their hands on what's in your guts right now.'

It could well be that there were other people on my trail. But who could I trust? If the CIA were prepared to have me killed for the information I was carrying, then presumably others would too. Maybe even MI6 would be prepared to allow me to conveniently disappear in order to recover the capsule and its contents? I must confess to have harboured a long-standing mistrust of Americans. Their brashness and vulgarity have always been anathema to my more modest sensibilities. Everything about Anna and her behaviour had only served to reinforce my low opinion of their character. But the thought that my own compatriots would also be prepared to sink so low was most disquieting.

It was barely two hours since the collision in the tunnel. I suddenly felt terribly alone. I had an overpowering urge to speak to Penny.

It is a source of constant bemusement to me that the entire population of the United Kingdom now seems unable to function without a portable telephone to gaze at on a regular basis. We seem to have fostered an entire generation of young people who live their entire life through the lens of the camera on their mobile phone. Regrettably, Jessica is no exception, and I have often had occasion to upbraid her for her addiction to this infuriating device. Unsurprisingly, I have never felt the need to own one myself. However, on this occasion I must confess that I would have given just about anything in order to be able to make a simple telephone call from my place of safety in the park. As it was, I was obliged to return to the streets of the town in order to find a public telephone.

This in itself proved to be a difficult undertaking. Judging by the number of people gesticulating wildly while talking into their phones, it seemed as if the infestation of these infernal devices was even more widespread in Italy. Eventually I found a pay phone at the local railway station, while continuing to look warily around me for signs of an inquisitive policeman, or of another sighting of the SVR man. I had plenty of change from my purchases at the bakery, and it was with trembling hands that I dialled my home number.

The phone rang for some time. I had never seen the need to invest in an automatic answering machine. I have always been of the view that if somebody had a pressing need to speak to me, they would always ring back, and continue to do so until I was able to respond. On this occasion I found myself hoping that Penny was in, and would answer the phone. Suddenly there was a click at the other end of the line. The ringing tone stopped, but nobody spoke.

'Penny. Are you there?' I enquired. And then added, rather unnecessarily: 'It's Colin.' I would have been disappointed had she not recognised my voice, after so many years of married life.

There was still no response, which I found rather unnerving: 'Penny, please say something. Are you alright?'

'Hello,' came a voice back down the line. But it wasn't Penny's voice. It was a man's. I wondered if perhaps I had dialled the wrong number.

'Is that Mr Colin Cavendish?,' continued the voice.

'Yes,' I replied. 'May I ask who to whom I am speaking? And what you are doing in my house?'

'Where are you Mr Cavendish?.'

I was about to tell him. To blurt out the whole story to this anonymous man. But the past thirty six hours had wrought a huge change in me. Without being overly paranoid, it did seem as if the whole world was on my tail, and wishing me harm. I would tell this man nothing until I knew more.

'Could I speak to my wife please?' I continued.

'I'm afraid that won't be possible.'

The blood froze in my veins. Had something happened to Penny? Was this man connected with Anna in some way? Had he made good Sergei's threat to have my wife killed?

'Why not?' I replied bluntly. 'What have you done to her?'

'She's quite safe,' said the man. He sounded British, which was vaguely reassuring.

'Who are you?' I insisted.

'My name is Detective Sergeant Arthur Bellingham. Metropolitan Police.'

The Police? What were they doing at my house?

'But you can call me Arthur. Perhaps you'd be so good as to tell me where you're calling from?'

'I'm telling you nothing until I've spoken to my wife.'

'There was an incident at your shop yesterday evening, Mr Cavendish. Shots were fired. You and a woman were seen running from the premises. Police were called, and following a search, a dead body was found in the back office.'

This news knocked me sideways. A body? It certainly wasn't Tweedledee, as I'd recently seen him with my own eyes. Could it have been his nasally-challenged companion, or someone else entirely? I was aware that Bellingham was talking again.

'The man in question was a Russian citizen. A Mr Mikhail Platonov. Was this gentleman known to you sir?'

Platonov? Anna and Sergei had mentioned someone with that name. Could this be the same man? And how on earth had his body ended up in my shop? One thing was becoming clear however. It seemed as if the Police were especially keen on talking to me.

'We do need to ask you a few questions,' Bellingham continued. 'And I'm sure your wife would be pleased to see you. She's very worried about you Mr Cavendish. We all are.'

I am, as I have previously indicated, not prone to excessive displays of emotion, but I must confess that this mild expression of concern on my behalf by an anonymous policeman did bring a tear to my eye. Events had proceeded at such a breakneck pace, I had barely had time to stop and consider the enormity of everything that was unfolding around me.

A dreadful though suddenly entered my mind: 'You're surely not suggesting I had anything to do with that man's death, are you?'

'I'm not suggesting anything sir. But the sooner we can talk to you, the sooner we can clear this up.'

I was suddenly filled with an overwhelming feeling of relief. Surely the Metropolitan Police could not be involved in this international conspiracy? I knew that I was innocent of any involvement in Platonov's death. I would even be able to tell them what I knew about Anna and Sergei. I wasn't sure I could trust the Italian Carabinieri, given the apparent connection between them and the SVR. But the British Police would surely protect me from further harm, if only I could get to them safely. I resolved to tell Detective Sergeant Bellingham everything I knew, starting with my exact whereabouts.

'I'm in a place called ….'

But before I could continue, a gloved hand was clamped firmly across my mouth while another knocked the receiver from my hand before grabbing my arm and twisting it firmly up behind my back. I half turned to see the face of the man who I now thought of as Tweedledum - the tall broken-nosed SVR man who had chased me from my shop. With practiced ease, he frog-marched me across the pavement towards a waiting black Audi saloon car. I could hear Bellingham's voice coming from the abandoned receiver.

'Mr Cavendish? Mr Cavendish? Are you alright sir?'

But then I heard no more. I was bundled into the back of the car. Sure enough, Tweedledee was at the wheel. The car door slammed shut and we drove quickly away.

The two men didn't speak a word to me as we drove down the main street. They seemed to have gone to the same school of Russian inscrutability as Sergei. I attempted to ask them who they were, and why they had kidnapped me, but answer came there none. The broken-nosed man made a phone call. A terse conversation in Russian ensued, before he hung up and muttered something to the driver before looking at me with an ominous smile.

The road led out of town and downhill. I could see the Mediterranean sea twinkling in front of me, and it soon became apparent that this was to be our destination. At the end of the road we passed through a pair of metal gates and entered a large Marina. On the far side, a cargo ship was being loaded with marble from the quarries. A number of smaller sailing boats were moored to jetties in the centre of the harbour, while a couple of much larger ocean-going yachts were sat in front of us. The largest of these sat at the far end of the jetty, and the car headed straight for it.

It was a magnificent looking vessel with a dark blue hull and two silver-coloured upper decks. I estimated it was some one hundred and fifty feet in length. From a low platform at the rear of the craft, a pair of staircases flanked a large Jacuzzi before leading up to the entrance to the interior. I could see the name of the boat and its home port emblazoned on its stern: '*Madeleine* – Monte Carlo.'

Tweedledum guided me up the staircase. I was aware of other crew members untying ropes and seemingly making preparations to cast off. He led me into the first cabin; a large, luxurious and well-appointed lounge. He searched me thoroughly, but all he could find were the bundle of Euros which I had stolen from Sergei. I was privately glad of my prescience in re-swallowing the capsule back in Carrara. The man motioned me to sit in one of the three large and comfortable leather sofas which were arranged around an enormous television screen. The engines roared into life and the *Madeleine* pulled slowly away from the jetty, passed through the entrance to the Marina and headed out into the open sea.

Chapter 6.

I have already mentioned my unhappy visit to France. It was not only my sojourn in that country which had proved disagreeable, but the sea passage on board the ferry. Being trapped on what had seemed like a large floating cafeteria full of overweight British people eating as much fried food as possible whilst consuming vast amounts of beer had been bad enough. But the rolling nature of our passage through the waves had proved equally deleterious to my sense of well-being, and I had spent a large part of the journey – in both directions – with my head bent low over a toilet bowl.

The gentle swell of the Mediterranean was nowhere near as unpleasant as the pitching and tossing which I had endured in the English Channel, but I nevertheless found myself feeling distinctly queasy. I was only prevented from succumbing to my urge to be sick by the sudden realisation that I had only recently swallowed the capsule. Were I to vomit, then it would surely come back up the way it had entered my body. I was also concerned about staining the rather expensive looking carpet, and so summoning up all my inner strength I resolved not to succumb. My captor must have seen that I was looking somewhat the worse for wear. He crossed to a large refrigerator, produced a bottle of mineral water and handed it to me. I sipped from it gratefully, and for the time being at least, my nausea faded away.

After some fifteen minutes, a door at the far end of the cabin opened, and a man appeared. He was around my age and dressed in a nautical striped t shirt, white shorts and a pair of open-toed sandals. His skin was tanned and healthy looking, but in my opinion his garb was not in keeping with that of a man in his sixties. He carried a slim briefcase which he put down on the glass-topped coffee table.

'Mr Cavendish,' he began. 'Welcome aboard the *Madeleine*. You will forgive me for not greeting you sooner, but I have had other matters to attend to.'

His English was perfect, although he spoke it with what sounded like a Russian accent.

'My name is Pyotr Vasiliev. It's a pleasure to make your acquaintance.'

He reached out and shook my hand, looking me straight in the eye as he did so. His grip was firm and vice like, and I quickly realised that for all his outward affability, this was not a man to be taken lightly.

'I see that you have some water. Would you care for something to eat?'

My stomach groaned at the prospect.

'No thank you,' I replied. 'I'm not hungry.'

'Very well. And so to business. What is your connection with Anna Orlov?'

I could only assume he was referring to the Anna who had been responsible for getting me into the precarious situation in which I now found myself.

'I don't really have a connection with her,' I replied. 'I only met her for the first time yesterday.'

Vasiliev seemed to find this rather amusing.

'Mr Cavendish. Before we continue our conversation, let me remind you of a few salient facts. You are on board my yacht, some kilometres from the Italian coast. To the best of my knowledge, nobody knows you are here. Your life is, quite frankly, of no consequence to me. However, I believe you may have some knowledge of the whereabouts of something that is very important to me. Help me find it, and there is a possibility I will let you live. Mess me about, and you will find yourself swiftly embarking on a one-way swim to the bottom of the ocean. Do we understand each other?'

'Perfectly,' I replied.

'Good' he said, reaching for the briefcase. He opened it, and produced a series of photographs. He tossed them onto the table in front of me.

'Is this always how you greet women on your first meeting?'

I looked at the photograph. It looked to have been taken from an elevated position and was rather grainy. But it clearly showed myself and Anna locked in a passionate embrace on the concourse of Victoria Station. There were more in similar vein, all taken from the same angle.

'We obtained these images from the station CCTV, after the event,' continued Vasiliev. 'A shame we didn't have access to them at the time. We could have avoided this tiresome chase.'

'Who is 'we' exactly?' I asked.

'Come, come Mr Cavendish. You know perfectly well that I am a senior figure in the SVR. I am sure your control will have told you all about me, or your CIA mistress.'

'Mistress!' I spluttered. 'My dear sir, I can assure you that ….'

'Spare me the protests,' said Vasiliev. 'We suspect that you are a British agent working deep under cover. We also know that Anna Orlov was sent by the CIA to London to purchase something which had been stolen from the Russian Government by a particularly unsavoury traitor called Mikhail Platonov. We were hot on Platonov's trail in order to recover our property, but arrived moments too late as he had already sold it to Orlov, for which he was paid one million US dollars, in cash. For his treachery he also subsequently received a Russian bullet in the head, courtesy of our friend here.'

He glanced at Tweedledum, who dipped his head slightly in acknowledgment. Vasiliev continued:

'Orlov fled with the information and our men gave chase, somehow failing to see you right under their noses at Victoria Station. Fortunately they were able to pick up the trail later, and with Platonov's body in the boot of their car, followed Orlov to your shop, where once again you managed to escape. Regrettably my men made something of a commotion while trying to detain you and the Police were called. They sensibly decided to leave Platonov at your work premises in order to throw the Police off the scent, while also blowing your cover as an MI6 operative. This goes some way towards mitigating their earlier blunders, but I have reminded them in no uncertain terms that further similar shortcomings will not be tolerated.'

Tweedledum looked away in discomfort. His boss was clearly not a man to be trifled with.

'For a while, the trail went cold, but the SVR has long tentacles, and we were eventually able to track you to a private airport near Carrara. A contact at the local police station subsequently informed us of a fatal accident at the quarry involving a vehicle containing Anna Orlov. While on their way to investigate, who should my men see at the station, but your good self? And so, Mr Cavendish, you appear to be the only living person who knows the whereabouts of a certain video, which, if it fell into the hands of the Americans or the British would seriously destabilise our country. Our intelligence suggests that this video has yet to be delivered to Washington or to your bosses at MI6. So please, would you be good enough to tell me where it is?'

I paused for a while, uncertain how to answer. I took a long swig from the water bottle to buy myself some more time. Vasiliev was labouring under several misapprehensions, most notably that I was employed as a secret agent, and – equally farcically – that I would ever consider being unfaithful to Penny. But he had also provided me with vital information which explained much of what had occurred since that fatal kiss at Victoria Station.

For a moment I considered making myself sick and handing him the wretched capsule and its mysterious contents. But I refrained from so doing for two reasons. The first was simple self-preservation. Vasiliev was clearly a ruthless man, working for an equally ruthless organisation. Once I handed over the flash drive, I would be of no further use to him. I had a strong feeling that if I followed that course of action, I would not make it off the *Madeleine* alive.

But another reason forced me to consider my response carefully. I was in possession of something which was clearly of vital national importance. Something which the British Government and our American allies were very keen on acquiring. Vasiliev had talked of a video. Could it be that he was unaware that it had been reduced to miniature size? If he had any notion that it was currently inside my body, then he would surely set about recovering it in the most expedient way possible. Anna had said as much. If I denied that Anna and I were lovers, then he would wonder why we were kissing so passionately. It would not take long for a man of his intelligence and perception to work out another reason for our oral interaction.

I found myself surprisingly moved to have Anna's death confirmed to me by Vasiliev. In spite of the horrors to which she had subjected me, I still harboured pleasant memories of our embrace at Victoria. Indeed, such was the passion Anna had shown as our lips and tongues were pressed together, I almost wondered if what was routine for Penny and I could even be called kissing at all. However, now was not the time for me to dwell on this.

I trust that I have conveyed the importance which I have attached throughout my life to telling the truth and always doing the right thing. However, I had already seriously compromised this moral code on several occasions since arriving in Italy, and it seemed clear to me that I would need to use my wits in order to have any chance of extricating myself from the dire situation in which I found myself. I looked Vasiliev in the eye and started to talk.

'I am impressed by your detective work Mr Vasiliev. Anna and I were indeed lovers and had arranged to meet at Victoria in order for her to hand over a DVD which she had recently acquired. I slipped it into my jacket pocket during our embrace and returned it to my shop for safe keeping.'

His eyes narrowed as he considered what I had just said.

'Why didn't you take it straight to MI6?'

He had me floored almost immediately. Surely that would have been the obvious thing to do, were I indeed an MI6 agent. However there was cause for optimism in his question, as he had not refuted my suggestion that the video was in DVD form.

'Anna asked me not too,' I continued, inventing desperately as I did. 'She said she had … other plans for it which she would discuss with me later, once she was certain that she had given your men the slip.'

'Go on,' said Vasiliev, seemingly satisfied by my answer.

'She arrived at my shop, as agreed, but before we could discuss her plans, your men arrived and we were forced to flee. We took refuge in a safe house in the East End of London and from there were flown in a private aircraft to Italy where Anna felt certain we were safe. Clearly she had underestimated the prowess of your organisation and your ability to track down your prey.'

Instinctively I had felt that some gentle flattery would make my story more believable and I was correct. Vasiliev was clearly a man with an enormous ego. He smiled briefly, as if to thank me for acknowledging his brilliance. I took another swig of water to allow myself time to come up with the next part of my increasingly preposterous story.

'It was there that we fell out. Anna revealed her intention to double-cross our respective employers. She had arranged to sell the documents on to a third party at a vast profit…'

'Who?'

'She wouldn't say. But she suggested we kept the proceeds for ourselves and run away together to start a new life at some secret destination.'

I was particularly proud of this latest piece of invention. For a brief moment I imagined myself and Anna alone on a beach in some exotic island, sipping cocktails as the sun slipped down over the horizon – a clear sign of the increasingly unregulated state of mind in which I found myself. Returning to the reality of the perilous situation in which I found myself, I continued with my tall tale.

'Obviously, as an honourable man, and a loyal employee of Her Majesty's government, I refused to countenance such a betrayal. We argued, and things turned nasty. She took the DVD from me at gun point. It was only our past association that stopped her killing me there and then. Realising that there was nothing more I could do, I made good my escape.'

'So she has the DVD?'

'I can only assume that is the case. It is quite apparent that I do not.'

'But you've seen its contents?'

I had to think quickly. If I said yes, he would ask me what they contained, and I would clearly be unable to offer him a satisfactory answer. I decided that in this case, honesty would be the best policy.

'No.'

Vasiliev looked at me intently: 'Do you really expect me to believe that?'

'It's the truth.'

'I don't believe you. You and Orlov risked your lives to get this information, and you didn't feel the need to look at it? How did you know it was the real thing?'

'Anna had seen it and was happy that it was genuine. I had no reason to disbelieve her.'

'So she told you what was on it?'

'No.'

Vasiliev looked at me for a while then came to a decision. He clicked his fingers at his subordinate.

'Champagne. We'll take it on deck. Then a spot of lunch I think. Our guest must be hungry.'

The man disappeared through the rear doors. My nausea had dissipated somewhat, and I must admit that the prospect of something to eat was a most favourable one.

Vasiliev led me through to the rear deck, where a bottle of champagne in an ice bucket had miraculously appeared, along with two glasses. The wake of the boat disappeared behind us, and the late September sun shone down from a clear blue sky. I could just make out the shore some miles away. I briefly wondered where we were heading and what lay in store for me when we arrived. But for the time being a glass of cold champagne would be most welcome. The boat seemed very well-equipped, and I felt sure that after lunch Vasliev would be able to provide me with a nice cup of tea. He filled the glasses and handed one to me.

'A toast,' he said. 'To Anna Orlov.'

We clinked glasses and I took a sip of the champagne. It was delicious.

'I am sorry that you and Ms Orlov fell out with each other, Mr Cavendish. I congratulate you on your choice of lover by the way. She was a very capable and attractive woman, as well as being an excellent agent, even if she was on the wrong side. It seems as if the DVD may well have been destroyed in the fire that also took her life. If that is the case, then the threat to our national security has been averted, particularly if I am to believe your claim that you have no knowledge of its contents.'

I breathed an inward sigh of relief and took another sip of champagne.

'Unfortunately,' Vasiliev continued, 'Although you may well be telling the truth, I cannot take that risk. As long as there is one person in MI6 who knows the truth about Yevgeny Rostov, then the security of mother Russia could be compromised. I do hear that Great White Sharks are sometimes found in these waters. I hope for your sake that your end, when it comes, is quick and painless. Goodbye Mr Cavendish.'

I knew then what was coming, but I was powerless to prevent it. He shoved me firmly in the chest and I pirouetted backwards over the low rail. I saw the sky spinning above me as the *Madeleine* sped away, and then the cold waters of the Mediterranean Sea closed inexorably around me.

Chapter 7.

I rose to the surface, coughing up the water that I had inadvertently swallowed during my sudden immersion. I watched the *Madeleine* receding into the distance as it turned and headed back in the direction from whence it came. Vasiliev stood on the deck, raised his glass to me and walked back into the cabin.

I looked around me in order to take stock of my surroundings. To the south, west and north I could see nothing but an empty horizon. Towards the east I could see the distant coastline. I had no real idea of how far away it might be, but I estimated it must be at least five miles, maybe more. I have already mentioned that I have always been a keen swimmer, and in my youth would have thought nothing of swimming a mile at my local pool. But this distance seemed insurmountable, particularly given my age and the privations I had endured over the past day or so. However, I was certainly not going to stay where I was and wait to be devoured by sharks, or allow the cold to seep into my bones until I gave up the struggle and sank beneath the waves, never to resurface.

Reluctantly, I kicked off my shoes and watched them sink out of sight. They had been a joint Christmas present from Penny and Jessica. It was the thought of my dear lady wife and my daughter that spurred me on. For their sake, I must do everything I could to stay alive. Easing into a gentle front crawl, I began to swim.
I had just turned forty when I met Penny. We found ourselves sitting in adjacent seats at a performance of King Lear at the Barbican Theatre in London. I had developed a regular theatre-going habit over the years. Usually I would go on my own, occasionally with my mother. Theatre-going had never appealed to my father, who harboured a deep-seated mistrust of actors, whom he considered without exception to be long-haired, effeminate wastrels.

Father had a similarly low opinion of anyone attached to the theatrical profession. He had died some two years previously following a sudden and unexpected heart attack. My mother found him face down in the dahlias while taking him his morning coffee. Although theirs had never seemed a particularly close relationship, she was heartbroken at his death – quite literally as it turned out. Some six months after burying my father, I found myself performing the same offices for my dear departed mother.

I was still living at home, and although our house in Overbury Avenue had never been the liveliest of domiciles, I found it difficult to adjust to the fact that I was now entirely on my own. I taught myself to cook, after a fashion, and took to visiting the theatre on my own. By this time I had been running my shop for five years or so, which was by nature a fairly lonely occupation. I had long since lost touch with anyone at the bank with whom I might have been on friendly terms, and so my weekly visits to the theatre had become solitary affairs.

It would be wrong to say that I was completely without romantic experience at this point. In my early twenties I had fallen head over heels in love with Maureen Sharples, a clerical assistant who worked at the bank. She was from an entirely different background to me, coming as she did from an extended East End family. I believe she had at least six brothers and sisters, although time has blurred my memory as to the exact number. She was lively and outgoing with a wicked sense of humour and an easy-going nature which I found entirely captivating. On the basis that opposites attract, and to the general astonishment of our work colleagues, we enjoyed six months together which were amongst the happiest of my life.

Unfortunately, our relationship was always doomed to failure. Her capricious ways and devil-may-care attitude to life, which had at first seemed fun and beguiling, became increasingly embarrassing for me to deal with. On reflection, I must also accept that although she had initially found my steady reliability a welcome change from the tumultuous nature of her home life, she soon found me dull and predictable. She broke things off over a vodka and lime in the Kings Arms in Bishopsgate – a public house I was never able to visit again without it invoking in me a powerful feeling of sadness. Soon afterward she left the bank and I never saw her again.

For the first time in my young life I had given my heart to a woman, only to have it broken. I resolved that I would never put myself in that position again.

And then, eighteen years later, during the interval at the Barbican, I found myself in deep conversation with a woman who actually seemed interested in what I had to say. Penny Morrison was some five years my junior, and lived at home with her elderly widowed father. Her mother having died when she was sixteen, she had devoted the next twenty years of her life to looking after her increasingly frail and demanding paterfamilias. Like me, she was an only child. We had similar interests – the theatre, obviously, as well as literature and the classics. The performance having concluded, I summoned up all my courage and enquired as to whether she would be interested in joining me on my next visit. Thankfully she said yes.

Within a year, I had formed the impression that a general understanding had grown between us that marriage would be the next logical step. Unfortunately, when I broached the subject with her, she declared that although she had developed a certain fondness for me, anything else would be out of the question due to her obligations towards her ailing father. I resolved to expedite the situation by calling on Mr Morrison and officially asking for his daughter's hand. His response will forever live in my memory. '

'Go on then,' he said. 'No other bugger'll have her.'

In spite of this admittedly less than glowing seal of approval from her father, Penny still declined to fix a date for our nuptials. Things were brought to a head by his not-unexpected (and in my case rather welcome) death. Following the sparsely attended funeral I followed the advice of Lady Macbeth, screwed my courage to the sticking place, dropped to one knee and in a rare display of emotion implored Penny to marry me.

'Might as well I suppose,' she replied, a chip off the old block, and six months later we walked down the aisle at Beckenham Registry office as Mr and Mrs Cavendish.

Although it took some time for both of us to readjust to married life after some years of independent living, I would like to think that Penny and I gradually developed an effective and companionable partnership as we settled into an agreeably steady existence. We continued our theatre visits, and Penny would occasionally help out in the shop when I was on buying trips. Although we continued to share a bedroom, moments of sexual congruence became increasingly rare. To be perfectly honest, I believe that suited both parties.

In the first year or so of our marriage, there had been some talk of children, although I never sensed it was of pressing importance to either of us. A few years passed, and as I moved into my fifth decade, the prospect of ever becoming a father was fast-receding, and I must confess that I was not over-vexed by this. It was therefore with some astonishment that I received the news from Penny – two months after her forty first birthday - that she was expecting our first child.

Although it has become very much the fashion for men to attend the birth of their children, indeed to play an active part in the whole mysterious process, I felt that this was not for me. So it was, that after a long night's pacing up and down the corridors of the Princess Royal Hospital, Bromley, listening to the fearful screams and groans which emanated from the delivery rooms, I was finally ushered in by a beaming midwife and set eyes on my daughter for the first time.

I have always faced life with a certain equanimity. I believe such a state of mind is what separates a true English gentleman from some of our more excitable continental neighbours. It has been with some distress that I have noted the gradual erosion of this state of *sang froid* amongst the young men of today. At an age at which my father's generation were fighting the Nazis or facing brutal incarceration in Far Eastern Prisoner of War Camps, the modern young man seems intent on mutilating himself with a variety of piercings and garish tattoos, while priding himself on being 'in touch' with his feminine side. What utter piffle.

However, when I first saw my rather tired and haggard looking wife nursing our baby daughter, I must confess to shedding a tear for the first time in my adult life. The sadness engendered by Maureen Sharples' termination of our relationship had failed to provoke me to lachrymosity, but the sight of the beautiful, perfectly formed little girl nestling in her mother's arms most certainly did. As I held Jessica in my arms, I knew that I would do anything in my power to prevent any harm befalling this tiny, red-faced child.

The change which motherhood wrought in Penny was amazing. It was as if she had been waiting all her life for this moment, and she loved Jessica with a passion and intensity which I sometimes found rather overwhelming. Although Penny remained a dutiful and caring wife, whatever passion she may once have felt for me was soon sublimated entirely into our daughter. The two of them formed a close and enduring bond from which I often felt excluded. I am by nature prone to self-isolation, and as my father had been to me, I soon became a remote and distant figure to Jessica. My love for her remains as constant as ever, and I am sure that in her own teenage way she still harbours some affection for me, but I am not sure she has ever fully understood me. Penny has not been the same since Jessica left to go away to University. Indeed, she had recently confided in me that she cannot walk past our daughter's empty bedroom without bursting into tears.

Thoughts of my dear wife and daughter occupied my mind for some time, as I slipped into a steady rhythmical swimming pattern. After a while, my arms tired, and I switched to breast stroke. I constantly scanned the horizon for signs of a passing boat, but save for distant craft some miles away, nothing came close. My arms felt like lead weights, and for a while I swam on my back, kicking out with my legs and letting my arms trail alongside. I looked at my watch. I had been in the water for one hour. I was feeling increasingly tired and cold. I turned to see how close to the shore I might be now, hoping against hope that dry land might be within reach. To my horror the shore seemed no closer. If anything, thanks to the tide and the prevailing current I had drifted even further out to sea.

I have never felt so alone as I was at that point. I could feel the cold seeping into my bones, despite the heat of the sun which was now directly overhead. I was exhausted. For all my determination, and my overwhelming desire to get back and see Penny and Jessica again, I knew that I would not be able to swim to the shore. It seemed as if I had reached the end of the road. The mystery of the contents of the capsule would perish with me. I had one more half-hearted attempt at swimming, but I knew it was useless. I resolved to lie back and wait for the waters to overwhelm me.

It was then that I heard the engine. Faint at first, then getting ever closer. Disoriented, I spun around in the water, and saw a small open fishing boat passing by some three hundred yards away. I could just make out two figures in the boat, but they were working on the far side, reeling in a large net as the craft continued its steady progress. In desperation I called out, but all that emerged was a feeble croak, which they would never have heard above the sound of their outboard motor. Summoning up my last reserves of strength I started to swim towards the boat, splashing the water as much as I could in the process, hoping that one of them would turn around and see me.

It was all to no avail. The boat continued to move slowly away from me as the fishermen hauled in their net. My throat was dry and parched, but I knew I had one last chance to attract their attention.

'Help,' I shouted. And then again, even louder: 'Help!'

But nobody heard me. The boat continued on its way. At that point I knew I was doomed. For the first time since Jessica's birth, I found tears running down my cheeks and mixing with the salt of the sea. What had I done to deserve this terrible end? One chance meeting at Victoria station, and a day and a half later I found myself on the verge of drowning in the Mediterranean. I was suddenly overcome by an intense feeling of calm. If this was how it was to end, let it end now. I trusted that Penny and Jessica would not be too upset by my death, and that enough of my body would be washed ashore to confirm my demise. I wondered if they would ever know the bizarre truth surrounding my abduction? At least I had left them both well-provided for. All fight left me, and with an air of resignation I slipped slowly beneath the waves, choking on my first mouthful of sea water.

Suddenly rough hands seized me. I was hauled bodily over the side of a boat and deposited on the deck, where I lay shocked and stunned, face-to-face with a rather surprised looking swordfish which lay twitching in front of me. I retched violently, then everything went black.

Chapter 8.

It was the cicadas that woke me. On my one and only previous visit to continental Europe I had been much disturbed by the noise of these insects and had found their constant chirruping infuriating and irritating. Much like the French. Now I found them strangely reassuring. It meant that somehow, against all the odds, I was still alive. I opened my eyes and immediately closed them again as they reacted to the bright glare of the sun which shone in through the open window. Cautiously, I half squinted around the room, taking in my current surroundings. A small gecko pattered up the white stucco wall in pursuit of a fly. I realised I was wearing a pair of old flannelette pyjamas which were slightly too small for me. I had no recollection of ever putting them on.

At least, this time, I was not in a coffin, but I did feel pretty wretched. My mouth was dry and my lips were cracked and peeling. A jug of water and a glass sat next to the single bed in which I found myself. With some difficulty I levered myself upright, poured myself a drink and gulped it down gratefully. For the second time on this bizarre adventure, I had no idea where I was. I thought to leave my bed and look out of the window, but when I tried to get up I found I simply did not have the energy to do so. I reached for another glass of water, but my trembling hand dislodged the glass and sent it tumbling to the floor, where it shattered on the hard terracotta tiles.

I heard a yelp of surprise, and moments later the door was opened by an ancient wizened old lady dressed entirely in black. She beamed at me, her teeth gleaming white against the background of her wrinkled walnut-coloured skin, and jabbered something in Italian. Of course I did not understand a single word of what she was saying, but she did seem pleased to see me awake.

'*Aspetta*,' she said, with another smile. '*Aspetta*.' Patting me fondly on the arm she left the room with some urgency.

I had a sense that she would not be long in returning, and I was right. Some two minutes later she bustled back into the room clutching a dustpan and brush and a fresh glass, and accompanied by a young lady who seemed to be not dissimilar in age to Jessica. She was of a similar complexion to the older woman, but her skin was smooth and unblemished.

'Thank God you are awake,' she said. 'My name is Emiliana. Please, what is yours?'

'Colin,' I replied, simply.

The old lady hurriedly scooped up the broken glass and left the room, jabbering away to Emiliana as she did.

'*Nonna* says she will bring you food. You must be very hungry.'

I realised that I was starving. Thirsty too. As if sensing this, Emiliana poured another glass of water and offered it to me.

'Drink slowly,' she said, and I did, relishing every drop of the cool water.

'Where am I?' I said. It was the obvious question. 'How did I get here?'

'You are in our home. In the *Cinque Terre.*'

I was none the wiser, but let her continue. She spoke tolerably good English, with a strong Italian accent.

'I live here with my mother and father, and my grandparents. My father is a fisherman. He was fishing with his brother, my uncle. They found you in the sea. You were very lucky. They had gone past you and were turning for home when my uncle saw you. We all want to know – how did you get to be there?'

I considered my response carefully. Emiliana seemed pleasant enough, but since being abducted from England, I had yet to meet one single person who I felt I could trust.

'I fell off a boat,' I said, non-commitally.

Emiliana looked at me, as if expecting me to tell her more, but I decided that discretion may well be my best policy until I discovered more about my circumstances.

'I see' she said.

'How long have I been here?' I asked.

'Three days.'

I was astonished at her reply, which she must have discerned from the expression on my face.

'Do you remember nothing since you arrived?'

I had to admit that I did not.

'You have been, how you say, delirious. One minute awake, then asleep. Talking very weird. Temperature very high. We thought you might die.'

I wondered who else knew I was here. I suddenly had a vision of Vasiliev raising his glass to me as I floundered in the water. If he and his men knew that I was still alive, it would surely only be a matter of time before they returned to finish the job properly.

'I will be honest with you *signore* Colin. It did not make sense finding you in the middle of the sea. My father thought you maybe want to kill yourself, but there was no alarm on the news for a missing English man. So we thought maybe someone want to kill you, or maybe you want to hide.'

I had clearly been rescued by some very astute people. I drained the glass of water without speaking. Emiliana continued.

'Old English man. Just wearing shirt and trousers. No ID. A thousand Euro in your pocket. We thought maybe you didn't want to be found. So we tell no-one you are here until we can ask you about yourself.'

A myriad of thoughts crowded into my head. Emiliana seemed honest enough. Maybe I should level with her. Tell her the whole outrageous story. Arrange for the family to make contact with the British Police. Surely they would be able to arrange my safe passage back to England? I could hand over the capsule and its mysterious contents. Then I would be safe.

It was at this point that a worrying thought struck me. If I had been asleep for three days, then what had become of the capsule? I realised that I would have to ask some rather strange questions in order to find out. Until I could be certain of the family's intentions, I simply could not risk them discovering that I was carrying anything untoward.

'Three days?' I asked. 'No wonder I feel so weak. Have I eaten anything?'

'Some soup. Plenty of water.'

'And what about …?'

I hoped that a gentle incline of the head and a gesture towards my nether regions might get my message across. Fortunately Emiliana seemed to understand the delicate nature of my enquiry.

'My mother help you with that. My grandfather is in bed all the time. He cannot walk. So she is used to help him to do what is necessary. She do the same for you.'

She looked across the room and for the first time I saw a plastic bed pan sitting on a table, partly covered with a cloth. Emiliana must have misunderstood my look of concern and attributed it to the delicate sensibilities of an English gentleman.

'Don't worry,' she said, with a friendly smile. 'She is a nurse, so no problem for her. And all flushed away in toilet now, so please not to bother yourself.'

I remembered little else of that afternoon. The old lady had returned with a plate of cheese, ham and bread which I had eaten with aplomb before drifting off to sleep again. When I awoke, I felt refreshed and ready to explore my surroundings. With some difficulty I tottered over to the window and looked out onto a most agreeable vista.

The house was perched half way up a steep hillside overlooking the sparkling blue sea. It must have been early in the evening, as the sun was about to set. A steep path, occasionally intercut with steps, led down to the water's edge where a wooden jetty protruded into the sea. As I watched, a small boat made its way carefully to the shore. A man, who I assumed to be Emiliana's father, tied the craft to the jetty and started to make his way up to the house. There was no sign of any fish. Either he had been unsuccessful that day, or had already dropped his catch off at a nearby port. Emiliana ran down the path to greet him and they both talked animatedly, occasionally gesticulating in the direction of the house. Presumably she was telling him that I was awake. I felt tired again, and sat down on the edge of the bed to consider my situation.

One thing seemed certain. The capsule had gone, lost in the Italian sewage system, and I would never see it again, nor learn of the significance of its contents. Vasiliev had implied that it contained information of vital interest to the Russian Government and its infamous President Yevgeny Rostov.

I took little interest in politics, but the whole world knew of Rostov. A fierce defender of Russian interests at home and abroad, he was incredibly popular in his home country and deeply mistrusted by everyone else. But whatever that information may have been, it was of no interest to me now. I resolved to throw myself at the mercy of Emiliana and her family, tell them as much of the truth as I felt was necessary, and get myself back to England at the first possible opportunity.

A short while later, there was a knock at the door and Emiliana entered, clutching a bundle of clothes. She seemed pleased to see me out of bed.

'You are feeling better?' she asked.

'A little.'

'Good. Can you please come downstairs? My father needs to talk to you.'

Emiliana led me to a small bathroom where I showered and put on the clothes she had brought: A pair of brown corduroy trousers with a pair of yellow braces, and a striped, collarless shirt. They presumably belonged to her bed-ridden grandfather. Although my apparel was faintly ludicrous, I was glad of the chance to wear some clean, dry clothes.

I was welcomed by Emiliana and her father, and my saviour, a small dark haired man by the name of Mario. Her mother and grandmother were still busying themselves in the kitchen. There was no sign of the bed-ridden grandfather. Mario shook me warmly by the hand and thrust a glass of beer at me. I am not over-fond of alcoholic beverages, but I must confess that I found it most palatable. Mario spoke no English, but Emiliana was able to translate. Her father welcomed me to his house, and said how delighted he was to see me so well. Indeed, he confessed that he had not been sure that I would survive.

Mario then spoke long and volubly to Emiliana. She listened intently, and when he had finished she turned to me.

'My father wants you to understand that he and my uncle make their living from the sea. Not all that they do is, how you say, within the law. For example, there are quotas for the *pesce espada* – the sword fish. He will sometimes take more than he is allowed to feed his family and our guests. He expects you not to ask questions of him about this. In return, we ask no questions of you, and where you come from.'

I was about to tell her that I was more than happy to volunteer this information, but before I could, she continued.

'Today my father was in the nearby town. People have been asking questions about an English man. A man who looks like you. These people seem very keen to find you.'

'People?' I said, with a calmness that belied the inner turmoil I was feeling. 'What people?'

'Bad people,' she replied. The serious expression on her face suggested to me that she was of the opinion that these people were very bad indeed.

I wondered who these 'people' could be. Vasiliev presumably thought me dead. As far as I was aware, Anna and Sergei had perished in the tunnels of Carrara. Who else could it be? Anna had told me that the whole world would be keen on securing whatever was in the capsule. The Chinese? The Israelis? The CIA, intent on avenging Anna's death? I resolved to find out more.

'Does your father know where these people are from?'

'They are local. Italians. But he thinks they are not acting alone. A reward has been offered for your capture.'

So that was it. Presumably Mario had given these 'bad people' the information they required in exchange for his thirty pieces of silver, or whatever the modern equivalent might be in Euros. There was no doubt in my mind that at this very moment they were coming to spirit me away to whatever gruesome fate awaited me. Anna was about to disabuse me of my most unworthy thoughts.

'My father is an honourable man. He does not betray a guest. He did not save you from the sea so as to give you up to criminals and gangsters.'

Mario seemed to be ignoring the fact that he was, by his own admission, also a criminal, but I did not feel that this was a good moment to point this out. Presumably he considered his level of illegal activity to be on a different scale to that of my would-be captors. Emiliana continued:

'But it is not safe to stay here. Not for you, or for my family. You must leave.'

'Can't you go to the police?'

Emiliana's nose wrinkled in disgust at the suggestion.

'My family do not trust the police. Some of them are bad people too. When you are away, you may go to them if you wish. But please do not tell anyone that you were here.'

I promised that I would not.

'And also, *signore* Colin, you must be careful who to trust. We do not know why these people seek you. We do not want to know. Tell us nothing, then we have nothing to tell other people, if they ask.'

'My dear young lady,' I replied, with a heartfelt sincerity. 'Your family have shown me great kindness. You can be assured of my utmost discretion at all times.'

Emiliana translated. Mario smiled in appreciation and replied with another stream of unintelligible Italian.

'My father thanks you. He says you are honourable English man. Tomorrow he will drive you to the City of *La Spezia*. From there you can get a train, or a boat to wherever it is you are going.'

She crossed to a dresser at the side of the room and pulled out a bundle of notes.

'This is the money you had in your pocket when we found you. It is all there. You will need it for your journey.'

I felt thoroughly ashamed of my earlier thoughts that Mario had betrayed me. I took some of the notes and offered them back to her.

'Please take this. As a thank you for saving my life.'

Mario spoke firmly in response to this gesture. Emiliana translated:

'My father says that you cannot put a price on a man's life. What we do for others, we do willingly. Otherwise, we don't do it at all. Dinner will be in one hour. Please join us.'

Chapter 9.

My previous experience of eating foreign food during our French holiday had not been a particularly satisfactory one. Every meal seemed to comprise of duck or fish, cooked in various forms, as well as a bewildering array of peculiar looking seafood and an over-reliance on garlic as a seasoning. By the end of our stay I was existing on a diet of bread, cheese and fruit, much to the chagrin of Penny and Jessica, whose palates proved to be considerably more adventurous than mine.

Whether it was due to the privations which I had endured over the last few days, the kindness of my hosts, or the simple fact that I was exceptionally hungry, the meal served up that night was quite simply the finest food which I had ever eaten. My previous scruples over garlic suddenly seemed base and ill-founded, as I tucked into a bewildering array of different courses.

We began with a plate full of cold meats, salty anchovies, artichokes, olives and sweet, sun-ripened tomatoes. Then came a simple bowl of home-made spaghetti seasoned with hot peppers, garlic and olive oil. This was followed by the most wonderful sword fish steak, accompanied by a simple green salad, all washed down with generous glasses of the local red wine. Juicy sweet peaches, almond-flavoured biscuits and strong black coffee rounded off the meal. I must confess that at no point during the evening did I long for some of Penny's toad-in-the hole or a portion of her tapioca pudding.

We were joined for the meal by Emiliana's mother and grandmother. There was still no sign of the bed-ridden grandfather. For the most part the family spoke amongst themselves, occasionally asking me simple questions, via Emiliana. They pointed out my location on a map, and I realised that I was some three hundred kilometres from the French border. As they chattered away, I could not help but contrast this lively, contented scene with meal times back in Beckenham.

When Jessica had deigned to join her mother and I for dinner, she would usually spend large parts of the meal sending typed messages to her friends via her mobile phone, continuing to do so even when I protested. Since Jessica had left home, Penny and I had enjoyed our meals in what I had always considered to be an agreeable silence.

I would certainly have no shortage of tales to tell once I got back home. I hoped that Penny was well. I could only hope that, in my absence, the Police were keeping her out of harm's way. I wondered if she had even told Jessica of my disappearance. I felt obliged to abandon my initial plan to tell all to Emiliana's family and throw myself at their mercy. I had no desire to compromise them by burdening them with information that might be useful to whoever the 'bad people' were who were looking for me.

My sketchy knowledge of European culture led me to believe that the Mafia were not operating in this part of Italy. However, there was no doubt that there were criminal gangs who would be happy to profit from handing me over to whoever it was who was hunting me. Despite the danger that its possession posed, I could not help but experience a pang of regret that I had lost something that may well have been of considerable significance to the British Government.

I was aware that voices around the table had been raised. Emiliana's mother was fanning the air with exaggerated gestures, while Mario had the familiar browbeaten air of a man attempting to defend himself from what he considered to be an unfair attack. I was also aware of a rather unpleasant odour in the room. Emiliana seemed rather amused by the exchange:

'My mother protest to my father. The smell is because of the *pozzo nero*. For one month he promise to empty it, and now she tell him it must be done tomorrow or else it is *divorzio!* Divorce!'

The grandmother cackled ferociously at this notion and Mario looked most put out. I was none the wiser.

'Forgive me Emiliana,' I replied, painfully aware of my total lack of knowledge of any language other than English. 'But what is a *pozzo nero?'*

Emiliana took out her mobile phone, which seemed to contain some sort of dictionary or translation device. She typed in a few letters until she found what she was looking for.

'Cesspit,' she replied. 'It is very old and does not work so well. Sometimes my father has to empty it with a bucket. It is not his favourite job.'

I am not always very quick on the uptake, even when things are laid out in a very simple way. Penny has often had occasion to upbraid me for what she considers to be a general lack of perception. On this occasion however, I suddenly became aware of the tremendous opportunity that had just presented itself. The house was serviced by a cesspit. Therefore the capsule had not been flushed away into a communal sewage system, but was still here, nestling somewhere in the midst of several months' worth of household effluent. There was something in that capsule which every major government in the world wanted to get their hands on, and it was my patriotic duty as a British citizen to deliver it safely back to London. I was also rather drunk, and I am sure this had some bearing on what I said next.

'You have been most kind to me,' I declared, rising unsteadily to my feet and looking Mario in the eye. 'Before I leave tomorrow, it would be a very great honour for me to assist you in this most unpleasant task.'

Emiliana smiled and translated. Her mother and grandmother applauded. Mario beamed from ear to ear, a tear in one eye, and to my intense embarrassment locked me in a fierce embrace and kissed me on both cheeks.

'You have made my father very happy,' said Emiliana, rather unnecessarily.

The next day dawned bright enough, although I could also detect an incipient change in the seasons. Even this far south, I sensed that Autumn was not too far away. The sooner I could get home the better, but by now I had resolved that I would not return without the mysterious information concerning Yevgeny Rostov. Such was my low opinion of all politicians, that I found it rather ironic that I was about to search for this information in the depths of a stinking cesspit.

The *pozzo nero* was a few yards from the house, and was accessed via a manhole cover which Mario prised back with expert ease. Emiliana had explained that her father normally carried out this job on his own, but would welcome the assistance of a second person. One of us would descend into the stinking black depths of the pit with a shovel, while the other would lower a bucket on a length of rope. The accumulated detritus would then be deposited in large plastic barrels and taken away to what Emiliana described as a 'communal facility.' For all I knew, that meant it would be dumped in the sea, but that was no concern of mine.

In spite of Mario's protestations, I insisted that I would be the one to descend into the pit. I felt it would give me the best chance of spotting the capsule. Emiliana suggested that I removed as many of my clothes as was decent.

'It is very hot in there,' she said. 'And very dirty.'

I looked down into the dark, fetid, brick-lined hole. Even up there in the fresh air, the stench was overpowering. I began to regret my wine-fuelled offer of the night before. There was another reason for my regretting last night's alcohol consumption. For the first time in many years, I realised I had a hangover.

And so, clutching my trusty shovel, and clad only in boxer shorts, wellington boots and a pair of rubber gloves, I eased myself through the hole and into the gloom below.

The boots immediately rendered themselves superfluous as I found myself thigh deep in largely slimy, but occasionally solid ordure which trickled down inside my footwear, making moving around something of a challenge. The smell was appalling, and that, combined with the heat and the lack of air, caused me to feel quite unwell. If ever there was a time for me to focus on the duty I owed to Queen and Country, this was it, and so I started to carefully fill the bucket.

Until this moment, I had never stopped to consider what it must actually be like to search for a needle in a haystack, but it was whilst labouring away in Mario's *pozzo nero* that I came to a greater understanding of that particular idiom. I realised that I was searching for a tiny object, which although metallic, would be smeared in the dark brown muck which I was loading into the bucket. Short of sieving through every shovelful, the chances of me finding the precious object were slim indeed.

After twenty minutes of this deeply unpleasant labour, I found myself feeling faint and giddy, so overpowering were the fumes and the heat in that particular hell-hole. Clambering out for a breath of fresh air, I saw Mario and Emiliana looking at my dung-smeared appearance with a new-found respect, Unsurprisingly, Mario declined to hug me this time. Via Emiliana, he did offer to swap places with me, but I declined. I had to find that capsule. And so, after recovering my equilibrium and taking a long draught of cool, fresh water, I once more eased myself below ground.

For almost two hours I laboured, occasionally coming up for air, but always declining Mario's offer to take my place. I lost count of the number of bucket loads which Mario hauled above ground, but eventually the pit was empty, save for a few inches of watery sludge still swilling round its base.

'*Basta,*' said Mario, looking down into the hole and beckoning me to come out.

'Enough,' said Emiliana. 'My father says it has never been so clean. You must stop now.'

I realised that were I to go on my hands and knees and sift through the sludge it would most certainly arouse suspicion. I must also confess, that by now I was entirely broken, both physically and emotionally. I had done my best, but the capsule was not there. It could only assume it was somewhere in one of the plastic barrels, and I had no intention of searching through them again. My entire body was smeared in filth which seemed to have leeched into every orifice. I could only hope that I had not contracted some horrible disease, but there was no sense concerning myself with that at this point. All I wanted to do was to get myself clean.

Emiliana handed me a large towel and pointed towards the sea.

'You must wash the worst of it off there.' She said. 'Then inside for a shower. We never felt that you owed us any debt, *signore* Colin. But if you thought you did, then please know that it has been paid in full. We will see you inside.'

I headed down towards the jetty, my boots making an almost comical squelching sound on the gravel path. There was a small cove behind a rock which sheltered me from view of the house, and I took the opportunity to remove my stinking shorts. I sat carefully and eased off my wellington boots, pouring their foul contents into the sea as I did. I had failed in my attempt to find the capsule, and although I knew that no-one could criticise me for lack of effort, I felt hugely disappointed. The world would never know what secrets the flash drive contained.

It was the noise that alerted me. As I poured the contents of the second wellington boot into the sea, I heard the unmistakable chink of metal against rock. I looked down and saw a glint of sunlight reflected against a tiny metallic object as it dropped into the water.

Without hesitation, I plunged in, determined not to lose sight of the precious object. For a while the water around me turned a muddy brown, but as it cleared, I could see the capsule nestling on the sea bed. I sensed I only had moments before it slipped into the sand, never to be seen again. I took a deep breath and plunged beneath the waves. The capsule had disappeared. In desperation I took a huge handful of sand in the location where I thought I had last seen it. Nothing. I tried again, and again, not daring to come up for air in case I lost track of the exact spot. Just as it felt as if my lungs were about to burst, I had one last try. With a huge sense of relief and triumph, my hand closed round something small and hard and I emerged into the warm sunlight, gasping for air. There in my hand, was the elusive capsule.

Chapter 10.

La Spezia is a busy sea port on the coast of the Italian Riviera, and home to a large naval base. It was comfortingly large and bustling, and I felt that whoever was looking for me would struggle to spot me in such a busy place. However, at Emiliana's suggestion, I had taken certain steps to change my appearance. In almost a week away from home I had started to cultivate a grey beard, and although I initially demurred, Emiliana had prevailed upon me to shave my head. When I looked at myself in the mirror, I was startled at the change that was wrought in my appearance.

Mario's wife embraced me fondly as I left, and handed me an overnight bag containing a change of clothes and some bread, cheese, water and fruit for the journey. I had decided against swallowing the capsule again. Instead I had carefully stitched the flash drive into the turn-ups of my corduroy trousers, using a needle and thread which I had found in the house. Just in case I had need to use it again, I slipped the metal capsule into my pocket – having first washed it carefully in boiling water to remove any last vestiges of the *pozzo nero*.

Following my near-death experience aboard the Madeleine, I had no desire to return to sea. With Emiliana's help I had plotted a route by train which would take me to Genoa, Lille and thence to Paris. To her credit, and that of her family, she never once asked me why I was on the run, and who I was running from.

My lack of a passport would not be a problem in crossing the border between France and Italy, but I would not be able to re-enter the United Kingdom without one. I therefore resolved to present myself to the British embassy in Paris, where I felt sure that there would be an official of sufficient seniority to accept delivery of the flash drive. I had considered Rome, as it was nearer, but I felt certain that my pursuers would come to the same conclusion, and could be waiting to intercept me there.

It was lunchtime when we arrived at La Spezia station. If all my connections were running on time, I should arrive in Paris late that evening, when my ordeal would be over. I gave Emiliana a handful of Euros and stayed in the car with Mario while she went inside to buy my ticket. While we waited, Mario scanned the passers-by carefully, but he saw no-one that caused him any alarm. Soon afterwards, Emiliana returned, clutching my tickets.

'Your train leaves in ten minutes,' she said. 'Come.'

I said my goodbyes to Mario, who once again embraced me fiercely. Embarrassing though I found such close physical proximity, I could not help but be moved by the generosity of this man who had not only saved my life, but taken me in and nursed me, with no thought of any reward for himself.

Emiliana led me through the crowds to the appropriate platform where the train was already waiting. A gaggle of school children were milling around on the platform, under the supervision of a harassed looking teacher who was trying to conduct a roll call as they filed on board.

'I think they are going to Genoa too,' said Emiliana. 'You have forty minutes to wait there for your next train. Travel safely *signore* Colin.'

'I will certainly endeavour so to do,' I replied. 'You and your family have been most kind – and remarkably discreet too.'

'It is our way,' she replied, simply. 'Do you have a wife back in England?'

'Yes. Penny.'

'And do you love her?'

Nobody had ever asked me this before. I was not used to discussing the notion of romantic affection with anyone, and certainly not a young Italian woman, but her unexpected question brought a lump to my throat and a tear to my eye.

'Very much,' I found myself confessing. 'It will be most pleasurable to see her again.'

'Most pleasurable,' she repeated, with a smile. 'Before I met you, I thought I spoke English pretty good. Now I'm not so sure. Please give my regards to Penny. She is a very lucky woman.'

'I'm not sure she sees it that way, but I will certainly pass on your best wishes.'

A whistle blew, as the last of the children scrambled frantically aboard. Emiliana squeezed me tightly and kissed me on the cheek.

'Goodbye,' she said. 'Don't forget us, will you?'

'Never,' I said. And I meant it. I clambered aboard and waved to Emiliana as the train pulled slowly out of the station. I fixed my eyes on her smiling friendly face until the train rounded a bend and I could see her no longer. Once again, I was alone, but this time I had a plan. With a following wind and no further mishaps, I should be back home within twenty four hours.

I made my way into the first carriage, which was full of chattering schoolchildren. I was rather taken aback when almost as one they rose to offer me their seats. Was it really less than a week since my embarrassing encounter on the 7.44 from Beckenham? I was also rather surprised to discover that good old–fashioned English manners seemed alive and well on this Italian train, even if they had died a lamentable death back home.

Pleased though I was at the gesture, I could not bear the thought of sitting amidst the noise and chatter of a carriage-load of school children, so with what I hoped was a polite shake of the head, I made my way to the next carriage which was mercifully half empty. I put my bag on the luggage rack and slid into the window seat. The journey to Genoa would take a couple of hours, with several stops along the way. I had my back to the engine, which was less than ideal, but I was sure that I could tolerate this for the relatively short duration of the journey.

We were only a few minutes out of La Spezia, when someone slid into the seat next to me. Given that there were plenty of empty seats in the carriage, I found this rather irritating. I glanced sideways at my new companion. He was an oriental looking gentleman, with slicked back dark hair and sunglasses. He wore expensive looking but casual attire – jeans, a checked shirt and a blouson jacket. He removed his glasses, smiled and greeted me cordially.

'*Bon giorno.*'

I had gleaned enough from my time with Emiliana's family to know that this was a standard Italian salutation, and I echoed the greeting with what I hoped was a passable Italian accent. Unfortunately this proved to be an incorrect assumption on my part.

'Ah. You are English,' he said. 'What brings you to this part of Italy?'

'Holiday,' I muttered. I was not keen on entering into a conversation, and hoped that if I kept my answers brief and to the point, he would stop trying to engage me in conversation.

'Me too,' he replied, proffering his hand. 'My name is Junjie.'

I shook it cautiously: 'Colin.'

'In Chinese, Junjie means Handsome and Outstanding,' he said, without any apparent sense of how boastful he sounded. What does 'Colin' mean?'

'Just Colin,' I replied, staring out of the window in the hope that he would take the hint. He did not.

'Are you going to Genoa, or stopping off in the *Cinque Terre?*'

'Genoa.'

He smiled broadly: 'Me too. It will be good to have an opportunity to practice my English. I stopped off at the *Cinque Terre* towns on the way. You must have seen them.'

I shook my head. 'Not yet.'

They are very beautiful. I am coming back from Pisa. That tower is crazy. It really leans, you know. Where are you staying in Genoa?'

'Just passing through,' I replied, in the most non-committal manner I could muster.

'Who is your favourite football team? I like Manchester United. Have you ever been to China? Are you married? I am married. I have two children – a boy and a girl.'

As the train made its way along the picturesque route Junjie continued this non-stop barrage of personal questions and random information about himself, seldom giving me time to reply, even had I wanted to. He paused occasionally to take a photograph while rhapsodising at the beauty of the view. Every few minutes or so, the train would stop at a station, the automatic doors would slide open and people would file on and off. Junjie would watch them intently, then as we got back under way, would resume his interrogation. After fifteen minutes or so I was slowly losing the will to live. I was not sure that I could endure this for the whole journey, and made to stand up, excusing myself as I did. The train was slowing as it pulled into a station.

'But you are not leaving the train?' he asked, concern written all over his face. 'It is still some distance to Genoa.'

'Not at all,' I replied. 'I simply need to stretch my legs, and avail myself of the gentlemen's facilities.'

'Of course,' he said, standing to let me out. 'When you return we can talk some more. I will keep your seat for you, Mr Cavendish.'

I nodded politely and walked forwards up the aisle of the train. I had recalled seeing a toilet at the front of the carriage containing the schoolchildren. If I locked myself in there for ten minutes or so, it would be ten minutes less of my life which I would have to spend listening to the inane chatter of Junjie. I passed through the door into the next carriage, but as I did, I came to a sudden realisation that was so profound, it was as if somebody had unexpectedly punched me in the stomach. Junjie had called me Mr Cavendish. But at no point during our rather one-sided conversation, had I volunteered that information.

With a sudden thrill of fear, I realised that Junjie was not the innocent tourist he appeared to be. Anna had mentioned that there were many people intent on recovering the information which I was carrying, and that this included the Chinese. I turned and looked back through the connecting door. Junjie had his back to me. He had reached up to recover my bag from the luggage rack and was rifling through it intently. Finding nothing, he replaced it on the rack, turning to look in my direction as he did. I tried to duck out of sight, but I was too late. Our eyes met. At that point I realised that he knew that his cover was blown. His open friendly smile was replaced by a look of intense purposefulness, and I knew that if I stayed on the train until Genoa there would be others like him waiting for me, and he would make absolutely certain that I was delivered to them.

I turned and headed back through the carriage full of schoolchildren. Other people had joined the train at the station and were heading down the aisle in the opposite direction. Although it went against every fibre of my being, I realised that now was not the time to play the English gentleman. If I were to allow each one of them to pass, Junjie would be upon me in no time. I pressed on regardless, aware that I had just seconds to get to the doors at the far end of the carriage before they slid shut, trapping me on the train with a Chinese spy who certainly did not have my best interests at heart.

I was almost at the door and a squat, black-clad priest stood blocking my way. Out on the platform, a whistle blew. With a sense of burning shame I elbowed the priest to one side, sending him flying into a couple of the schoolchildren who were sitting in a double seat. There was immediate uproar, as the priest gasped in outrage while the entire carriage full of children gathered round to see what the commotion was, blocking Junjie's way in the process.

'I'm most dreadfully sorry,' I muttered over my shoulder, and just squeezed through the doors as they closed. The train pulled away. Inside I could see Junjie battling his way back down the carriage, pushing children out of the way. He took out a mobile phone and dialled a number, gazing murderously at me as he did, and then the train was gone.

I looked at the station name. Vernazza. Once more I was on the run, and I knew that if I stayed where I was, it would only be a matter of time before I was captured. I had to get away, and without really knowing what I was going to do next, I ran down the steps which led to the street below.

Unfortunately, it was my desire to make good my escape which also proved to be my undoing. In my haste to get as far away as possible, as quickly as I possibly could, I lost my footing on the smooth steps. The whole world turned on its head as I tumbled forwards. My head cracked against the hard concrete pavement, and I suddenly found myself lying in a crumpled heap amidst the litter and detritus of the main pedestrian thoroughfare.

Chapter 11.

It took me a few seconds to gather my senses. I did not appear to have broken any bones, but as I attempted to get to my feet, my knees buckled beneath me and I sank back to the ground. I was dimly aware of a young man in his late-twenties crouching beside me.

'*Stai bene?*' He enquired.

'I'm fine' I muttered.

'Well you don't look fine,' he replied, producing a handkerchief from the top pocket of his immaculate suit and soaking it with water from a bottle he was carrying, He dabbed the handkerchief on my forehead and I was perturbed to see blood as he took it away.

'Looks worse than it is,' he said, reassuringly. 'You've got a nasty graze, that's all.'

'You're English,' I stated, rather obviously.

'Correct. Wayne Adams. How do you do?'

'Colin,' I replied instinctively, but then thought it might be best if I did not reveal my real name. 'Colin Smith.'

Wayne helped me to my feet. My head was aching, but I did not appear to have suffered any lasting damage from my fall.

'You were in a right hurry going down those stairs. As if somebody was after you.'

I hesitated before replying. I could be reasonably certain that Wayne was not a member of the multi-national force who appeared to be pursuing me through Italy, but it would clearly be inappropriate to tell him the real reason, gratifying though it was to meet a fellow countryman.

'You looked scared out of your wits,' Wayne continued.

I decided that a degree of honesty might be the best.

'I was indeed anxious to leave the train unexpectedly. Fortunately my pursuer is still on it. However I am concerned that he may alight at the next station and return to find me.'

Wayne looked concerned.

'We can't have that, can we? Where are you heading?'

'Genoa. Though I may have to change my plans.'

Wayne clapped his hands together with childish glee.

'Looks like I may have stumbled on a little adventure. I'm driving to Milan. That any good?'

I had no idea if Milan would be any good or not. I was unsure of its whereabouts, its distance from my current location, or what I might do when I got there. But I also reasoned that if I had no idea where I was going, it might also serve to confuse Junjie and whoever else might be pursuing me. I had told him that I was heading to Genoa, so a detour might be in my best interests.

'You are most kind,' I replied. 'May we leave immediately?'

'Five minutes to the car and we're on our way,' said Wayne with a beaming smile. 'Can you walk?'

I assured him that I could, and we set off up the winding cobbled street.

Although I have led a fairly cloistered life, I am not entirely innocent when it comes to the ways of the world. It has not been possible for me to have spent so many years working in the heart of Theatreland without recognising a homosexual male when I see one. It was therefore immediately clear to me that Wayne was most certainly of that particular persuasion. Indeed, he made little attempt to hide the fact.

I am well aware that there are many homosexual men who do nothing by their speech, mannerisms or conversation to betray their private proclivities. Indeed I have often suspected that my late Uncle Bernard was so inclined. However, there are a large number of men who, by their intonation, mode of expression and loose limbed physicality express their sexuality in a more demonstrative way. Wayne was of that ilk, and was of such a sunny disposition and good heart that the word 'gay' could be applied to him in both its modern and more traditional meanings.

Although the thought of any form of physical intimacy with another man makes me shudder, I have certainly never been one to judge others for pursuing a lifestyle different to my own. As we drove along the winding road which snaked through the mountains, he told me a little about himself.

He worked as a translator, and lived in Milan with his partner, an Italian by the name of Alessandro. He had been visiting a client in Vernazza, having driven down from Milan that morning. The return journey would take some three hours or so, and would take me 150 kilometers north of my original destination of Genoa.

'To be honest,' he said. 'I'm glad of the company. So come on then – out with it. I've told you all about me. What's your story?'

At this point I was faced with some difficulty. I had been most fortunate that Emiliana had not pushed me for an explanation as to how I came to be floating in the middle of the Mediterranean. But I sensed that Wayne would not be so easily appeased and that I would need to come up with some story to explain myself.

'I had an unfortunate encounter with a man on a train,' I began.

'I've had a few of those too, 'retorted Wayne with a wicked smile. 'Join the one yard high club did you? Quick fumble in the toilets?'

I must have looked embarrassed at the notion, which Wayne had the good grace to notice immediately.

'Sorry. Can't stop myself sometimes. To be honest, you don't look the type. Not in those trousers anyway.'

I realised that the rough fisherman's clothes which I was wearing did not exactly show me off to my best advantage.

'He was trying to steal something from me. I caught him looking through my bag.'

'Then I guess he was successful. As you haven't got a bag.'

'I left it on the train.'

'If that's what he was after, why was he still chasing you?'

For some reason, the words of Sir Walter Scott sprang to mind: 'Oh what a tangled web we weave, when first we practice to deceive.' I decided that my best course of action would be to tell the truth – or at least as much of the truth as was necessary, just as Anna had done. I reached down and removed the flash drive from my trouser turnup.

'He was after this.'

'A flash drive? Why?'

'It contains information which seems to be of interest to a large number of people.'

'What sort of people?'

'On the evidence of my experiences during the last few days, some rather dangerous people from a collection of foreign governments.'

'Oh. I don't really do politics.'

I inwardly bemoaned the complete lack of interest from the youth of today in world affairs. Rostov was hardly 'politics.' He was one of the most important men in the world, and one of the most feared.

'I believe it has something to do with Yevgeny Rostov.'

This made him sit up and take notice.

'The President of Russia?'

'The very same.'

Wayne's face wrinkled in disgust.

'I've got a couple of friends from Moscow. They had to leave. Not a good place to be gay since he's been in charge. So what's on that thing then, if everyone's so keen to get their hands on it?'

'I honestly don't know. I have not had the opportunity to peruse it.'

The car screeched to a halt. Fortunately we were on a straight stretch of road at the time, and there was no vehicle immediately behind us, but I was still rather taken aback by this sudden manoeuvre.

'OMG!' he pronounced, dramatically. 'You mean there's a bunch of gangsters chasing you through Italy, and you don't even know why?'

I had to admit that this was the case, which only served to increase his curiosity.

'And how did you get involved in the first place?'

I had been on the run for some time now. There was something about this young man which I trusted, and almost before I knew what I was doing, I had told him the whole bizarre story: my disagreement with Penny, the unexpected kiss, the flight from my shop, my subsequent drugging at the undertakers, the explosion in the tunnel, my capture by the SVR, being pushed off Vasiliev's yacht, my rescue at sea, the unpleasant experience in the *pozzo nero* and my escape from Junjie.

When I had finished, his jaw was gaping so wide open I wondered if he had accidentally dislocated it. Eventually he spoke:

'Bugger me. And that's an expression by the way, not an invitation. You are a dark horse, aren't you?'

'Hardly. I have simply been a victim of a remarkable and unexpected turn of events.'

'You can say that again. Right. First thing is, we're going to get you back to my place and into some decent clothes. Then we're going to have a look at what's on that drive.'

Chapter 12.

It was late afternoon by the time we arrived at Wayne's flat in a modern apartment block in the suburbs of Milan. The flat itself was furnished in a modernist style which was not remotely to my taste. The colours were rather garish, and the walls were adorned with paintings which purported to be art, but to my eye were simply random splashes of colour which could have been administered by a five year old. It transpired that Alessandro was away on business for a few days, and so we had the place to ourselves.

'He's roughly your size,' said Wayne. 'Clothes-wise at least,' he added with a wink. I was not amused, but felt it would be rude of me to express displeasure at his continued feeble *double-entendres*. He disappeared into a bedroom and soon returned with a handful of clothes.

'See what takes your fancy from this lot and freshen yourself up. I'm nipping out. I'll need a special adapter to view that drive on my PC. I shouldn't be long.'

I locked myself in the bathroom and studied my reflection in the mirror. There was a graze on my forehead where I had fallen. A thin stubble was already beginning to grow on my recently shaved head, and greying whiskers continued to proliferate around my face and chin. Penny would barely recognize me when I returned home. I wondered how she was, and whether or not I should attempt to telephone her again.

I showered and changed into a pair of beige slacks, a rather bright shirt and a light blue pullover. They fitted me tolerably well, and it was certainly a smarter look than the fisherman's shirt and corduroy trousers, from which I had been careful to retrieve the flash drive.

No sooner had I emerged from the bathroom than Wayne returned. He looked at me approvingly.

'That's better. You look almost normal. I've got the adapter, so let's have a look, should we?'

I handed over the flash drive. He inserted it into the adapter and plugged it in to his computer.

'Right' said Wayne. 'Let's see what all the fuss is about.'

I must confess that at that moment, I experienced a thrill of excitement the like of which I had seldom felt before. I had been pitched into an unlooked-for adventure, all thanks to whatever it was that I was about to see on the screen. Given the urgency, ferocity and murderous intent with which certain people had sought to recover the flash drive, I was agog to learn exactly what this was.

A window opened on the computer screen to reveal a darkened room containing several indistinct figures. The images appeared to have been filmed on a portable telephone, and judging by the shaky camera work and the oblique perspective, it appeared as if the operator had gone to some lengths to film covertly. At first it was difficult to make out what was happening, as the pictures were indistinct and blurred. Then the images suddenly clicked into focus, and Wayne and I were finally able to see exactly what was going on.

I could not be considered, in any way, shape or form, a man of the world. My own sexual interactions have been restricted to just two women: Penny and Maureen Sharples. Three if you include a brief but passionate kiss with Anna Orlov at Victoria Station.

What unfolded on the screen were a series of sexual acts and practices the like of which I had never imagined possible, and certainly never experienced. Some required a degree of physical dexterity which I found quite astonishing, and of which I would never have been capable, even in my youth. Suffice it to say, that the film provided me with an explicit, eye-opening and occasionally eye-watering introduction to homosexual sexual activity. Most remarkably, at the centre of this sybaritic and debauched orgy was the unmistakable, naked figure of the World's most powerful demagogue, a man whose name was a byword for repression, extreme nationalism and the brutal suppression of gay rights in his own country: Yevgeny Rostov.

The film came to an end, and Wayne and I gazed at the screen for a while, unsure as to what we should say next. I noticed that he was breathing slightly faster than he had been when he sat down and pressed 'play.' Given that I cannot sit in the same room as Penny and watch a man and a woman kissing on TV without suffering a severe pang of embarrassment, the whole ghastly experience of sitting with another man and watching President Rostov and his male companions had presented a serious challenge to my normal stoic equanimity. I really did not know what to say. Eventually, Wayne broke the rather awkward silence.

'Oh. My. Days,' he said, finally, with an exaggerated pause between each word. 'As orgies go, that is right up there, so to speak.'

I was still lost for words. If anything, I felt a little sick,

'That's Rostov isn't it?' Wayne continued. 'The world's most anti-gay man being just about as gay as it's possible to be. No wonder everyone wants to get their hands on this.'

He was right of course. It was hardly surprising that the CIA had sent Anna to recover the footage. With this in their possession, they would be able to exert all manner of diplomatic pressure on Russia. As would Junjie and his Chinese overlords, and every other major foreign power intent on weakening Russia's position in the world. No wonder Vasiliev and the SVR were so keen to get it back.

'Do you think this is the only copy?' Wayne asked.

'So it would seem.' I replied. 'Why else would everyone be so keen to recover it?'

'We have to get it to the Police or someone. As soon as.'

'I would advise caution in that regard. The tentacles of my pursuers reach far and wide. Regrettably, I do not entirely trust the Italian Police. It is my intention to personally deliver this information to the British Embassy in Paris.'

'Why don't I just email it to them?'

His suggestion was so brilliantly simple, I wondered it had not occurred to me before. Although not well-versed in computers, I was aware that it was possible to do such a thing. Wayne continued:

'We'd have to find the right address, obviously, but that shouldn't be too difficult. Then it'd be out there, and you'd be in the clear.'

I thought this most unlikely. I felt certain that Rostov would take great pleasure in exacting vengeance on me for revealing his dark secret. It began to strike me that I may never be 'in the clear.'

'I cannot ask you to expose yourself to such obvious danger,' I said. 'The email would no doubt be traced back to you. I think it best that I take the drive and stick to my original plan. I would also suggest that you erase this footage from your computer, and tell no-one that you have seen it. I did not ask for this burden, but it seems to have come my way, and I must bear it with whatever fortitude I can muster.'

'Hark at Frodo' he replied, with a cheeky grin. 'But I do take your point about the email. I must say, I'm not mad keen on a visit from a bunch of Russian boot boys, and don't think Allesandro would be over the moon about it either.'

'In that case, I must resume my journey to Paris as soon as possible.'

A sudden thought struck Wayne, and I swear he jumped a full foot off his chair with a squeal of delight.

'Why go all the way to Paris? There's a British Consulate here in Milan! We could be there in fifteen minutes! I'll check and see when it's open.'

As he typed into the computer, I considered his proposal. The prospect of being able to get rid of the vile pornography which I had unwittingly been carrying was irresistible. But as I thought about it further, I realised that we must exercise caution.

'We are dealing with dangerous and desperate adversaries. Having lost my trail on the train, there is every chance that they will have cast their net far and wide in order to find me again. Any bastion of British influence would be an obvious place for them to start looking. Where I to attempt to surrender myself at the Consulate, they may well be lying in wait for me.'

'Then let me take it in!' said Wayne, enthusiastically. 'No-one knows who I am.'

I considered his suggestion for a moment. It was certainly most tempting, but I realised that, in all conscience I could not allow him to take the risk.

'That is most kind,' I replied. 'But I would rather deliver it myself.'

Wayne looked rather hurt, but recovered himself manfully as the necessary information came up on his screen.

'It's closed now. Opens again in the morning. So, here's the plan. First thing, we'll get in the car and head down there. I'll drive round the block a few times, and you can check it out. If there's no dodgy looking men hanging around, I'll drop you right outside and you can dive in.'

I could see no flaw in his plan, although I did have some reservations about remaining in the flat overnight.

'Are you quite certain no-one followed us from the station?'

'Positive. No-one knows you're here.'

He was right of course. Providing I continued to keep a low profile, there was no way that anyone could possibly know my whereabouts. Including Penny. Once again my thoughts turned to my dear wife. Who knows what agonies she would be going through now?

'What's up Col?' said Wayne, as if reading my mind, and with an obvious concern for my well-being which I found unexpectedly affecting.

'I was thinking about Penny,' I replied. 'We have never spent this long apart before. I hope she is alright.'

'If she's got half your spirit, she'll be fine. You got any kids?'

It was a sign of the changes that the last few days had wrought in me, that I barely noticed his appalling grammar, let alone felt the need to comment on it.

'A daughter. Jessica. She is at University, so her mother will be all alone.'

'Why don't you give them a call?' he said, indicating the telephone on the coffee table.

'Nothing would give me greater pleasure. Unfortunately, I have no way of knowing who might answer, and whether or not they would have the wherewithal to trace my call. Much as I long to hear her voice again, it must wait until I have safely disposed of the drive.'

Wayne removed the drive from his computer and handed it over to me. He pressed a button on his keyboard and the final frozen image from the video disappeared from the screen.

'That is well and truly deleted from my PC.' He said. 'Although there are one or two images that will be forever stored in my brain. Suffice to say, Alessandro's in for a treat when he gets home.'

I decided not to dwell on this rather unsavoury image. Instead, I took the capsule from my pocket, unscrewed it, and placed the drive carefully inside.

'You going to swallow it again?' asked Wayne.

'Not unless it is absolutely necessary.'

'Right, I'm going to make you up a bed in the spare room and rustle up some dinner. What d'you fancy while you're waiting? Cuppa, or a glass of wine?'

A week ago, I would certainly have plumped for a cup of tea.

'Wine would be perfect, thank you.'

Chapter 13.

Considering the stress under which I was labouring, I slept surprisingly well. The bottle of wine which I had consumed with dinner certainly helped with that. I am ashamed to say that I locked my bedroom door, in case Wayne became unduly amorous during the night, but I had no need. He remained a perfect gentleman throughout.

The next morning dawned bright and fresh. It was approximately 9.45 as Wayne's car drove down the Via San Paolo past the modern concrete building where the British Consulate is situated. From studying their website, it appeared that their offices were on the 5th floor. There would presumably be some security at ground floor level which would allow me access to the building. I had only to cross the street and enter the building and I would be safely under the protection of her Britannic Majesty's Consular Officials.

A line of cars was parked on the other side of the road. I asked Wayne to drive slowly past, so I could check for any obvious signs that someone was watching the Consulate. He had lent me a baseball cap and dark glasses, which along with my burgeoning beard provided a ready disguise – or so I hoped. The street was busy with traffic and pedestrians. I could see the door that led into the building. Everything seemed normal.

At the end of the street Wayne turned the car and headed back towards the Consulate. He had given me his telephone number, and I had promised to call him once I was safe inside the building.

'Happy?' he asked, as the car approached its destination.

My hand closed round the capsule in my pocket, to make sure it was still there. I had one last look up and down the street. Everything seemed as it should be. The car drew to a halt. I estimated it would take me twenty seconds to reach the safety of the building, following which my awful nightmare would be over.

'Thank you once again for everything you have done,' I said, sincerely. 'I will make sure the authorities are aware of the tremendous service you have rendered Queen and country.'

'Us queens got to look out for each other, don't we?' he replied with that familiar twinkling smile. I thought for one terrible moment that he was going to kiss me goodbye, but instead he patted me on the knee. 'Now off you go, and give my love to Penny.'

I opened the door to step out of the car and put one foot onto the pavement. As I did, I automatically glanced to my left. To my horror, just a few yards away and heading straight for me was Tweedledee - the SVR agent who I had last seen dropping me off to board the *Madeleine*.

'Drive!' I shouted, pulling myself back into the car, slamming the door as I did. The man was next to us now, looking angrily through the window, clawing at the door handle. 'For God's sake man!' I repeated. 'Drive!'

Wayne needed no further prompting. Pressing hard on the accelerator, he sped away. I turned to look behind me, and could just make out Tweedledee as he climbed into a car which had pulled up alongside him. It was the same black Audi in which I had already made one almost fateful journey. I was not keen on making another.

'What's going on?' said Wayne as he sped down the street, narrowly avoiding a man on a bicycle who hurled a volley of abuse at us as he wobbled in our slipstream.

'One of the Russian agents. Somehow they must have learned that I did not perish at sea.'

Wayne looked in his rear-view mirror.

'They're gaining on us. What are we going to do?'

He was frightened. Knowing what I knew about my pursuers, I must say that I could not blame him. I realised that I had placed this young man in a dangerous situation that was none of his making. We were driving through streets full of pedestrians. By going on foot, there was a good chance I might be able to lose myself in the crowds, as I had done before.

'Stop the car!' I shouted.

'Are you mad? They'll get you.'

'That is a risk I am prepared to take. I cannot allow you to expose yourself to danger.'

'Too late. I'm exposed already. I'll lose them, then we can work out what to do next.'

'I really do think ...'

'Oh shut up will you? I'm driving.'

His hands gripped the wheel as he weaved the car through the traffic, pressing the horn as he did. Even given the more casual adherence to sensible road usage that seemed to pertain in Italy, it was a reckless and yet impressive piece of driving. I looked over my shoulder and could see that the Audi was falling behind. It seemed as if we might yet elude our pursuers. But my hopes were dashed as I looked forward again. The traffic was slowing to a halt, held up by a red light at a busy crossroads.

'Hold on tight,' shouted Wayne. 'In fact, you might want to close your eyes.'

With that, he turned the steering wheel violently to the left, just as it looked certain that we would collide with the slowing vehicle ahead of us. We were on the wrong side of the road now, racing along at high speed as oncoming cars veered to one side amidst a plethora of blaring horns and shouted insults. Still Wayne raced on, past the queue of traffic and straight through the red light. Now we were ploughing across a stream of traffic that passed from right to left in front of us. A motorcyclist swerved at the last minute, and I can still see the look of astonishment and fear on the rider's face as we sped past him.

'I really am most dreadfully sorry' I yelled to no-one in particular, as we passed the busy intersection, pulled back to the right side of the road and pressed on down the now vacant highway. I looked behind. There was no sign of the Audi.

'I think we have lost them,' I shouted triumphantly.

'Thank Christ!' yelled Wayne. 'Let's head back to the flat. I need a drink.'

Although it was only ten o'clock in the morning, I could not blame him. Unfortunately a terrible thought struck me – one which meant that for me at least, a return to Wayne's apartment block would be quite impossible.

'The Russians will have seen your registration number. There is no doubt that they will be able to work out where you live. If we return there, I fear they will be waiting for us.'

'But I've got to go home at some point. Allesandro's back later. We've got a table for dinner.'

Once again I realised that I had visited a most unwelcome danger into this young man's life.

'Drop me at the railway station. I will take my chances from there. I suggest you present yourself to the local Police Station and tell them everything. Once I am no longer on the scene, I am sure you will be safe.'

'But you won't be! They're bound to have the station covered.'

'That is a risk I must take. I do not really have an alternative.'

Wayne though for a while as he realised the impossible situation in which he now found himself. A broad smile suddenly lit up his face.'

'There's always an alternative,' he said.

'And what might that be?' I exclaimed. 'I must get to Paris as soon as possible, and hope that they are not lying in wait for me there. I cannot travel by aeroplane. The train is the only solution.'

'No it isn't. Because I'm going to drive you there'.

I was astonished at this unexpected offer. It was also clear that I could not possibly accept, and I said so.

 'Why not?'

'It's too dangerous.'

'No it isn't. You travelling on your own, not speaking a word of Italian or French, with the world's intelligence community out to get you, that's dangerous. You wouldn't last five minutes,'

I bridled at his inference.

'I have managed to get this far.'

'More by luck than judgment. And because you've had people helping you. I reckon it's about eight hours drive. If I put my foot down, we should be there by early evening.'

'But your dinner engagement…'

'It's only food. This is far more exciting. Now stop moaning, because I am so giving you a lift to Paris, whether you like it or not.'

And with an air of absolute finality, he turned the car and headed out of the City.

■■

Although I had tried to dissuade Wayne from driving me to Paris, I must confess that I was somewhat relieved at his most kind offer. We stopped at a small shopping mall on the outskirts of Milan, where he filled the car with petrol, as well as purchasing a road map and some food and drink for the journey. Thankfully he did allow me to pay for them.

'There's one more thing I need to get,' he said, disappearing back into the mall. He returned fifteen minutes later and presented me with a mobile telephone.

'It's got a month's credit on it. Just in case we get separated.'

I reached for more money, but he stopped me.

'Please. It's a present. Something for you to remember me by. Now let's get going.'

We had discussed various possibilities for the route. I had favoured a more circuitous option, but Wayne was dead against it:

'The longer you're at large, the greater the risk. From what you've said there's only a handful of people chasing you. They can't cover half of northern Europe. The biggest risk will be once we get to the Embassy. So let's just get there as quickly as possible.'

He was right of course, and so we headed west out of Milan, before taking the A24 northwards towards the Mont Blanc tunnel. At first I glanced fearfully at every passing car, convinced it would be full of pistol-wielding secret agents intent on forcing us off the road. But as the Alps grew ever-closer, I began to relax, convinced that for the time being at least, I was safe.

'Why are you doing this?' I asked, after half an hour or so of silence. 'Putting yourself in danger in order to help a complete stranger?'

'I fancied an adventure,' he replied, simply. 'Life as a translator's interesting enough, but it's not exactly edge of the seat stuff.'

'I would have though there were plenty of other adventurous opportunities of which you could have availed yourself. Why me?'

'You're about the same age as my dad.'

'I see. So my predicament invokes some filial obligation on your part?'

'Not really. I hate the bastard. We haven't spoken in almost ten years.'

I was rather taken aback by this revelation. I may have had a distant relationship with my own father, but at least it was a cordial one.

'I am sorry to hear that.'

'I was, at first. Broke my heart. Spent ages trying to patch things up, but he didn't want to know. So I thought, sod him. Moved to Italy, met Allesandro – the two best things that ever happened to me.'

'May I enquire as to the reasons for your falling out?'

'Guess.'

My natural reticence in discussing anything of a personal nature had precluded any prior reference to his sensual urges, but it seemed as if there was only one obvious answer to this question.

'Would it perhaps have coincided with his discovery that you were homosexual?'

'Got it in one. I was seventeen. I'd known for ages. Tried to fight against it. Gave football a go, joined the scouts. Quite enjoyed that actually, and not just because it was all boys. Turned out I was quite good at the outdoorsy stuff. I tried kissing girls, but it didn't really do anything for me. So I had a go at kissing boys instead, and I discovered I had a bit of a flair for it. I couldn't find the right way of telling my parents, then my dad came home early from work and found me in bed with a rather nice boy called Adam. He hit the roof. Then he hit me. Told me to get out and never come back.'

'I am truly sorry to hear that.'

'Thanks. You said you had a daughter at Uni. Jessica?'

'That is correct.'

'Straight, or gay?'

I pondered the question for a moment, and to my shame realised I had absolutely no idea,

'I believe there may have been boyfriends, although she has never brought any of them home to meet myself or her mother.'

'And what if she was gay? What if you came home and found her in bed with another woman?'

We were venturing into hitherto unexplored territory here. I was not used to having this sort of conversation with anyone, particularly when it concerned the sexual proclivities of my own daughter.

'I think I would very swiftly draw a veil over the whole sordid business.'

'Because it was a woman?'

'No. Because it was …. business. Her own business, and certainly none of mine. However, if she did turn out to have Sapphic tendencies, it would in no way diminish the affection I have for her. She would still be welcome in my house, as would her …. partner.'

'Of course she would,' he replied, with a smile. 'And that's why I'm driving you to Paris. Because, you're brave, and decent, and you're not a bit like my dad. Now get your money out – we'll need it for the tunnel toll.'

Chapter 14.

The long stretch of the Mont Blanc tunnel safely negotiated -
without, I am glad to say, any headlong collisions with marble–laden
lorries - I found myself back in France. Mont Blanc towered behind
us, and I was much taken by the verdant beauty of the surrounding
Alpine countryside. It was now early afternoon, and Wayne stifled a
yawn.

'Time for a stop.' He said. 'And something to eat.'

A few kilometres further on we pulled in at a roadside parking area
fringed by thick woodland. In the distance I could hear the sound of
rushing water. Wayne pulled up next to the trees at the far edge of
the car park. I was reassured by the fact that we were the only car
there, although by now I felt reasonably secure that we were not
being followed – or indeed that anyone knew where we might be.
Wayne produced the bag of provisions he had purchased in Milan:
some bread, ham and pastries. I suddenly realised I was very hungry.
I was also in pressing need of relieving myself, and headed into the
woods while Wayne prepared our picnic.

The woodland was still, quiet and dark. I headed down a narrow
path. Somewhere ahead of me I could make out the sound of fast-
flowing water. After a few metres I headed into the trees and found a
suitably quiet spot to go about my business. Some minutes later, I
headed back towards the car. I was very much looking forward to
assuaging my hunger before we resumed our journey to Paris.
Wayne had estimated it might take another six hours or so – longer if
we stopped again. I had no idea if the embassy would be open in the
evening, so we might need to stay somewhere overnight and present
ourselves there the next morning. I wondered if we should find
somewhere in Paris, or stop along the way. I resolved to ask Wayne,
who seemed well versed in the art of travel.

I emerged into the parking area and noticed that a car with an Italian number plate had parked next to our vehicle. I was relieved to see that it was not a black Audi. There was no sign of its occupants, or indeed of Wayne, who seemed to have completely disappeared. I supposed that he too had gone to answer the call of nature. I could see the bag of food sitting on the passenger seat of the car, and tried the handle to see if he had perhaps left the car open. Unfortunately, it was locked.

'You'll be looking for these I expect, Colin,' came a familiar voice from behind me. I spun round in surprise. It was Junjie. In his left hand he held Wayne's car keys. In the other, a gun, which was pointing straight at me. He was still wearing his back-pack.

'Where's Wayne?' I found myself asking, much to my surprise.

'You mean the faggot? He tried to put up a fight and I had to deal with him. I'm sure you won't make the same mistake.'

'What do you mean, 'deal with him?''

'I shot him. He's dead. Now, we're not on a train full of kids this time, so let's get straight to the point. I believe you have something I want. Information relating to Yevgeny Rostov. Please hand it over.'

I was struggling to take everything in. This man had killed Wayne, in cold blood, and seemed totally oblivious to the enormity of his actions. He would presumably despatch me with similar callousness once he had obtained what he was looking for. The capsule was in my pocket. I wondered about swallowing it again, but there was something about the cold glint in Junjie's eyes that led to me to suspect he would not hesitate to cut me open in order to recover it.

Another car swung into the other side of the parking area. A man got out and lit a cigarette. I wondered about making a run for it, but Junjie was ahead of me.

'Let's go for a walk in the woods. After you.'

He motioned towards the path I had recently taken. I had no choice but to start walking. As we entered the trees, Junjie indicated an area of thick bushes to the left:

'Your friend's in there. The rats will take care of him. Or the wolves – I believe there have been a few sightings. Keep walking.'

We carried on down the path, towards the sound of cascading water. The trees loomed oppressively on either side of the path. Sometimes I had to push the branches to one side in order to pass by. I was filled with a sense of foreboding. I felt sure that as far as Junjie was concerned, I would not be making the return journey. I wondered about making a bolt for it through the trees, but reason got the better of me.

'Are you going to kill me too?' I asked.

'Possibly.'

My blood froze.

'May I at least know to whom I will be surrendering the information?'

'The People's Republic of China. It will give us significant influence over the Russians. Although if their intelligence service is anything to go by, they shouldn't pose too much of a threat to our worldwide interests.'

'How did you track me down?'

'More Russian incompetence. We had been monitoring their communications, and so were aware of the car in which you had escaped. It was a simple matter to log into Italian number plate recognition systems. Presumably even they will have managed that, so we need to complete our transaction as quickly as possible. They won't be far behind.'

The path was broadening out now, and the noise of the water had become even louder. We emerged from the trees into a small viewing area bounded by a graffiti covered concrete wall some four feet in height. I looked cautiously over the side at a teetering cliff face which dropped several hundred feet into the raging torrent of a river which ran through the valley below.

'Pretty, isn't it?' said Junjie as I turned to face him. All traces of the garrulous simpleton on the train had disappeared now. I could see that he was in deadly earnest. There was no escape down the cliff, and my way back along the path was barred by a gun-wielding killer. Things did not look good.

'And now. The information, if you please.'

I reached into my pocket and produced the capsule. I briefly considered flinging it into the gorge below, but I reasoned that if I did that, he would most certainly kill me. If I handed it over, there was a possibility that he might let me live. With the awful realisation that my adventure was over, and that I had failed in my quest to see the damning video safely delivered to the British authorities, I gave it to him.

He unscrewed the capsule to reveal the flash drive.

'Have you seen what's on this?' He asked.

I nodded. There seemed no reason not to tell the truth.

'I hope you won't mind me checking to see that it's what you claim it is.'

With that, he slipped off his backpack and produced a small laptop computer. He loaded up the drive, squatted on his haunches and started to play the video. I could hear the grunts of pleasure and pain emanating from the computer as Junjie watched it keenly. As he did, I saw a flicker of movement over his shoulder. I was astonished to see Wayne emerging stealthily from the trees. His shirt was drenched in blood and he held a large heavy stick in his hand. So intent was Junjie on watching the video, that he failed to see my flicker of surprise. Wayne put his finger to his lips as he slowly edged towards Junjie. I remained rooted to the spot.

Junjie had seen enough. He slammed the lid of his computer shut, stood up and pulled out his gun.

'I'm feeling rather soiled now Colin, and I'm afraid I hold you personally responsible. So it looks like I will have to kill you after all.'

Wayne was just feet behind him now, raising his rudimentary club slowly above his head.

'President Rostov eh?' continued Junjie as he levelled the gun at my forehead. 'Who knew that the world's most powerful man was a faggot? Those perverts are everywhere.'

'Too right we are,' said Wayne, as he brought his club crashing down. Junjie half turned at the sound of Wayne's voice and the blow caught him flush on the temple, knocking him back past me and into the wall. His knees buckled but he steadied himself and raised his gun slowly at Wayne. I knew I needed to act fast and with a sudden downward chopping movement I knocked the gun from his shaking hand. As I did, Wayne charged forward. His impetus carried Junjie up and over the wall. The spy teetered on the edge, clawing at thin air, trying to find purchase where there was none. Then soundlessly he fell back, and I watched him bounce off the rocky cliff face before being swallowed up by the river some hundreds of feet below.

I turned to Wayne and found him slumped to the floor, blood oozing from a wound in his chest. It must have taken a huge amount of energy and determination for him to drag himself through the woods and now I could see that he was in a bad way. I took Junjie's abandoned backpack and fashioned an emergency pillow for him to rest his head on.

'You saved my life,' I said.

He looked back up at me. A faint smile flickered over his drawn, pale face: 'A man's gotta do, what a man's gotta do.'

I reached for the mobile telephone which he had given me back in Milan.

'How do I call an ambulance? I don't even know where we are. Will they speak English?'

He put his hand on my arm: 'Just leave it for a minute, will you?'

'But you need help.'

His breathing was getting shallower and I suddenly noticed he was deathly pale. He looked very calm – almost serene.

'To be honest Col, I think it might be a bit too late for that.'

'We have to do something.'

The pool of blood around him was growing ever larger. I pulled out the handkerchief from his top pocket and desperately sought to stem the flow. But he was right. It was too late.

'There is something you can do,' he said. 'Would you hold me, please?'

I eased my arm under his shoulder and cradled him gently – just as I had Jessica when she was a small child.

'Don't cry,' he said, as a tear ran down my cheek and fell on his face. 'It's all been a fantastic adventure.'

'But it shouldn't have ended like this.'

'Who says it's ended? Make sure you get that video to the right people. For Penny. For Jessica. And for me.'

With that, Wayne let out one last breath – a rattling sigh – and then he breathed no more. To my shock, I realised that he was dead. I held him in my arms for a while and I am not ashamed to say that I shed tears: tears of sadness for his death, tears of guilt for my part in it, and tears of utter desolation as I realised that I now had the blood of two more people on my hands. I do not know how long I sat there holding him closely. After some time, I laid his body to rest on the hard ground and considered what I should do next.

I think I have never been at a lower ebb than I was at that point. I seriously considered turning myself in to the French Police and hoping that they would allow me access to a responsible British official before the Russians, the Chinese, the Americans or some as yet unidentified secret service managed to infiltrate them. On reflection, this may well have been the best thing to do, but at the time I was not thinking straight. I had been on the run for so long now that I was suspicious of everyone. I resolved to keep on running. Somehow, I must make my way back onto British soil, and it seemed that I must do it alone.

Wayne's car keys had disappeared over the cliff with Junjie, but even if I did have access to them it was clear that his was a marked vehicle. I would not get far. According to Junjie, the Russians were also hot on my trail. They knew my route now, and if I were to stay on the same road, no matter in which vehicle I travelled, it was only a matter of time before they tracked me down. I needed to head in a different direction. Descent into the gorge was impossible, and I had no desire to lose myself in the mountains that rose up on the other side. I reasoned that if I crossed the main road on which we had been travelling and struck out in the opposite direction, I would not only stand a better chance of shaking off any pursuers, but would also be heading downhill.

I was now faced with another dilemma. What should I do about Wayne's body? Were I to telephone the authorities it would simply alert them to my presence. There was nothing anyone could do for him now, and although this spot did not look as if it was frequented that often, no doubt someone would stumble upon the body at some point. I closed his eyes, kissed him gently on the forehead, and vowed that once I was back in England I would seek out Allesandro and tell him how brave Wayne had been. Assuming I made it back myself, of course.

I recovered the drive from Junjie's laptop and replaced it in the capsule. I had no idea if the video had been saved onto his computer, so I set about the laptop with a nearby rock, before depositing the shattered fragments over the side of the cliff. I also took Junjie's now empty backpack. I felt sure it may come in handy on my journey.

Without a backward glance I headed back up the path to the parking area. The other car had gone, and I could still see the modest picnic which Wayne had prepared as it sat invitingly on the car seat. With the keys to the car somewhere at the bottom of the gorge, my only hope of food in the foreseeable future was to break in. A week ago, the thought of smashing my way into a vehicle would have been total anathema to me, but such were the straits in which I now found myself, I thought little of finding the nearest rock and smashing the side window.

I bundled the food and a bottle of water into the backpack, along with the road map which Wayne had purchased at the shopping mall. It was on a very large scale, but at least it would give me some idea of where I was, and where I should be heading. In the boot I also found a thick anorak and a torch, both of which would be most welcome as the night drew in. Such was the altitude, the weather here was noticeably colder than it had been in Milan.

I swiftly made my way across the dual carriageway to a heavily wooded slope on the far side. A stream ran parallel with the road before turning off into the trees. Reasoning that whatever else may befall me, I would at least have water to drink, I followed the stream as it plunged downhill into the forest. It was late afternoon now, and I needed to find somewhere where I could sleep before night fell. I was not sure where that might be, but as I could not stay where I was, or continue along the main road, it was my only option.

Chapter 15.

At first, my route was fairly straightforward. There was a path of sorts which ran alongside the stream, and once I was safely away from the main road I stopped, ate some of my food and drank from the ice cold running water. Eventually the path petered out, and I was no longer able to follow the stream. Making sure that I continued to travel downhill, I struck out through the woods. Although there was no obvious path, the trees were sufficiently widely spaced to afford me a relatively easy passage.

I must have walked for at least two hours, and in all that time, I saw no-one. Although I was reasonably confident that any pursuers would have no idea in which direction I was heading, for the time being I was more than happy to stay off the beaten track. It was difficult to judge distances from my map, but I estimated that I should reach a minor road before too long. From there I aimed to head for the nearest small town or village, and find a bed for the night. The Russians had already proved themselves to be persistent – if rather inefficient – in their pursuit of me. I wondered if Junjie was acting alone, or whether I could expect more Chinese agents to be out there looking for me. Following Anna's death, I also wondered whether or not the CIA had despatched others to continue the hunt for the Rostov video.

As I considered the various foreign intelligence services who were hunting me, I must confess to feeling somewhat disappointed that I had yet to be tracked down by anyone from MI6. I had assumed that British Intelligence would be operating in conjunction with the Metropolitan Police, and that Sergeant Bellingham would have informed them of my telephone call. If the Russians and the Chinese were able to pinpoint my location in both Italy and France, it was surely not beyond the wit of Britain's finest to do the same.

Several days had passed since my last attempt to speak to Penny, and I wondered once again how she might be managing without me. Unsurprisingly there was no signal on my mobile phone, wandering as I was in the depths of an alpine forest. It also seemed clear that telephone calls could be traced, and I was loath to do anything which would alert my enemies to my location. I decided to bide my time, and wait until I was properly on the move again before risking another call to home.

More time passed, and still the hoped-for road failed to materialise. Afternoon passed into early evening, and the light was starting to fade. The trees were becoming more tightly spaced, and my progress was becoming increasingly difficult. I was also very tired. I stopped and listened, hoping that I would hear the distant sound of a road, running water or any sign of human activity. But the forest was deathly quiet now. The birds had stopped singing, and pretty soon I would need my torch to continue any further.

I am not a superstitious man. Nor do I frighten easily. But there was something about the impenetrable stillness and incipient darkness of that place that disturbed my equilibrium. I would be glad to get out from the trees and into some open space, from whence I might be better able to determine my exact location. Taking the torch from my pocket, I pressed on.

It was barely five minutes before I heard the howl for the first time. A distinctive sound which I had hitherto heard only on wildlife documentaries. It was the unmistakable cry of a wolf. I stopped dead in my tracks. Such was the density of the trees it was impossible to determine how far away the sound had been, but there was no doubt in my mind that it came from a wolf. Junjie had said that there were such beasts in the area, and I dimly remembered reading tales of wolf attacks on French sheep. I had no idea if their animosity extended towards humans, but I was not keen to find out. Shining my torch ahead of me, and despite my growing fatigue, I redoubled my pace.

I heard another howl, and was reassured that it seemed no closer than the previous one. But my relief was short-lived, as it was almost immediately answered by another much louder call which came from the woods just to my left. A frisson of fear surged though my body as I shone my torch in the direction of the second howl. It was not yet pitch black, and through the gathering gloom I could just make out a large grey shape as it flitted through the woods no more than twenty yards from where I was. It seemed to be keeping pace with me, without getting any closer. I wondered if it was waiting for the other wolf to arrive before mounting an attack. It howled again, and this time the answering call was noticeably closer and louder than before.

I was tired now, and scared. I had no chance of outrunning these beasts. My only hope was to get to a place of safety where they could offer me no harm. The branches of one of the surrounding trees seemed to be my only hope, assuming that I could reach them. The trees were evenly spaced, with tall straight trunks which thrust skywards. So gloomy was it beneath the forest canopy that the bulk of the trees' growth was concentrated towards the top of the trunk. In the main, the lower branches looked flimsy and would certainly not bear my weight. The stronger load-bearing boughs started some ten feet or more above the ground, and were well out of my reach.

I scanned the forest to my left, looking to see if the first wolf was still shadowing me, but I could see nothing. It was too much to believe that it had disappeared completely. I imagined that it was in there somewhere, stalking me carefully, waiting for the opportunity to pounce. I shone my torch in the upper branches of the trees, and there, directly ahead of me, I saw a tree with branches which looked low enough for me to reach. The silence in the forest was even worse than the sound of the eerie howling, and I headed towards the tree, knowing that it could offer my only hope of survival.

As I neared the tree, I heard a noise behind me. I looked over my shoulder and saw a large grey wolf emerging from the trees in hot pursuit. The beam of my torch illuminated its fierce face. I could see the beast's bared fangs as it bore down on me. I looked forward again, and to my horror saw the other wolf standing at the foot of the very tree I had hoped to climb. It's head was down, and it's front legs planted wide apart as it glared malevolently at me. I was left with no doubt in my mind - if these two caught me, they would rip me to pieces. Jamming my torch in my pocket, I took one last sighting of the lowest branch of the tree ahead of me. As I did so, the leading wolf crouched down, as if ready to pounce.

Fear lent me wings, and as the wolf bowed its head, I leapt skywards, taking the animal totally by surprise. My foot came down on the back of the startled beast's neck and I sprang forwards, reaching out for the branch as I flew through the air. My hands caught the bough firmly, and I prayed it would not give way beneath my weight. As I hung there, the second wolf leapt into the air, grabbing at my trailing leg and sinking its teeth into my trouser cuff. Somehow I managed to shake it free and scramble frantically upwards, as both wolves leapt at me, redoubling their efforts to bring me down before I could escape their slavering jaws. I reached for the next branch and desperately hauled myself a few feet higher until I was some ten feet off the ground, seated on a branch and clinging onto the trunk of the tree for dear life. I was gasping for breath, trembling with fear, and my trousers were torn. But at least I was alive.

It was almost completely dark now, but there must have been a bright moon above, as there was sufficient light for me to see the wolves pacing beneath me. For the time being, I was quite safe. Even if they were to slink away, there was no way I was descending from that tree while it was still dark —once day broke they could still be lying in wait for me. Even as I struggled to regain my breath, I was reminded of a quotation from Timon of Athens, one of Shakespeare's lesser known plays: 'and still though liv'dst but as a breakfast to the wolf.' It was going to be a long night.

I took stock of my surroundings. The branch on which I sat was broad and fairly robust. There were some even thicker ones just above me, and for a while I considered climbing even higher, but I soon discounted the notion. I was safe enough where I was. It was very dark now, with just enough light from the moon for me to be able to make out the two menacing grey shapes at the base of the tree. It was also getting rather cold, and I was glad that I had the foresight to take Wayne's coat from the boot of his car. I wondered if anyone had found his body yet. It occurred to me that there might even be other members of the wolf pack who had stumbled upon poor Wayne. I hoped that the vicinity of the busy road would keep them away.

I had no such reassurance here in the depths of the forest. I had no idea how far from civilisation I was, and when, if ever, the wolves would leave the scene. I wondered if they were actually that ferocious at all. They had followed their hunting instincts by chasing me through the trees, and had probably become emboldened by the fact that I ran away. I recalled an early evening cliff top walk on a family holiday in Devon where my mother, father and I had been pursued across a field by a herd of cattle. My father had surprised me by suddenly turning on his heels and charging towards the startled beasts, waving his arms and shouting, whereupon they turned tail and ran. I wondered if a similar trick would work with wolves, but I must confess that as I looked down at the snarling face of the largest of the two animals as it sat looking up at me, I was not tempted to give it a go.

The best I could hope for was to sit it out and hope that they would tire of waiting and head off in pursuit of easier prey. As I sat in the branches, shivering with cold, my posterior going numb and my legs cramping up, one thing was certain. I would get no sleep that night. I made myself as comfortable as I could and waited for the dawn.

■■■

I think I must have woken up a fraction of a second before I hit the ground. Despite the discomfort of my situation, I must have nodded off and lost my balance. As I came too and realised what had happened, I looked around me in a wild panic, half expecting to find a yellow-fanged wolf standing over me, ready to rip my throat out. But I was alone. I stood up carefully. Miraculously I seemed to have received no injury from my fall, and as I looked about me, I saw with some relief that the first streaks of dawn were beginning to permeate the night sky.

I was briefly tempted to return to the safety of the tree, but instinct told me that my safest bet would be to escape from this forest as soon as possible. I looked at my map again. Assuming that I was travelling in the right direction, I was bound to reach human habitation before too long. Logic suggested that where there were people, there would be no wolves. I ate the last of the pastries, took a mouthful of water from my bottle, and continued my journey, stopping every minute or so to make sure that I was not being stalked.

My route continued downhill through the forest, and after some half an hour's steady walking it seemed to me that the trees were beginning to thin out. It was then that I heard the welcoming sound of bleating sheep. I reasoned that if there were sheep, then people could not be too far away, or at the very least a friendly shepherd who could point me in the right direction.

Sure enough, a few minutes later, I finally emerged from the darkness of the forest into wide open pasture land where a large flock of sheep grazed a few hundred yards further down the slope. The sun was just rising above the snow-capped mountains which towered above me in the distance. I could see a river snaking its way through the base of the valley, with a road running alongside it, and although they were still some way off, I could see houses and what looked like a small town. I would need to approach with caution, and avoid any contact with people until I had found a way to rest and smarten myself up a little. If Wayne's body had been found – or even that of Junjie – then it would surely be the talk of this small alpine community. The emergence of an unshaven, exhausted Englishman would inevitably lead to speculation which, if my experiences so far were anything to go by, would soon bring more trouble my way.

I made my way down the slope and was brought up short by the sight of a dead sheep which lay on the ground. Its throat had been torn open, and huge chunks of flesh had been ripped from its side. The wound looked fresh, and was surely the work of the wolves. With a chill I realised that were it not for the welcoming boughs of the pine tree that had served as my bed for the night, this could well have been my fate.

Down below me I saw that the flock of sheep were suddenly looking anxiously in my direction. At first I thought they must have been alerted by my presence, but as they started to spread out and run away down the slope I realised that they were fleeing from someone or something far more sinister than me. I looked over my shoulder, and to my horror I saw that one of the wolves had broken cover from the trees and was heading down the hillside towards me.

There was no way I could make it back up to the trees. My only escape was to follow the sheep and hope to find some refuge before the wolf caught me. I started to run down the steep slope, hoping that the pursuing beast would lose interest or head off in another direction. I looked over my shoulder and to my horror saw that the wolf was not pursuing the sheep which were now some distance away. He was heading straight for the nearest quarry and easiest pickings – and that was me. I redoubled my efforts to escape, and this proved to be my undoing. The combination of my increased momentum and the steepness of the slope sent me cartwheeling head over heels. I lay sprawled on the ground, and had barely turned to see where the wolf was before it was upon me. I could smell its putrid breath. Saliva from its mouth flecked across my face as it pinned me to the ground, ready to strike.

A shot rang out, echoing round the valley. I was face to face with the wolf now, and it looked faintly startled at the sound. As it glowered down at me, its eyes suddenly glazed over, and it collapsed on top of me, blood pouring from a bullet wound in the side of its head as a hideous gurgling sound came from its throat. Pushing its dead weight off me, I rose unsteadily to my feet and looked round to see a man striding purposefully towards me, clutching a shotgun. He was overweight with a ruddy complexion and a large black moustache, and he had most certainly saved me from certain death.

'Thank you' I said, instinctively, then remembered that I was now in France. '*Merci*,' I repeated – one of the few French words I had remembered from my previous ill-fated visit to the country with Penny and Jessica. '*Merci*.'

The man did not say a word, but walked straight past me to survey the stricken wolf. It was still breathing. He cocked his rifle one more time, squeezed the trigger and put another bullet through the beast's head. Up close, the noise was deafening. He then reached into his pocket, slipped two more cartridges into his shotgun and pointed it straight at me.

'*Haut les mains,*' he snarled.

I may have been deficient in my understanding of the French language, but his meaning was entirely clear and I put my hands in the air with some alacrity. Jamming the barrel of the gun between my shoulder blades, he marched me down the hill towards the town.

Chapter 16.

As we processed down the hillside, I tried to engage my moustachioed captor in conversation, but received nothing in return apart from an occasional grunt and the barrel of the gun shoved into my back when my pace faltered. It was still very early in the morning, and no-one else was about. Eventually we arrived at a small farm house. He motioned me towards a stone- built outhouse which abutted the main building. With one last shove I was propelled inside as the thick wooden door slammed shut behind me. I heard a heavy bolt sliding into place, and a key turning in the lock for good measure.

Straw lined the floor, and a glimmer of light filtered in through a high, narrow, barred window at the rear of the hut. The room stank of animals, but judging by the rustling sound which I could hear coming from the straw, the only current occupants were of the rodent variety. A thousand thoughts filled my brain. Why had the man captured and imprisoned me? Did he think I was some sort of burglar or sheep rustler? Had Wayne's body been found, and was my sudden emergence from the woods being linked with his death? Most importantly, where had my captor gone, and who could I expect to walk into the hut when next the door was opened?

I felt in my pocket. The capsule containing the drive was still there. Once again, the enormity of the burden which I carried weighed heavily upon me. I was my patriotic duty to preserve this sordid information as well as I could, and make sure it did not fall into the wrong hands. With no idea what might happen next, I reasoned there was only one thing to do. For the third, and I hoped final time, I popped the capsule into my mouth and swallowed hard.

I wondered what Penny was doing, and how she was bearing up in my absence. Much as I wanted Jessica to do well at university, I hoped that she had been able to return home and offer her poor mother some comfort and companionship. With a sudden thrill I remembered the mobile telephone which poor Wayne had bought me back in Milan. I had tucked it away in the zippered pocket of his jacket, which I was still wearing, and with trembling hands I sought it out. All fears of being tracked down via its signal had long disappeared. I just wanted to hear my wife's voice again. I pulled the phone out and dialled the familiar Beckenham number. Nothing happened. I tried again. Still no response. I peered at the display on the phone. To my crushing disappointment, it showed that I was receiving no signal. This was hardly surprising, given the remote and mountainous nature of my location, but I was immediately plunged into deep despondency.

I suddenly felt very alone and very tired. I had enjoyed precious little sleep overnight, and with total disregard for whatever might emerge from the straw, I lay down and almost immediately fell asleep.

I am not sure how long I slept, but I was rudely awakened by the door being opened with just as much force as it had been shut. Given the aggressive muscularity of my gaoler, I was surprised that it had not long-since fallen from its hinges. He stood there once again, still with his shotgun pointed at me. But this time he was not alone. Standing either side of him were two uniformed policemen. One was also pointing a gun at me, while the other one brandished a pair of handcuffs.

'Stand up slow and careful please *monsieur*,' said the second policeman in heavily accented English.

I did as I was told. Approaching me cautiously, while his colleague and the farmer continued to train their guns on me, he clipped the handcuffs over my wrists and carried out a careful search of my body. He found little, other than the phone and the remainder of the Euros I had acquired in the mountain hut at Carrera. How long ago that seemed now! I was pleased that I'd had the foresight to swallow the capsule. Satisfied that I was not carrying any weapon, the officer led me outside. A car was parked in front of the Farmhouse, with the letters 'Gendarmerie' spelled out on the side. I was guided into the back seat and the policeman with the handcuffs slid in next to me. The other took his place behind the wheel, and with what I presumed were a few words of thanks to the farmer, we sped off down the dusty track which led to the main road.

'Where are you taking me?' I asked.

'The Police station, to see my boss. He will ask you a few questions.'

'What about?'

'You will find out, very soon.'

The car continued on its way, following the winding road as it snaked through the valley following the course of the river. I wondered if this was the same stretch of water where Junjie had met his fate. After ten minutes or so a roadside sign told me we were entering the town of Saint-Antoine. Almost immediately we pulled into the yard behind the local gendarmerie. I was escorted into the building, and immediately led into a small room at the rear of the building and invited to sit on one side of a large desk. The English-speaking policeman stayed with me, while the driver disappeared, presumably to fetch his 'boss.'

Some ten minutes later the door opened and a small, wiry man entered the room. His dark hair was plastered firmly backwards over his head in an unsuccessful attempt to conceal a large bald patch. He carried a bundle of papers which he slammed onto the desk with what I considered to be unnecessary showmanship. My previous visit to France had not left me well-disposed to either the country or its people, and little had happened in the last few hours to disabuse me of this notion.

'Good morning,' he said tersely, in a tone so condescending that it was difficult to believe that he considered there was anything good about it, or indeed that it was actually morning at all.

'I am *Inspecteur* Delrieu. What is your name?'

'Cavendish. Colin Cavendish.'

He looked at the file which lay on the desk in front of him. I noticed that the other policeman was scribbling in his notebook as we spoke.

'And may I ask what you were doing in the forest above our town?'

I had thought long and hard about this during my time in the farm outhouse and during my drive to the Police Station. Now that I was in Police custody, I reasoned that I was certainly safer than I would have been out in the woods, pursued by murderous spies and ravenous wolves. But my suspicion that the SVR had been in cahoots with the Italian Police led me to a certain circumspection where the authorities were concerned.

'I respectfully request that you contact the nearest British Consulate. I have important information which I need to pass on.'

His eyes narrowed as he looked at me scornfully.

'What sort of information?'

'It's classified.'

He looked at me blankly. 'Classified?'

'Secret. And highly important. I must insist ….'

I jumped in my seat as his fist slammed suddenly down on the desk. I noticed that his colleague did not flinch at all. This was clearly part of his boss's well-established interview technique.

'You will insist nothing! You are In France now, under French jurisdiction, and you will answer for crimes committed on French soil. Then, maybe, we will contact the British and you can give them your 'classified' information. And so, I ask you again, what were you doing in the forest?'

My first instinct is always to be polite and honest in response to any question, particularly those posed by those in authority. But a combination of my natural caution concerning the information I was carrying, and this irritating man's rudeness and irascibility led me to an untypically truculent response.

'I was taking a walk.'

He glared at me.

'A walk from where, to where?'

'I was taking the mountain air.'

'Mr Cavendish, I must warn you, this is no light-hearted matter. If Jules Deschamps had not killed the wolf when he did, you might not be here to tell your tall tales. Up until today, we have had no recorded cases of wolves attacking humans. It seems that in choosing you for their first human victim, they have chosen wisely.'

'I am indeed grateful to the gentleman for saving my life. However, I am at a loss to understand why he then sought it necessary to frog-march me down the mountain …'

'Frog march? What do you mean. *Frog* march? Are you insulting the French people *monsieur*?'

I realised that my use of the phrase could have been open to misinterpretation, but I was in no mood to explain. He looked at me with ill-concealed loathing.

'You were fortunate that Jules was there to save your life. What a shame he was not present when you killed this man.'

From his dossier he produced a photograph and slammed it down on the desk. It was a picture of Wayne, smiling broadly, arm in arm with a man who I assumed to be Alessandro. Tears sprang to my eyes as I remembered the sacrifice that brave young man had made in order to help a perfect stranger. Inspector Delrieu studied me carefully.

'I see you at least have the grace to regret your savage act. A bullet in the back or so it seems. And what can you tell me about the death of this man?'

He produced another photograph. It was the lifeless body of Junjie. His face was battered and bruised down one side, either from his fall down the cliff face or from his body's progress through the rocky ravine.

'He was found in the river this morning. The first man we know to be Wayne Halliday, a resident of Milan in Italy. The Italian police have given us some very interesting information about his movements in the last 24 hours, in the company of an Englishman with your name. This oriental man we do not know, but we are making enquiries. But it is curious, is it not, that you should emerge from the forest just a few kilometres from where they were murdered?'

'You're not suggesting I killed Wayne?'

'I am suggesting exactly that. I have been in touch with your Scotland Yard. It seems as if casual assassination is something of a specialty of yours. They tell me that they are very keen to question you concerning the murder of a Russian national by the name of Mikhail Platonov.'

Reeling though I was from the suggestion that I had anything to do with Wayne's death, I sensed an opportunity.

'Then surrender me to the British authorities. Send me back to London for questioning.'

'Alas *monsieur,* that will not be possible. First you must answer for the crimes you have committed on French soil. Crimes which carry a long sentence.'

'But I am innocent,' I cried.

'That is what they all say. We will let the court decide the truth of the matter.'

He put the photos back in his folder and slammed it shut dramatically.

'Colin Cavendish, I am arresting you for the murder of Wayne Halliday, and of this other person, as yet un-named. You will be held in custody while we make further enquiries.'

He nodded towards his colleague.

'Read him his rights, Arnaud. Though is it was up to me, he would not have any.'

With that, the *Inspecteur* strode from the room, leaving me with the dawning realisation that I faced the very real prospect of spending the rest of my life incarcerated in a French prison.

Chapter 17.

The next hour passed in a whirl. I was read my rights; informed that I could have an interpreter if necessary, and see a doctor if I required one. I asked if I could make a telephone call, but was informed that due to the severity of the charges this would not be possible. Arnaud, the officer who had detained me at the farm, did say that he would make a call for me, and I requested that he contact the nearest British consulate immediately. He promised that he would, but in such a way that led me to believe that this was unlikely to happen any time soon.

Soon afterwards, *Inspecteur* Delrieu returned to take my statement, with Arnaud once again in tow.

'So, *Monsieur* Cavendish. Now you have had time to consider, I need you to tell me exactly what you are doing in France, your connection with the two men, and your part in their deaths.'

I was in a real quandary. I had the perfect opportunity to tell my story in all its unlikely complexity. Despite my suspicions of Italian Police collusion with The SVR, I had no real reason to suppose that Russian tentacles extended as far as this small Alpine town. For all his unpleasant demeanour, Delrieu and his team offered me the best possible protection, as long as I remained in their custody. And yet I hesitated. The information that was once again passing through my digestive system was undoubtedly of global significance. As long as there was a chance that I would be seeing someone from the British Consulate in the next 36 hours or so, then I resolved to save the full explanation for them.

'I've told you. I was on holiday,' I replied.

'Holiday? Where?'

'Here.'

'And how did you get here?'

'I walked?'

'Where from?'

'England.'

He looked at me with thinly disguised contempt.

'We know that you left London a week ago, after the sudden and unexplained death of the Russian, Platonov. on your premises. You then disappeared for some time, until you made a call to your home in London. The call was traced to Carrara in Italy, and was made not long after the mysterious death of two people after their car collided with a vehicle carrying explosives to the mines. Such was the force of the explosion we have not yet been able to establish their identities. A man answering your description was seen fleeing the scene on a *velomoteur*. Again, you disappear, until surveillance cameras pick you up passing through the border with Italy in the company of a British man living in Milan by the name of Wayne Halliday. Soon afterwards, Halliday is also found dead with a bullet in his back. The next morning the body of a man who we now know to be a Chinese citizen by the name of Junjie Chen is dragged from the river. Our forensic scientists tell me that it is likely he fell from the cliffs close to where the body of Halliday was found. So, in the space of seven days, you have been closely connected with the suspicious deaths of five people. That is some fucking holiday, *Monsieur* Cavendish.'

I had to admit that he had a point. I was shaken to hear of the circumstantial evidence which had stacked up against me. The need to explain all to one of my own countrymen, rather than to this overbearing Frenchman became even more paramount. I decided to stall for time, and try a bit of flattery in the process.

'Your English is very good *Inspecteur*. Including your grasp of the vernacular and the profane.'

'I am married to an English woman. We lived for five years in Peterborough.'

'Then you have my commiserations.'

'*Monsieur* Cavendish. We are not here to discuss my marriage or the lamentable state of provincial Britain. You are accused of two very grave crimes, and if you continue to refuse co-operation, then it will go all the worse for you in court.'

He was sorely testing my resolution, but I knew that I had to persist.

'Find me someone from the British Consulate, as is my right, and I will happily tell them everything I know. Until then, I have nothing further to add.'

I folded my arms in what I hoped would be a gesture of finality. Delrieu glowered at me contemptuously.

'So be it. You will appear in court tomorrow. It is unlikely that we will be able to find somebody from the Consulate before then. As you are refusing to co-operate or provide a statement, then the *Procureur* will have no choice but to remand you in prison while we make further enquiries, or until you come to your senses. I believe the average remand time pending trial is currently around eighteen months.'

This was shocking news. I may even have let out an audible gasp. Delrieu smiled grimly.

'I promise you, *Monsieur* Cavendish, that five years in Peterborough is infinitely preferable to five weeks in a French prison. Lock him up.'

■■

The cell in which I was incarcerated was a small room, about eight feet square with twin bunk beds and a foul-smelling hole in the ground situated in the opposite corner, which I assumed was to be used for my daily ablutions. There was a tiny barred window above eye level and a neon electric light on the ceiling which flickered and buzzed annoyingly. Two burly policeman deposited me in this tiny room quite unceremoniously without any indication as to how long I might remain there, or when – if ever – I might expect something to eat, or an opportunity to take some exercise.

I sat in the lower bunk and contemplated the dire circumstances in which I now found myself. If I thought my original visit to France had been unpleasant enough, then it seemed as if this one would outdo it in every department. I still held onto the hope that once I was able to explain the truth to a responsible British official and hand over the earth-shattering information which I carried with me, there was still a good chance that I would be set free. I longed for the simplicity and predictability of my former existence. The daily commute to London, the familiar routine of my domestic life and the comforting presence of Penny all seemed so far away now.

But even if I was set free – what then? Assuming that I was able to get the vile video of Rostov to the British authorities, the SVR would be fully aware of my unwitting part in its procurement. If the Russian President's position was compromised as a result, surely swift retribution would follow? Had they already threatened Penny and Jessica? I felt helpless and alone. I may be temporarily safe in this stinking French cell, but the thought of my wife and daughter in the hands of Vasiliev and his minions made me feel physically sick.

I have always had a strong mental character, and I believe it was this inner fortitude that got me through the next few hours. The thought of Wayne's innocent, trusting face and the immense sacrifice he had made to save my life, haunted me. To make matters worse I was now being charged with his murder. My only hope rested with Arnaud. Had me made the call to the British authorities as promised? I longed to see one of my countrymen, in the hope that they would be able to extricate me from the dreadful mess in which I found myself.

After some time, my spirits were briefly raised by the sound of the door being unlocked from outside and I sprang from the lower bunk where I had been resting. It was Arnaud.

'You have company,' he said simply, and stepped back as his two colleagues ushered in my new cellmate. He was black, with close-cropped hair and wore a garish t shirt, multi-coloured training shoes and frayed jeans which were ripped at the knees. I had first spotted this bizarre 'fashion' in London some months earlier. I could not help but think that those who chose to display their kneecaps in the depths of an English winter were asking for arthritis to come calling in later life.

'He doesn't speak English. In fact, he barely speaks French,' Arnaud continued.

He barked something in French to the young man, who glowered back at him, sucking his teeth in disdain as he did.

'*Terroriste,*' snarled Arnaud in a parting shot as he and the other policemen left the cell. Once again, the metal door was slammed shut, but this time I was no longer alone. My new companion stood immobile for a few seconds, then suddenly started to hammer on the door with his clenched fists. The echoing sound reverberated chillingly around the closed cell. After a few minutes he stopped, wringing his hands in pain. He glared balefully in my direction, cleared his throat, spat in the general direction of the rudimentary lavatory and took my place on the lower bunk.

'Actually, that's ....' I began. But a glowering stare stopped me in my tracks. It was only a bed, after all. I resolved to try and strike up a relationship with the young man. If we were to be incarcerated together for any length of time, it would help if we could be on good terms.

'Cavendish,' I ventured, thrusting out a hand. 'Colin Cavendish.'

He stared at my hand, and then at me, with ill-concealed hatred. With another suck of his teeth he turned his back on me and faced the wall. Rebuffed as I was, there was little else I could do other than climb awkwardly up onto the top bunk, keep well out of his way and hope that this violent young terrorist would not murder me in my sleep.

A further hour or so passed in awkward silence. I had little else to do other than watch the slow progress of a cockroach as it made its way across the ceiling immediately above my bed. After some time, I became aware of a faint sound coming from the bunk beneath me. The bedstead rattled slightly, and I realised that events had taken a most unexpected turn: the young man was sobbing quietly into his pillow.

Cautiously I climbed down from my bunk. He was still where I had left him, but his heaving shoulders and muffled sobs suggested that he was gripped by a deep melancholy which I found most affecting. Cautiously I perched on the edge of his bunk, reached over and placed my hand on his shoulder.

'There, there old chap,' I said, in as soothing a voice as I could muster. He arched his shoulder away in a dismissive gesture so I removed my hand, but remained in my seated position.

'It seems like we're both a long way from home,' I continued. 'I know I certainly shouldn't be here. Maybe you shouldn't either. My name is Colin.' I searched my memory for a schoolboy French phrase. '*Je 'm'appelle* Colin.'

'Yacine,' he replied, between sobs, and without removing his face from the pillow. I assumed that he was telling me his name.

'Pleased to meet you Yacine. *Parlez vous* English?'

'Some. A little.'

'Why are you here?'

'Because I African.'

I was not aware that simply being African was a criminal misdemeanour in France, although having been subjected to time in the company of *Inspecteur* Delrieu, I could well believe it.

'Which Country?'

'Senegal. I live here three year. I sell bracelet in *la ville.*'

I thought I would try again to establish why he was in the cell.

'So why have they arrested you?'

He turned to face me. His face was wet with tears and he suddenly seemed a lot less threatening.

'Because I African! *La racisme.* They say I steal bread from shop. But another man, he do this. White man friend of police. Then give bread to me. Then tell police I steal it! And that I am *terroriste! La racisme!*'

I was at a loss to know how to respond. A week or so previously, I would not have believed that an officer of the law – even a French one – would collude in the false arrest of an innocent man. But if my recent escapades had taught me anything, it was that the world was a far more venal and complicated place than I had ever imagined. I was inclined to believe young Yacine, even if there was little I could do about it.

'I am sorry,' I said, and meant it. 'What will happen next?'

He jumped from the bed and paced the room angrily. 'Prison? They send me back to Senegal? *Je ne sais pas.*'

With that he resumed his furious drumming on the cell door with such force I was concerned he might break his hands, and gently tried to restrain him. He rounded on me, pushing me away violently.

'*Ne me touche pas*! You all the same. *La racisme!*'

I felt this to be very unfair criticism. Admittedly, my rather cloistered life had not put me into contact with many people from other races, but I liked to think that I was a fair-minded person. I have always taken as I find, and the colour of a man's skin is of little significance as far as I am concerned.

'We are not all the same,' I replied, gently, but he sucked his teeth and glared back at me.

'You don't know what it's like. Only black face in a white town.'

'Indeed, I do not. But my experiences of the last few days have given me some insight into what it is like to be hunted and persecuted for crimes I did not commit. On that level at least, we have more in common than you might imagine.'

'Why you here?' He asked. 'Why old white English man in France prison?'

'They say I killed a man. Well, five people actually. Four men and one woman.'

His eyes widened with a mixture of respect and fear.

'Five peoples? You kill five peoples?'

'No. I didn't do it.'

'Not one of them?'

I had to think about this for a moment. I had certainly been complicit in Junjie's death, although it was Wayne who had tipped him over the edge of the cliff. But on reflection, my conscience was clear.'

'Not one of them, no.'

It was clear he did not believe me. He climbed effortlessly onto the top bunk and sat with his back to the wall, staring down at me suspiciously.

'Five peoples? Five peoples!'

It seemed as if by default, I had reclaimed possession of the lower bunk. With conversation, seemingly at an end, and nothing much else to do, I clambered into the bottom bunk, turned the pillow damp-side down, and stared glumly at the wall.

Chapter 18.

Now that he was convinced that I was a murderer, Yacine treated me warily, and there was little further conversation between us. At some point in the evening, trays of food were brought into the cell, but my request for some fresh air and exercise were answered with a shake of the head. So, with little else to do, I closed my eyes and drifted into a fitful sleep. At one point I was aware of Yacine relieving himself in the corner, but I pretended to be asleep so as not to invade his privacy.

I was awoken by the unlikely sound of birds singing outside the cell window. The door opened and Arnaud entered, accompanied by two policemen. He thrust a towel and a change of clothes at me, and I was escorted to a simple shower room just down the corridor. It was clear that the Police Station was small and provincial, and not really set up for the long-term incarceration of prisoners.

I showered as best I could, and changed into the grey tracksuit and t shirt which looked as if it had been hurriedly purchased from a local shop. Arnaud was waiting for me outside.

'We take you to court soon. My boss ask if you want to make a statement yet?'

I shook my head.

'I will only talk to somebody from the British Consulate. Did you call them as I asked?'

'Line was busy. I try again later.'

The man was clearly talking absolute poppycock. I could only hope that the French Justice system provided Judges of a higher calibre than their small town Police officials. I could only stall for so long, and once I managed to speak to somebody from the British Consulate, I hoped that my ordeal would finally be over, and that I would be able to demonstrate my innocence of all charges against me.

Once I was safely back in the cell Yacine was taken away for a shower. After a simple breakfast of bread and coffee, Arnaud arrived, and I was taken out to the front office where I was reunited with *Inspecteur* Delrieu. He looked as if he had enjoyed a better sleep than I.

'So, *Monsieur* Cavendish,' he began. 'Very soon, we will take you to the court, where the *Procureur* will decide what is to be done with you. It will be easier for him to make that decision if he is armed with all the facts. I am hoping that a night in the cell with our terrorist friend will have focused your mind, and that you are now ready to make a statement.'

I paused for a moment, weighing up the pros and cons in my mind.

'Yes,' I said. 'I would like to make a statement.'

His eyes lit up. Arnaud prepared his notebook, as Delrieu switched on his desktop voice recorder.

'I knew you would come to your senses,' he said, with an arrogant smile. He licked his lips in anticipation and ran his hands through his receding hair.

'And so, *Monsieur* Cavendish. Concerning the deaths of Wayne Halliday and Junjie Chen, what have you got to say for yourself?'

I stared back at him levelly, and began to talk.

'Before I come to the demise of those two gentlemen, I would like to say something about my cellmate.'

'Ah, the terrorist. Do you wish to make a complaint about his behaviour towards you in the night?'

He smiled sardonically.

'I hope he was not too rough with you.'

'On the contrary. He told me all about your attempts to frame him, the false accusations of theft, the planting of evidence and the accusations of racism. All matters which I shall be relaying to the authorities, once I have had my meeting with the British Consulate, as I believe is my right. You are recording this, I trust?'

That certainly wiped the smile off his face. He pulled out his old party piece and banged his fist on the desk.

'Enough of your games Cavendish. Now tell me what you know of your part in the deaths of Halliday and Chen!'

'I have said everything I have to say to you. What time do we leave for court?'

He glared at me, his face a picture of fury.

'I have tried to help you Cavendish. But you seem to think this is one big game. However, if this is the way you want to play, so be it. I hope they lock you up and throw away the key. Get him out of my sight.'

It was to be an hour's drive to the regional court where my case would be heard, and it seemed as if Yacine would be coming with me too. Despite his protestations, the young Senegalese was handcuffed to me and we were put in the back of a police car, with two policemen up front, neither of whom appeared to speak any English. I had decided that the best thing I could do was to say as little as possible until such time as I was able to talk to someone from the Consulate.

'You did call them?' I asked Arnaud again as we were loaded into the car.

'They are aware,' he replied, enigmatically. 'But they must come from Marseille. It is a long way.'

'Will they be at court?' I asked. But he simply shrugged in annoyingly Gallic fashion and walked back inside the Police Station. I was left to ponder my fate as we drove out of town and along the narrow tree-lined road.

Yacine was still not speaking to me, however he continued to direct a volley of complaints to the officers in front. Although I did not speak the language, it was clear that I was the target for his vituperative remarks.

Despite my sleepless night in the cell the impossible situation in which I now found myself, I found that I had somehow found new courage. I reasoned that I had sunk to such depths, that things could not possibly get any worse. The evidence against me was purely circumstantial, and once the right people were aware of the momentous information which I was carrying, it could only be a matter of time before I was reunited with Penny.

I wondered how the shop was managing in my absence. Miranda certainly knew enough about the business to keep it ticking over, but without my input and expertise it would not be long before stock would dwindle to the point at which the very survival of Cavendish and Daughter would be jeopardised. Maybe the crisis would persuade Jessica to temporarily abandon her studies and take over the running of the shop which bore her name, just as I had always hoped? Even as the thought entered my mind, I realised I was being unduly foolish. Jessica had made it quite clear that her ambitions lay elsewhere. Whether I returned or not, I had no real hope that she would ever take her rightful place behind the counter.

I was disturbed from my reverie by the realisation that the car was slowing down. I looked up and saw that a car had stopped in the middle of the road, coming in the opposite direction. The bonnet was up, and the driver was bent low, tinkering with the engine.

The policeman seated in the passenger seat wound his window down and shouted something in French. I assumed he was telling the other driver to get his car out of the middle of the road. But he appeared to take no notice. With a sigh of exasperation, the officer opened his door and walked towards the stranded vehicle. As he did, the driver lifted his head from underneath the bonnet and I saw him properly for the first time. It was Tweedledum – my old adversary from the SVR. He had already tried to kill me twice. I felt certain he would not fail this time.

'Get out of here,' I barked urgently to the driver. 'It's a trap.'

Although I doubt he understood what I had said, he clearly understood the urgency in my voice and saw the panic in my face. He stepped quickly out of the car and fumbled for his holstered gun, calling out a warning to his colleague as he did.

Tweedledum suddenly produced a gun and levelled it at the driver, who sadly did not have the sense to stop reaching for his. It was barely half-removed from his holster before a shot rang out and he collapsed to the ground, blood oozing from his chest. From my vantage point in the rear of the car, I could see his lifeless eyes staring back at me. The other policeman had more sense. On seeing his stricken colleague lying on the floor, he raised his hands in surrender.

My experience with the SVR had shown that they tended to hunt in pairs, and sure enough Tweedledee emerged from the rear of the car, his gun also pointed at the surviving policeman. I was aware of Yacine cowering next to me. I was curiously unmoved. In a few hectic days, such displays of unexpected violence had become almost normal.

Tweedledum walked carefully over to the Police Car and motioned for me to get out. Yacine had no choice but to follow. He cried out in fear as the SVR man pointed his gun at him, motioning him to stay in the car. I brandished our handcuffed wrists.

'I'm afraid where I go, he goes too,' I said, and we both climbed carefully from the car.

Tweedledum motioned to the policeman and to our handcuffs. His meaning was clear, and with trembling hands, the officer produced a key and released us. Tweedledee gripped him roughly by the neck and forced him into a kneeling position, and indicated to Yacine that he should do the same. I started to follow suit, but Tweedledum stopped me. It was the first time I had heard him speak English.

'Not you. You know what we are after.'

I had to think fast.

'The DVD? I told Vasiliev on the boat. Anna had it.'

'Then why are you still running? We don't know how you survived at sea, but why not go straight to the Italian Police?'

'I did. That's why I'm in protective custody.'

He chuckled deeply. It was an eerily disconcerting sound.

'You killed the Chinese spy. And the queer. Nearly killed us trying to chase you through that traffic in Milan. I think you still have what we need.'

'I swear, I don't.'

Tweedledum nodded to his colleague, who placed his gun in the back of the policeman's neck and pulled the trigger. I was sprayed with a film of blood and splintered bone and flesh as the dead man slumped to the ground, his head a shattered mess. Yacine was crying with fear.

'Tell me where it is, or we will kill this man too. Then we will kill you.'

Tweedledee levelled his gun at Yacine. His finger tightened on the trigger. I could see the veins standing out in fear on the poor man's sweating brow.

'No!' I shouted. 'That's enough!'

And for me, right then, that was enough. It was all over. I was convinced that they would kill me anyway, but I wasn't prepared to let another innocent man die because of my ridiculous belief that I could somehow outwit the World's intelligence agencies and get the Rostov video back to the United Kingdom.

'I know where it is.' I said. 'Let him go, and I'll tell you.'

Tweedledum looked at me suspiciously.

'Why should I?'

'Because if you don't release him, I won't tell you. Then you'll kill me. I suspect that once I have told you, you will also kill me. So, if I'm going to die anyway, I'd rather it was without Yacine's death on my conscience.'

Tweedledum gave me an odd look.

'You Brits are crazy.'

He placed his gun against Yacine's temple. I thought the poor man was going to pass out with fear.

'We know who you are, and we know how to find you,' he said to Yacine. If you tell anyone what happened here today, you will be dead in an hour. You have thirty seconds to get out of my sight.'

Yacine could not believe his luck. He rose carefully to his feet, still terrified, wondering what the catch might be.

'That's ten seconds,' said Tweedledum, menacingly.

Yacine didn't need a second invitation. He turned and hared away through the woods.

'So,' said Tweedledum. 'Where is the video?'

I was in a desperate situation. I still had a few hours to play with before nature took its course. But I also knew that if I was to buy myself more time, I would have to tell the truth.

'I swallowed it.'

A dark shadow passed across Tweedledum's face.

'You swallowed a DVD?'

'There is no DVD. It's on a flash drive. In a capsule. Somewhere inside me. It should emerge later today. Tea time, I'd say.'

'Tea time? We can't wait until fucking tea time. I've had enough of your bullshit. You say you swallowed it? Only one way to find out.'

He reached down inside his trouser leg and produced a long hunting knife.

'I have had a shit week Cavendish, and I blame you. I'm going to cut you open. That's a lot of guts to look through, but you know what? I'm kind of looking forward to it.'

Tweedledee moved round behind me. His strong arms grabbed me, pinning my arms to my sides. With an evil smile, Tweedledum ripped open the front of my shirt. I felt the point of the knife pricking my skin.

'I think you've had your last cup of tea, Cavendish.'

The next few seconds passed in a blur. I was aware of a shot ringing out. A look of surprise flitted across Tweedledum's face as a round red hole suddenly appeared in the side of his head. His knees buckled, as he slumped lifelessly to the floor. Tweedledee released me and spun round as another shot echoed through the woods. He took the bullet between the eyes, took a couple of staggering steps and collapsed in a heap on top of his colleague.

From the bushes a man emerged. He looked to be in his mid-forties, with brown hair parted neatly to one side. He wore a well-cut suit and a pair of shiny brown shoes. In his right hand he held a gun. Smoke was still seeping from the barrel. He crossed cautiously to the two men, his gun pointed at them. It did not take a genius to ascertain that they were both quite dead. He tucked his weapon inside his tailored jacket and extended his hand.

'Sorry it's taken a while to catch up with you Mr Cavendish.' He said, in a crisp, Home Counties accent.

'Jolyon Turnbull. British Intelligence. I've come to take you home.'

Chapter 19.

I must have stood open-mouthed for some seconds at this latest development. Turnbull broke the silence.

'Stop trying to catch flies Mr Cavendish.'

He surveyed the scene of carnage with a practiced eye.

'We need to get rid of these bodies, ASAP. This isn't a busy road, but someone's bound to come along before too long. We need to buy ourselves a little time in order to get well away.'

He looked at me with some concern. I was still rooted to the spot. I noticed that I was shaking a little. Even everything that had happened over the last few days had not prepared me for the suddenness and brutality of what had just passed.

'Mr Cavendish,' he repeated, with an edge to his voice. 'Do you want to see your wife again? Soon?'

'Yes,' I replied. In fact, at that moment, there was nothing in the world I wanted more.

'Good. Then you need to snap out of it, and give me a hand. Okay?'

'Of course,' I mumbled.

We moved the two policemen first. Turnbull took their arms, while I grabbed them by their feet. We half-dragged and half lifted them across the ground, and I suddenly appreciated the true meaning of the words 'dead weight.'

'Shouldn't we be contacting the authorities?' I asked.

'These are the authorities,' replied Turnbull with a grim smile. You were already looking at a twenty year stretch. And now you've been involved in the death of two Police Officers, I don't think they're going to be letting you go any time soon, do you?'

'Yes, but …'

'There are no buts Colin. If you want to get back home without a long intervening spell in a French prison, just do exactly what I tell you.'

And so I did. We bundled the two policemen into the boot of their car. Their lifeless forms lay on top of each other in a bizarrely lewd configuration.

Turnbull jumped behind the wheel of the Police Car and drove it off the road where thick bushes screened it from view. He did the same with the Russians' car, but instead of bundling Tweedeledum and Tweedledee into the boot, he leant their bodies up against the doors of the car, where they sat in a pool of their own blood.

'Just wait till their friends see that,' he said – rather unnecessarily I thought. Indeed, there was something about the casual callousness of the act which sent a shiver down my spine – and also felt somewhat familiar, in a way I couldn't quite explain.

'This way,' he said, breaking into my reverie, and set off through the trees at the side of the road, forging a path through the dense shrubbery.

I was still trying to come to terms with the sudden onslaught unleashed by my saviour, and the calm way in which he had dealt with its gory aftermath, when I suddenly tripped over a trailing root. To my horror, as I hit the ground, I found myself face to face with the wide, staring, lifeless eyes of Yacine. I jumped to my feet as Turnbull stared dispassionately at my erstwhile cellmate.

'God knows why the Russians let him go,' he said. 'Unfortunately for him he walked straight into me.'

I was appalled. I had put my own life on the line to save this innocent man, and now a British agent had snuffed his out, with little apparent thought. Turnbull must have read the disgust on my face:

'This is no time for sentimental mawkishness Mr Cavendish. The more people that know of my existence and my involvement in your rescue, the less likely it is that I can get you back to safety. Now let's get moving.'

Unfortunately, I found I could not move at all. First Wayne, and now another innocent young life ended too soon because of my deadly cargo. I remained rooted to the spot. Turnbull seized me roughly by the shoulders and stared hard at me.

'The car isn't far away. We need to go.'

'I'm not sure I ...'

But before I could finish the sentence he had slapped me hard across the face. I recoiled with the shock and pain caused by this unexpected blow.

'For God's sake man. Pull yourself together and get off your arse. Now!'

The blow to the face focussed my mind sufficiently, and I staggered to my feet. Turnbull grabbed me by the arm and half dragged, half steered me on through the bushes. After ten minutes or so we came upon another road, lower down the valley, where his car was parked: a blue BMW with French number plates.

'Get in,' he barked, tersely. Still in a daze I automatically headed for the passenger seat.

'Not there,' he snapped. 'The entire French Police force will be looking for you soon. In here.'

He opened the boot of the car and indicated that I should climb in. Accustomed though I was to the many privations which had been forced up on me over the last few days, I felt the need to protest at his outlandish suggestion.

'I would prefer to ride in more comfort.'

He stared at me with cold eyes.

'This isn't about your comfort Mr Cavendish. It's about your survival. Get in.'

There was a stark finality about his words which hit home. I climbed reluctantly into the admittedly capacious boot of the car and lay on my side. The lid was slammed unceremoniously shut, and I found myself in total darkness. Having spent a night in a coffin – how along ago that seemed now – I was at least used to being confined in such a manner. I heard the driver's door slam. The engine kicked in, and we set off. Not for the first time since leaving England, I had absolutely no idea where I was going, or what awaited me when I got there.

After what seemed like an eternity, the car pulled to a halt and the engine stopped. I heard the muffled sound of Turnbull talking on the telephone, but was unable to hear what was being said. The boot opened, and I clambered stiffly out, blinking in the unaccustomed sunlight.

We were parked on a quiet track, surrounded by woodland, some distance from the road. My right knee ached abominably.

'How long was I in there?' I asked.

'A couple of hours,' Turnbull replied, casually, as if being locked in the boot of a car was an entirely normal occurrence. 'My apologies for the inconvenience, but I can assure you it's nothing compared with what will happen if the French Police get hold of you. Not to mention the SVR. I can't imagine they're going to be too pleased at the death of two of their best men.'

I shuddered as I recalled the casual way he had dealt with Tweedledum and Tweedledee.

'Was that entirely necessary?' I asked.

'What did you expect me to do? Reason with them in a logical manner? Appeal to their better nature? Ask them politely to let you go?'

There was a certain logic to his argument, and I decided not to pursue my objections.

'Where are we?'

'On the road to Lyon. I've arranged a meeting with some colleagues who will arrange for your safe passage back to England. I expect you'll be looking forward to seeing Penny again.'

Tears sprang to my eyes at the mention of my dear wife's name.

'How is she? Is she safe?'

'She's fine. Under police protection for her own safety, until such time as we can get you back to England and recover the video clip which is in your possession. I take it you still have it? You're not carrying anything, so you've either lost it, or necked it. My guess is the latter. You strike me as being a pretty resourceful chap, and I can't imagine you'd give it up that easily.'

I tried to remember how long it had been since I last swallowed the capsule. Everything was somewhat of a blur, but I reasoned it must be some 24 hours. My eyes moistened again as I realised that I was almost safe. If I could stay under Turnbull's protection for a little while longer, I would be able to hand over my unwelcome burden. Once I made the British authorities fully aware of the events of the last week or so, I felt sure that my innocence could be proved and I would be free to resume my previous uncontroversial existence. But first I needed to be sure of my rescuer's *bona fides*.

'I have indeed,' I replied. 'And will be able to hand it over in the fullness of time, once nature has taken its course. But first, I would be grateful if you could furnish me with some evidence that you are indeed who you say you are.'

He looked at me again with his cold, grey eyes, then burst out laughing. I must confess, I failed to see exactly what he found so amusing.

'And what if I'm not?' he said, simply. 'We're in the middle of nowhere. I've got a gun, which I have already demonstrated I am more than happy to use. You'd hand it over whether you wanted to or not.'

He was, of course, entirely correct.

'True. But having come this far, it would at least reassure me to know that the information I am carrying was to end up in British hands.'

'Your patriotism does you credit. Unfortunately, we secret agents tend not to carry ID around with us. It's all rather inconvenient if we get captured. However, let me try and convince you that I am indeed who I say I am. Along with every other major intelligence agency, we have been aware for some time of the existence of, shall we say, compromising video featuring President Rostov. As far as we are aware, there is only one copy of this video, and it was smuggled out of Russia by a man called Platonov. He sold it to a woman called Anna Orlov at Victoria Station ...'

'I met her. She claimed to be working for the CIA.'

'Is that what she told you?'

'She told me many things.'

'I'm sure she did. She was indeed a CIA operative, and the US taxpayers will no doubt be delighted that it was their tax dollars which paid for the video. Unfortunately we also suspect that she had no intention of passing it on to her superiors.'

'What else could she do with it?'

'We don't know. That information died with her in the quarry tunnel. That was quite an explosion by the way.'

I thought back to the searing heat of the blast, and the strange pang I once again felt at the death of this mysterious woman, and my part in it. Turnbull continued:

'From then on, things got a bit sketchy. For an amateur, you did a pretty good job of disappearing for a while, until you resurfaced in Milan. Once we got word that you were in custody, we knew it was time to act. I was sent to recover the video before the French got their hands on it.'

'But why go about things in such an underhand way? Why not go through official channels?'

Turnbull sighed.

'Your naivety does you credit Mr Cavendish. The country which possesses that video will be able to bring much pressure to bear on the Russian government. It could result in trade deals which would be worth billions of pounds to the UK. I am sure that the Chinese, the Americans and the French will feel exactly the same. You are sitting, quite literally as it turns out, on a goldmine, and we will stop at nothing to make sure that it is the United Kingdom who gets to exploit that particularly rich seam.'

My heart soared at the prospect of finally being rid of the accursed video. But I had one more question to ask.

'This 'we' of whom you speak. Who is that exactly?'

'British Intelligence. MI 6.'

'And once I've handed it over, you'll get me safely back home?'

'There's a plane waiting in Lyon. You'll be back with Penny within 24 hours.'

Everything about Turnbull's story made sense. It seemed as if I had indeed been rescued by a guardian angel – albeit a rather ruthless and bloodthirsty one.

'Let us continue on our way then,' I said, heading back towards the boot of the car. I was willing to endure more discomfort if it were to lead to my being reunited with my darling wife.

'There's no rush,' he replied. 'In fact, if it's all the same to you, I think we should wait here until you're able to hand the information over. It might be safer in my possession.'

I could see the logic in what he said. By now, the entire French Police force would be looking for me. I was keen to get rid of the video as soon as it was physically possible. It seemed as if he had read my mind:

'How long do you think that might take?'

Recent events had rather played havoc with the regularity of my bowel movements.

'I am afraid I cannot be certain of that. However, I would anticipate that it will be sooner rather than later.'

'Excellent. In that case, I suggest we take it easy until you're good and ready. Would you care for a cup of tea?'

To my astonishment he produced a flask from the car, and two plastic cups. He motioned me to sit on a grassy bank.

'I'm afraid it might be a little stewed by now, and it's hardly the best china, but at least it's warm and wet.'

With that, we both sat down, and I savoured what I suddenly realised was the first cup of tea I had enjoyed since leaving England. Turnbull stretched out on the bank, his head resting on his hands. He seemed very relaxed for someone who had recently completed a triple murder. I found myself intrigued by his apparent insouciance, and sought to make conversation.

'How long have you been in your current … employment?'

He smiled, briefly.

'As a spy, you mean? I was recruited at University. English Literature. There was some unpleasantness over a rival for my girlfriend's affection. My bosses offered to hush it up in return for my entering their employment. I had planned to go into teaching, but I must confess that this kind of work suits me better.'

He produced a nail file and started to clean the dirt from underneath his fingernails. He noticed my look of surprise.

'Haven't had a chance for a proper shower today.' He explained. 'I can't abide dirty hands.'

I reflected that he probably had the blood of many people on those hands, judging by the casual way in which he had disposed of the three men earlier.

'How many men have you killed?' I asked.

'Enough.' He replied simply. 'A few women too. It goes with the territory.'

'My limited exposure to the world of international espionage certainly suggests that life is held cheaply in your world.'

'It's kill or be killed. You don't really have a choice.'

'That has never really presented itself as a dilemma in my line of business.'

'Then you're very lucky.'

I wondered if I would ever be able to return to my previous life in the bookshop, and communicated my concern to Turnbull.

'Notwithstanding your pledge to return me safely to Penny, I am now implicated in so many deaths, I wonder if the French authorities – not to mention the international espionage community – will just sit back and let me resume a normal life.'

'You'd be surprised at what can be arranged. Once you're back in the UK, there are wheels within wheels. All we have to do is get you safely on that plane. Once you've handed over the video.'

'I will be delighted to be rid of the infernal thing. At least I can say that in some small way I have done my patriotic duty.'

He smiled briefly: 'Indeed you have. It isn't always about killing people. And anonymity can be arranged. How do you think I've managed to stay undercover for so many years?'

'That must have been difficult. Do you have family? A home? Children?'

He shook his head briefly. 'Maybe when I pack it all in. Until then, I need to keep a low profile. There's a lot of people out there who would love to see me dead, if only they knew who I was and how to find me.'

'But you told me your name the moment we first met.'

'I told you *a* name. I have several.'

'But you must have some form of identity within your organisation?'

'I have a codename. We all do. They change all the time, but currently we're all characters from Shakespeare. Now, if you'll excuse me, nature calls.'

He got up and headed for the bushes, leaving me to speculate as to which of the Bard's characters could best describe this cold, calculating yet impeccably mannered killing machine.

And then it hit me, like a slap in the face.

Back in Carrara, while I was in the coffin, I had heard Anna and her colleague talking. They had mentioned a British agent who had gone rogue. A traitor, whose name was Aaron.

There is a character in Titus Andronicus called Aaron The Moor. He is widely held to be Shakespeare's most vile creation – one who had always fascinated me with his unswerving commitment to evil, sometimes just for its own sake. I recalled a stanza from the play.

'Oft have I digg'd up dead men from their graves,
and set them upright at their dear friends' doors.'

Turnbull had said something very similar, as he propped up the dead bodies of Tweedledum and Tweedledee next to their car. 'I wonder what his friends will think when they see this.'

As an English graduate, he would certainly have read Titus Andronicus. he could well have chosen the name himself as a sinister nod to his own sadistic proclivities. of course, I had no way of knowing is this was true, but if it was, then it seemed ineluctable to me that once I handed over the flash drive to Turnbull, I would swiftly become yet another victim of this callous traitor. if my reasoning was correct, the flight from Lyon was almost certainly an invention, and I would end my days in this tranquil spot, murdered by one of my own countrymen.

I realised I needed to act fast. I did not know for certain that Turnbull was out to betray me, but I instinctively knew that it was safer to work on that assumption, and apologise later if my fears proved to be unfounded.

My first thought was to make a run for it. I headed for the car in case, by some good fortune, Turnbull had left the keys in the ignition. To my dismay, this was not the case. I wondered about striking out across country, but reasoned that with all his training and undoubted superior fitness, it would only be a matter of time before he caught me. I swiftly inspected the interior of the car to see if there was anything that I could use to aid my escape. It was then that I saw the gun. It was a small, black pistol, and it sat in the side pocket of the driver's door.

As you will have surmised from my account of my adventures, I have led a secluded existence. Nothing about my life to date had prepared me for the madness of the last few days and weeks. I had been interred in a coffin, kidnapped, almost drowned, shot at, and threated with violent death on more than one occasion. But in spite of the reasoning of *Inspecteur* Delrieu, I was confident that at no point had I been directly responsible for the deaths of the many people whose lives had been cruelly curtailed around me. However, I also realised that if my suppositions concerning Turnbull were correct, I may need to be prepared to defend myself if I was ever to see Penny and Jessica again. I swiftly slipped the gun into my pocket, stepped away from the car and returned to the grassy bank.

No sooner had I taken up my previous position, than Turnbull returned, fastidiously wiping his hands on a pocket handkerchief.

'Mission accomplished,' he observed, with a wry smile. It seemed as if he was oblivious to my visit to the car, and there was certainly no reason for him to suppose that I suspected anything.

'I don't suppose you're any closer to delivering the goods?' he continued.

I had barely had time to plan my next move, and saw that this would provide me with an opportunity so to do.

'I rather think I might be,' I said, as calmly as I could. 'If I may be excused for a few minutes.'

'Take as long as you like,' he replied. indicating the thick bushes. 'And then we can get you back to your family.'

I headed towards the undergrowth, my heart pounding. I moved well into the bushes until I was confident that I was out of sight and earshot. I slipped the gun from my pocket and examined it more closely. It was black, with the manufacturer's name printed on the side. 'Glock. Made in Austria.' I had to assume it was loaded. And would I be prepared to use it on Turnbull, should the occasion demand such a serious course of action?

'It seems as if I may have underestimated you, Mr Cavendish.'

The voice came from behind me. I turned, and there was Turnbull, just a few feet away. He had another gun in his hand, and it was pointed straight at me.

Chapter 20.

'Hand it over,' said Turnbull, waving his gun in the direction of the one that I had removed from the car. I was about to do so, until something inside me stayed my hand. If my suspicions concerning Turnbull were correct, then by surrendering my weapon I could well be saying goodbye to my one last chance of survival.

'I think not,' I replied, and to my own astonishment I found myself pointing my gun back at him. There we stood, like two characters in a Western film. I believe it is referred to as a Mexican stand-off. Turnbull's eyes narrowed in annoyance.

'Don't be a bloody fool.' He said. 'Have you ever fired one of those things before?'

He took my silence for the confirmation he was seeking.

'I thought not. Not really your cup of tea is it?' There was a mocking tone in the way in which he phrased the words *cup of tea* which I found rather offensive. 'But more to the point, why on earth are you pointing a gun at me? I've come to take you home.'

'How can I be certain of that?'

'You can't. You'll just have to take my word for it.'

'Once I've given you the flash drive?'

'Precisely.'

'I think I'd rather wait until we're back in England, if that's all the same to you.'

A flicker of annoyance passed across his face.

'Why? Don't you trust me.'

'Quite frankly, after everything I've gone through over the past few days, I'm not sure I trust anyone any more. Particularly someone who is as cold and calculated a killer as you are. And whose soubriquet is Aaron.'

I saw the quick look of surprise at my unexpected use of this name. I could see that it had hit home, even though he affected ignorance.

'I don't know what you're talking about.'

I tried to remain calm. Inside, my heart was pounding nineteen to the dozen, but I knew that if I was to get out of this alive I would need to keep a very clear head. I returned his stare, making sure that the Glock was still pointing in his direction.

'You forget that I am something of an expert on The Bard, and am especially well versed in some of his more villainous creations. I have also picked up certain information on my travels, particularly relating to an MI6 traitor who goes by the name of Aaron. It does not take a genius to come to the conclusion that you are one and the same.'

He eyed me coldly, with a look of grudging respect.

'Ten out of ten Mr. Cavendish. You are a resourceful man.'

I nodded my head slightly at the unexpected compliment.

'I am in no doubt that it is your intention to kill me once you have recovered the information I am carrying,' I replied.

'Once again, ten out of ten. You may have noticed that I'm not big on mercy or compassion.'

'And may I ask what you intend to do with the information once you have it? Sell it to the highest bidder I presume.'

'I reckon the Russians would pay anything to have it safely back in their possession. Then I can retire a happy man.'

'Knowing that you have betrayed your own country?'

He shrugged. 'I've never been big on nationalism either. Money, on the other hand ….' He raised his pistol and pointed it towards me with cold intent. 'Now I suggest you get on and do what you need to do and hand over the drive. I promise I'll make it quick. You won't feel a thing.'

I felt a sick feeling in my stomach. There was no doubt that he intended to kill me, given the opportunity. The man was a cold calculating professional killer. I stood no chance. I felt an overwhelming desire to drop my own gun and surrender to the inevitable. But something stopped me. I had a sudden image of Penny and Jessica weeping at my grave. Of Mario and Emiliana who had risked everything to help me. Of Wayne who had died selflessly saving my life. Of Yacine, brutally murdered by this vicious, traitorous thug. If I was to die at Turnbull's hands, I had no intention of making it easy for him. I raised my gun and pointed it straight back at him.

'You forget that I too have a weapon.' I replied. 'And I must assume that it is loaded, otherwise you would have taken it from me by now. You may well choose to shoot me. But I promise that I will shoot back. It may well be that we will both die, but I have no intention of surrendering this video to you without a fight.'

Turnbull looked back at me coldly.

'Bravo,' he said, sardonically. 'Tell me, have you ever fired a gun before? I'm guessing not, judging by the way you're holding it. You need to be careful of the recoil, particularly on the Glock. Got a hell of a kick to it if you're not used to it. And is the safety catch off? No point trying to shoot me if it won't fire. I, on the other hand, finished top of the class in target shooting. There was even some talk of me representing the UK at the Olympics. Couldn't be bothered in the end though. There's far more satisfaction to be had in killing a man than dangling a medal round your neck on a bit of cheap ribbon. So I would say the odds are very much in my favour. Wouldn't you agree?'

I had to admit, he had a point.

'There's another thing to consider,' he continued. 'I don't suppose you've ever killed anyone before. Not in cold blood anyway. If push came to shove, I don't reckon you could do it. In fact, I'd stake my life on it. I bet you don't even know how to fire the fucking thing.'

And with that, he placed his gun down on the ground in front of him.

'Looks like the odds have shifted in your favour, wouldn't you say?' he asked, his voice once again dripping with sarcasm. 'Except of course, they haven't. Because you're too much of a fucking gentleman to kill me. The guilt would be too much. Gunning down a defenceless man? You could never do it. You'd rather die with your precious honour intact, than kill me, even though you know I'm going to kill you and make your precious Penny a widow. You prick.'

I am sure that had he not added the casual reference to my wife and that personal insult at the end of his supercilious tirade, I would have given up the ghost. But in all my years, no-one had ever spoken to me in that way before. I had been incredibly fortunate so far to survive the vicissitudes of the past week or so, but I was damned if I was going to let this smug, patronising man insult me in such a vile and coarse manner. And so, aiming my Glock carefully at his chest, I shot him three times through the heart.

I will never forget the expression of surprise, bordering on amazement, that flashed across his face as he looked at the red stain that spread across his chest.

'You are indeed the first man I have ever shot.' I told him. 'I very much hope that you will be the last. But I used to shoot at school. I too, was top of the class. I also happen to know that the Glock pistol's safety catch is released by a simple squeeze of the trigger. Goodbye.'

And those were the last words he heard as he slumped forward to the ground, quite dead.

It was perhaps symptomatic of the many privations I had endured since leaving England, that I could have killed a man in cold blood. A week previously, the very thought of committing such an act would have brought me out in a cold sweat. Such were the straits to which I was now reduced, that I felt barely a flicker of remorse at what I had just done. 'Kill or be killed' - this was Turnbull's self-confessed mantra, and thanks to his arrogance and hubris, one which had ultimately led to his own death.

I dragged his body into the nearby bushes. It seemed as if few people passed this way, and I was confident that it would be some time before it was found. Trying not to look the dead man in the eye, I made a cursory examination of his pockets. I found a handful of euros, a mobile telephone and the keys to the car, all of which I stuffed into my own pockets, along with the Glock. I hoped that I would not need to use it for a second time, but I resolved once again that I would get my deadly cargo back to MI6 if it was the last thing I did.

I assessed my situation.

I was some distance away from where Turnbull had killed the policemen, the Russians and Yacine, but there was no doubt that the bodies would have been discovered by now, and every police officer in France would be looking for me. I was a marked man, and following my treatment at the hand of *Inspecteur* Delrieu I had no confidence that the French authorities would look kindly on the notion of returning me to the safekeeping of the British authorities. My only hope was that no-one would associate Turnbull's car with the deaths. If this was the case, and providing there was sufficient petrol in the tank to obviate the need for me to refuel, there was a good chance I could get to the Channel coast and somehow secure safe passage back to England. Exactly how I could do this was unclear, but it seemed like the best plan I could come up with, given the circumstances.

I was suddenly aware of an urgent need to defecate. This was hardly surprising, given recent events. Once more I was able to retrieve the precious capsule, but this time, after giving it a good clean, I resolved to slip it into my pocket.

I returned to the car, and was gratified to see that the tank was almost full. There was also a road map of France on the passenger seat. I had no idea where I was, but Turnbull had indicated that we were heading towards Lyon. I resolved to hit the road until I found signs pointing towards that City, and from there proceed in a North Westerly direction towards the Channel coast, travelling whenever possible by minor roads. I was by no means out of the woods, but at least I felt in control of my own destiny.

I eased myself into the driving seat of the BMW, taking some time to familiarise myself with the left hand drive and the positioning of the controls. Taking a deep breath, I swung onto the main road and set off in what I hoped was a northerly direction. The next stage of my adventure had begun.

I soon established my location. I was some hundred kilometres South East of Lyon, heading in the right direction. My mind was in turmoil. Had I really just killed someone in cold blood? Had the privations I had suffered really transformed me from a man who would run with embarrassment at mis-ascribing a pregnancy, to one who would calmly shoot a defenceless man? Evidently so. And yet, although I knew that I had committed the ultimate crime, that of taking another man's life, there was a more rational and logical part of me that realised I had been faced with no other choice. Turnbull would have killed me, without hesitation, then gone on to betray his country. I was more determined than ever that I would get this video back to London, and into the safe-keeping of the British authorities. But this was only part of what drove me on. The sneering way in which Turnbull had referred to my good lady wife had only served to remind me of the fondness which I felt towards her, and how much I was missing her stable, comforting presence. I was doubly determined to do whatever it took in order that I might see her and Jessica again.

I have already suggested that my relationship with Jessica was a distant one. There is certainly no doubting the strong affection I have for my daughter, and deep down I believe that my feelings are reciprocated. However, I think it would be more than fair to say that we have never really understood each other.

Through her teenage years, she made it increasingly clear that she had no interest in taking over the bookshop once I retired. To my dismay, she had little interest in the theatre, or indeed any form of artistic endeavour. She was altogether more practical, and developed a keen interest in physics, chemistry and the natural sciences. At the age of sixteen, she joined a local sailing club. I spent many a windswept Saturday at South Norwood Lake, waiting to collect her. She always seemed pleased enough to see me once her session had finished, but the car journeys home were usually spent in what I hoped was a congenial silence. Her mother had privately confided that she hoped that joining the Sailing Club would give Jessica the opportunity to meet suitable members of the opposite sex, but she seemed to show little interest in the motley collection of young men who frequented the place, preferring instead to spend time at home in her room, devoting herself to her studies.

Both Penny and I were extremely proud – and not all surprised – when Jessica sailed through her examinations with straight As, and won a place at University. I hoped that the tentacles of the SVR did not stretch as far as Plymouth. Even if they did, I could see no reason why anyone would be interested in harming my beloved daughter. I wondered what she was feeling now, and how she would be reacting to the news that her father was wanted on several counts of murder? Suddenly, I realised that I need not speculate as to this. I had Turnbull's mobile telephone and I knew Jessica's number off by heart. I could call her!

I realised I needed to be careful. The very act of using the telephone would put me at risk of being traced. I had no way of knowing whether or not anyone was interested in Turnbull, but once they found his dead body, there was no doubt that the authorities would take every possible course of action in order to track him down. The sooner I telephoned her the better. I could then put as much distance as possible between me and any potential pursuers.

I veered off the road at the next convenient stopping place. With trembling hands I dialled the number. After a few rings, the call was answered. I recognised her voice immediately.

'Hello?'

I found my voice trembling unexpectedly at hearing my dear daughter's voice.

'Jessica. It's your father.'

There was a long pause.

'Jessica?'

'How dare you call me? I don't ever want to see you again. I hate you, you bastard.'

And with that, the phone went dead.

I was stunned. Never before had Jessica spoken to me in that way. Nor had I ever heard her use profane language. It was hardly surprising, given the notoriety that I must have attracted back home. Tears sprang to my eyes. Now even my own daughter had turned against me. And once news of Turnbull's death reached her, and my part in it, any hope of a reconciliation would be dashed. I was suddenly overwhelmed by the futility of my position. For days now I had battled against the odds in my attempts to make it safely back home, and it had been the thought of seeing my wife and child again that had spurred me on. If this was the sort of welcome which awaited me upon my return, the whole exercise suddenly felt pointless. There was only one thing for it. I must head to the nearest police station, surrender myself to the French authorities, hand over the blessed flash drive, and abandon myself to the French penal system.

My heart felt suddenly lighter at the prospect of an end to my lonely flight. I would argue my case in court and plead innocence to all the crimes of which I stood accused, save that of the murder of Turnbull. Penny and Jessica would have the shop, the house and my modest savings. Even if I never saw them again, they would not be left wanting. I dried my eyes, took a deep breath, and prepared to rejoin the main road. However, before I could put the car into gear, I was startled out of my self-pitying reverie as Turnbull's telephone suddenly started to ring.

Chapter 21.

My first week at Plymouth had been a bit mixed. I'd said goodbye to Dad on the Saturday morning. True to form, he'd not said much. Gave me a hug, muttered about having something in his eye, then carried on sorting out his books. He was always sorting out his books. Used to drive me up the wall. Mum too, I think, though she never said anything. She's always been very loyal where Dad's concerned. Me, I just think he's a bit of a pain, to be honest. Recently, I've started wondering if Mum thinks the same. Not that I'd ever ask her, or that she'd ever tell me, come to that. I thought of saying something as she drove me down to Uni, but the opportunity never arose. So I didn't.

My room in Halls was OK. A bit smaller than I expected. Mum made all the right noises about it being bright and clean, with a nice view, but I could tell she wasn't that impressed. I was at the end of a long corridor with nine other rooms coming off it. At the other end was a shared kitchen, which was pretty big. Mum said that was clean too. Things being clean is a big thing with her. God, if she could see it now, she'd have a fit. A week on and there are dishes in the sink which have been there since day one.

We unpacked my stuff and went to the kitchen to see who was around. There were just two others who'd arrived before me; Will and Andy. Both their parents had already gone, and they were jabbering on about football. They asked me who I supported, and I said 'no-one,' which is the truth, and they both went a bit quiet. I hate football. Mum tried to make polite conversation, but it was all very awkward, and I found myself wishing she'd just leave. Eventually she looked at her watch and said it was about time she was heading back. I walked her down to the car. She gave me a great big hug, and held on to me for a bit too long. At last, she got into the car and drove off. And there I was, at Uni, a proper adult, all on my own, not knowing anyone.

Back at the flat, Will and Andy had been joined by a girl called Amy. It turned out she was from Norwood, which isn't far from Beckenham, and she was on my course too, which was great. Soon we had a flat full. Five boys and five girls. There was a Freshers Meet and Greet at the Student Union that night, and we all decided that we'd go along. To be honest, if I'd been at home, I'd have probably just stayed in and watched a bit of TV. But I knew that if I was on my own in that flat while everyone else was out partying, I'd end up feeling pretty sorry for myself, which is something that happens to me quite a lot. So I made myself go out with the others.

Actually, it wasn't too bad a night. Not at first anyway. We had a talk at the Union from a third year student called Alice. She was quite tall, with long blonde hair, grey blue eyes and a piercing in the side of her nose. I reckon she was a mature student, as she looked a lot older than twenty one. She told us about all the good places to go, and the ones to avoid. After the talk, me and Amy decided to buddy up and we headed for the Vaults, which was a pub on Campus. I decided I'd just drink water. I've never really been one for too much alcohol. Mum and dad don't have it around the house that often, and I guess I've never really got the taste for it. But after an hour or two, Amy had already drunk most of a bottle of wine, and Will, who had tagged along, was on his third pint of beer, so I decided I might as well have one after all. I was about to head for the bar, but Will got all old-fashioned on me (he's from Bolton) and said he'd get them in. He asked me what I wanted, and I honestly didn't know, so he said he'd surprise me.

While he was at the bar, Amy got all confidential. She reckoned Will fancied me, and I was quite shocked. Don't get me wrong – he was quite good looking and very friendly, even though I couldn't understand what he was saying half the time, what with him being from up North. It's just that I hadn't really had that much to do with boys. My mum was always asking if I'd met anyone nice, but the truth was, I hadn't. At least, not nice enough for me to want to have sex with them. And nice though Will was, I couldn't really imagine wanting to have sex with him either. He came back with the drinks. More wine for Amy, another beer for himself, and a tall glass with a colourless liquid in it for me.

I asked him what it was, and he said I had to guess. I took a sniff and it smelt of bacon. Seriously! He laughed and told me it was crispy bacon flavoured vodka, with tonic. He suddenly looked embarrassed and asked if I was a vegetarian. I told him I wasn't, but I wasn't sure if I liked the sound of bacon-flavoured vodka. Amy said I was being a bit of a wuss, and if I didn't drink it, she would. I reckoned it probably wouldn't do her a lot of good to be necking a vodka on top of the best part of a bottle of wine, so said I'd give it a go. To my surprise, it tasted all right, and it left me with that nice warm glow you get when you've had your first drink. In fact, it was so nice, that I soon found myself heading back to the bar to get my round in, which is what Will said was the done thing.

I have to admit, everything got a bit blurry after that. We stayed at the Vaults for a while, then headed into town to a club which was full of other students. Amy disappeared off with some guy and I found myself dancing with Will. After a while, I said I had to sit down, and he headed off to the bar to get more drinks. I told him I'd just have a water as I was starting to feel really drunk. But I'm not sure he heard me, because he came back with another vodka; just regular this time, as they didn't do the bacon flavour. I knocked it back anyway. All of a sudden, the room started whirring, and I realised I needed to be sick quite urgently. I stumbled through the crush, not quite able to put one foot in front of another in a straight line, and just got into the ladies' in time. The cubicles were all taken, so I ended up bending over one of the sinks and throwing up. Some girl said it was disgusting, and that I shouldn't drink if I couldn't hold it, and I got quite upset. But then Alice turned up. The older student from the Meet and Greet. She was really nice. Helped me freshen up and made me drink a load of water from the tap. She asked if I was here with anyone, and we went to find Will.

We caught up with him outside. I immediately felt better, thanks to the fresh air. Will had been worried about me, and was wondering where I'd got to. Alice checked that we knew the way back to our Halls, and he said he thought he did, but he mustn't have sounded too sure, so Alice said she'd walk us back. And she did, which was really kind of her. She left us at the front door, and told us to take care, and that she hoped she'd see us both again some time. We staggered back into the flat. Andy and one of the other guys were chatting in the kitchen. Will asked if I was OK and did I want a cup of tea? I said I thought I'd better be getting to bed and thanked him for taking care of me. I stumbled into my room, locked the door and collapsed onto my bed. As I drifted off to sleep, I could hear the sound of squeaking bed springs and a low moaning noise coming from Amy's room next door. I wondered how Mum and Dad were managing without me, and wished that my Mum was there to look after me. Or if not Mum, then Alice.

■■

After that mad first night, I decided that staying in on my own was preferable to getting drunk and partying every night, though it didn't seem to stop the others. Amy was the worst. The next night she was out again, and ended up coming back with an entirely different guy. Once again, I was lulled to sleep by the sound of her testing out her bed springs. By the time it got to Wednesday, I was getting a bit bored with just staying in to be honest. Lectures didn't start till the next week. I'd been to the Bursar's office and got my University Card, filled in all the paperwork to do with my student loan, and phoned mum and dad every night at eight to let them know I was alright. It was always Dad who answered the phone. He must have known it was me calling, because I called at the same time, but he always sounded surprised that it was me, and immediately passed me on to Mum.

I've never really worked out my Dad. He's very different from all my mate's Dads. He's a lot older for a start, and incredibly old-fashioned. It's almost like he lives in the wrong century. He's not a bad man, and I know that in his own way he cares about me. But we've never really been able to talk about stuff, unless it's Shakespeare, who I do quite like to be fair. And then it's always him that does most of the talking. I know he's disappointed that I don't want to take on his shop when he retires, but I know I'd die of boredom. Science has always been the thing that's excited me. I don't know where I got that from, as both Mum and Dad are more arty. By the time I was thirteen they weren't able to help me with my homework anymore, so I just got on with it. I never really knew what I wanted to do after A levels, until I'd seen this course in Marine Biology. It sounded really interesting, and Plymouth was far enough away from Beckenham for me to feel that I was getting away from home and seeing a bit more of life.

Unfortunately, I wasn't seeing much of life stuck inside my room. So, on the Thursday I decided to head into the Student Union again to see what was going on. There was a load of stalls set up from all sorts of different societies, trying to get people to join. Most of them were sporty: football, netball, rugby, swimming and the like, which isn't really my thing. There was drama, wargames, computers and other nerdy stuff which didn't really do it for me either. Just as I was about to give up, I saw something that really caught my eye. The Sailing Society. I'd done a lot of sailing at South Norwood Lake, but it had never occurred to me that this was something I could carry on at University. And to make it even better, when I got closer to the stall, who should be there, but Alice.

I said hello, not sure if she'd remember me, but she did straight away, and asked how I was doing and was I fully recovered. I must have blushed – something I'm in the habit of doing when I'm embarrassed or nervous - and she told me not to be silly. She confessed she'd been just as bad on her first night too, and I should just forget about it and put it down to experience. Turns out she was really into her sailing, and when she told me all about the stuff they did, I knew I had to join. They even did powerboating too. I signed up there and then. She was really pleased and asked how I was settling in. I said it was alright, but that I was getting a bit bored and couldn't wait to start my course. She said there was plenty of time for that next week, and how did I fancy going out powerboating on Saturday? I was a bit nervous at this, but she said that she was a bit of an expert and she'd look after me. Of course, I said yes. I hardly knew Alice, but something told me that with her, I'd be in very safe hands.

Saturday couldn't come soon enough. I was up far earlier than I needed to be. Unusually, Will was up early too, as he was playing football that morning. He was impressed when I told him what I was doing, and said it was a shame we hadn't seen much of each other that week, and did I fancy going out for a drink that evening? I remembered back to the first night we'd arrived and Amy saying that she thought he fancied me, and although I wasn't sure that I fancied him back, I did like him, and I thought it would be good to have someone to talk to about my day powerboating, so I said yes. He seemed really pleased, and said he'd look forward to it.

Alice had given me directions to the marina where the boats were stored. It was a still, sunny day, and as I looked out over Plymouth Sound I could see countless people out in sailing boats and motor boats, enjoying the early autumn sun. There was a light breeze blowing, and the water looked pretty calm.

Alice was waiting by the quayside, next to a small grey rubber RIB with a massive engine at the back. There was an upright helmsman's console at the front, and a bench seat behind that looked like it could fit three people at the most. She said that there should have been two other newbies joining us, but they'd cancelled, so it would just be the two of us today, and was that alright? I said it was. She fitted me out with a life jacket, and went through a basic safety drill. She warned me that once we were out in the open, we might be going pretty fast, and it would be my job as the only crew member to keep an eye out at all times for any other boats, or obstacles that might get in our way. She settled into the helmsman's seat, fastened a thick red cord around her leg and plugged the other end into a slot on the console. She explained that this was the kill cord. If she lost her balance while she was at the helm and fell into the boat, or even worse, overboard, it would automatically switch off the engine. Then it would be down to me to manoeuvre the boat round to rescue her. I hoped that wouldn't happen, and she said it never had yet, but it was better to be safe than sorry. I agreed.

She switched on the ignition and the engine roared into life. I unfastened the mooring ropes, something I'd done hundreds of times before, when I'd been sailing. Alice was very complimentary and said it looked like I knew what I was doing. Slowly we eased away from our mooring and headed for the open water. She asked me a bit more about myself. Where I was from and what had made me choose Plymouth? I told her about my dad and his shop, and she said he sounded very interesting. I didn't want to be too disloyal, but I did say that of the many words you could use to describe him, interesting wouldn't be one of them. She was in the third year of her English degree, and was actually from Plymouth and still lived with her parents. She'd not known what to do when she finished school and had spent a year working as an au pair in the south of France, then another year helping out in a nursery. Eventually she'd decided to do something a bit more positive with her life and had applied for Uni. She was twenty three.

After about ten minutes, we were out into open water, and she asked me if I wanted to see how fast the RIB could go? Of course, I said yes. She told me to hold on tight, and eased the throttle forward. The roar of the engine got deeper and louder, and the boat started to surge through the water. There was a very light sea, and soon we were skimming through the top of the waves, as the base of the RIB slapped into the water as it leapt forward from wave to wave. My hands gripped the side of my seat, the salty spray washed across my face, and I felt a sense of freedom and excitement that I'd never experienced before. Alice piloted the boat round in a steady fast arc, expertly banking the boat until I thought I might fall out, and I clung on even harder, screaming with fear and exhilaration. Then she eased back the throttle until the boat slowed almost to a standstill. She turned to face me. Her face was happy and shining, and wet with the salt water, and I could see that she'd enjoyed it as much as I had. And it was then that I did what seemed like the most natural thing in the circumstances. I kissed her, full on the lips.

She held the kiss for a moment then broke away, a strange look on her face. I could see I'd made a terrible mistake. I hadn't even thought about whether or not she'd wanted me to kiss her, and now here I was, stuck in an open boat far from the shore having made a complete idiot of myself. There's no way she'd ever take me out again. She might even sue me for assault or something. At the very least I might get a slap in the face. She looked at me, with a strange expression, like she didn't really know what had just happened.

'Have you done that before?' she asked.

'Kissed someone? Of course.'

This was partially true. I had snogged a couple of boys at school, but on each occasion we'd both been very drunk, and after a bit of pointless fumbling, things had kind of ground to a halt.

'Have you ever kissed a woman?'

I thought I'd better be honest.

'No.'

'So why me?'

This was a good question. I wasn't sure I entirely knew the answer.

'Because you've made me very happy, and you've been so nice to me. And ….'

I couldn't say the next bit at first. It seemed wrong somehow, and I wasn't sure what she'd think of me.

'And what?'

We were alone in the middle of Plymouth Sound. There was no-one there to judge me. No-one to laugh at me. No-one to tell my parents. So I came out and said it anyway.

'Because I fancied you.'

She smiled. It was the smile of someone who'd been paid a compliment and liked it. Not a condescending smile - you know the sort of smile that makes you wish you'd never opened your big fat mouth in the first place. She kissed me gently on my forehead and I thought I was going to melt. But then she pulled away, with a much more serious expression on her face.

'Are you gay?' She asked.

'I don't know. I think I might be.'

'You think?'

'I mean, I've been with a couple of boys. Just kissing. But I didn't really like it.' But just then. With you….'

I leant in to kiss her again, but she pulled away, a serious expression on her face.

'Listen Jess. I really like you. But I don't think this is a good idea.'

'Why not?'

She thought for a while, like there was something really important she wanted to say.

'I just don't, that's all. Come on. We should be getting back.'

We returned to the Marina in silence and moored the RIB. It was getting dark now.

'Do you want me to walk you back to hall?' she asked.

'No thanks. I know the way now. Maybe I'll see you around.'

And with that, I turned and walked quickly away, holding back the tears, feeling I'd made a complete idiot of myself and not wanting Alice to see. I realised that I was late for my evening call back home. That would have to wait until I was at the flat and feeling a bit calmer.

When I got back, I immediately came face to face with Will, and to my horror I realised that I'd arranged to go out with him that night. I felt really guilty and started to apologise, but he cut me short and said it didn't matter. He said there was someone there to see me, and almost pushed me into the kitchen, There was a police woman sitting at the table, drinking a cup of tea. God knows where Will had managed to find a clean mug.

She stood up.

'Jessica Cavendish? My name's Claire Peters, from Devon and Cornwall Police. I'm here about your father, Colin.'

Chapter 22.

I wasn't sure what to do or say at first. We stood there; me, Will and the Police Woman - Claire. No-one said anything. Claire looked at Will, and then back to me.

'Is there somewhere we can talk?'

'You'd better come to my room,' I said, hoping I hadn't left it in too much of a mess.

'Do you want me to come too?' Asked Will.

I didn't know what Claire was going to say, or how I might react. I suddenly felt physically sick, like someone had tied a great big knot in my stomach. I knew I needed to do this on my own.

'No thanks,' I said.

I walked down the corridor with Claire following just behind. The rest of the flat was quiet. Everyone else was out, which was a bit of a relief really. We went in. I moved some clothes off the back of the chair which was next to my desk and motioned to Claire to sit down. I perched on the edge of the bed. I could see that Claire was looking nervous. She didn't look that much older than me. Mid-twenties maybe.

'What's happened to dad?' I asked.

'There's been an incident.'

'What sort of incident?'

'Shortly after six o'clock this evening, our colleagues in the Metropolitan Police received reports of a disturbance at your father's shop in London …'

'What do you mean, a disturbance?'

'There were reports of shots being fired.'

I felt the blood rush to my face, and my stomach turned upside down.

'Shots? Is he alright?'

'When officers arrived at the premises, they found a body.'

'Oh my God. Is it dad? Is he dead?'

Claire shook her head and looked at her notebook.

'We've yet to identify the body, but it's not your father's. He was seen running from the rear of the premises with a woman.'

'That was probably Miranda. His assistant.'

'We have spoken to Miranda Newton. She had left the shop an hour earlier. Your father was alone at that point. She had no idea of the identity of the body, or your father's female companion.'

'So where is he now?'

'We don't know. But we are anxious to speak to him in connection with the body found in his shop.'

'You're not suggesting Dad did it? Killed somebody? That's ridiculous!'

'Maybe so. But we do need to speak to him as a matter of urgency. Has he been in touch with you at all?'

'I don't think so. I've been out.'

I checked my phone. There were ten missed calls from mum, and two from Will. Nothing from Dad. I showed Claire.

'He never rings me – he doesn't have a phone. I don't think he even knows my number. But mum's been trying to call.'

'So I see. Who's Will?'

'My flatmate – the one who let you in.'

'And there's nothing more you can tell me about your father's disappearance?'

'He doesn't disappear. That's not what he does. He's regular. Reliable. He doesn't shoot people or run off with strange women.'

'Maybe not' said Claire. 'But if he does try and get in touch, you will let us know, won't you?'

'Of course.'

A horrible thought struck me.

'Do you think he's alright?'

Claire paused briefly before replying.

'At this point, we really don't know. But the sooner we can find him, the sooner we can clear this up. We may need to speak to you again. Are you planning on going away anywhere?'

'My course starts on Monday. I'll need to speak to my Mum. See how she is. I suppose I might have to go home. I don't know.'

She patted me reassuringly on the arm.

'I've got your number, and here's mine.'

She handed me a card with her details.

'I'll see myself out. Now why don't you give your mum a call?'

I got straight on the phone to mum. She didn't know much more than the Police had told me. She'd cooked shepherd's pie, like she did every Saturday, timing it to be ready twenty minutes after dad got home. But he hadn't turned up. She hadn't worried too much at first, thinking that his train was running late, which was not that unusual. But then two hours had gone by. She'd rung the shop, and Miranda, but got no answer from either of them. Just as she was wondering what to do next, the police had come knocking at the door. They were carrying guns!

I said I'd come straight home, but she wouldn't hear of it. She was sure there was an innocent explanation for all this, and she didn't want me to miss out on the start of my course. Dad would be back soon, she was certain, and she was looking forward to hearing exactly what had been going on. She asked me my news, and wondered if I'd 'met anyone', in that casual but annoying way that parents do so very well when they're trying to find out stuff you'd rather not tell them. I suddenly felt very lonely, and wanted to tell her everything. Alice, the RIB, the kiss and my confusion about exactly what had happened. But mum and I didn't really have that sort of relationship, so I just said no. We agreed to talk again the next day.

I hung up and wondered what I should do next. I suddenly felt very alone and very scared. There was a gentle knock at the door.

'Jess? It's Will. Are you OK?'

'Not really,' I said, in a tiny voice, trying to hold back the tears and failing completely.

'Can I come in.'

'Yes.'

I must have looked a right state, sitting on the side of my bed, the tears streaming down my face. Will came and sat next to me, and put his arm around me, holding me close to him and letting my tears soak his shirt.

'Why don't you tell me all about it?' He said. So I did. Not the stuff with Alice, that was too embarrassing. But about my dad disappearing. Shots being fired. The strange woman.

When I finished he was quiet for a while. Then he said:

'I thought you said your dad was really boring.'

'He is. Or at least, I thought he was.'

He asked me if I was planning on going home, but I told him about what mum had said about the course being important. And to be honest, now I'd had a good cry, and told Will all about it, things didn't seem quite so bad. I liked it here in Plymouth, and having finally got away from my boring life in Beckenham, I wasn't really in a hurry to go rushing back.

'Does that make me a bad person?' I asked.

'Of course not. Go home if you need to, but as long as you're here, don't forget you've got friends who'll look after you.'

I thought about this for a minute. The truth is, I didn't really have any friends here. I thought that Alice might be one, but after today, it didn't look as if that was going anywhere. In fact, I was so confused about what had happened out in the RIB, I wasn't sure that I knew where I wanted it to go anyway.

'I'm not sure I have, really. Apart from you.'

'Will I do to be going on with?' he said, with a great big smile.

'Yes' I said, meaning it.

Things were suddenly a bit awkward. He still had his arm around me, and my face was pressed against his tear-stained shirt. I thought for a second that he was going to kiss me, and I decided that if he did, I would probably let him. But instead, he disentangled himself gently and stood up.

'It's late. I should be getting off to bed. Will you be OK?'

'Yes.'

'Great. I'll see you in the morning. Let me know if you hear anything more from the Police.'

'I will.'

'Great. Sleep tight.'

And he left, closing the door gently behind him.

■■

Considering everything that had happened, I slept really well that night. When I woke the next morning it wasn't dad I thought of, or Will. It was Alice. I hadn't set out meaning to kiss her. It had kind of just happened. And in those few seconds, it had seemed like the most natural thing in the world. But when I was in Will's arms, that had felt good too. I wasn't entirely sure what was going on, but I did come to the conclusion that as far as my sexuality was concerned, I was officially confused.

I phoned mum to see if there was any more news, but the phone was answered by a man whose voice I didn't recognise. I told him who I was, and he passed me straight on to mum. She hadn't heard anything. She said the stranger was a Police Officer - a very nice man called Sergeant Bellingham, and that they were screening all her calls. One again I offered to come home, but mum insisted it wasn't necessary. Once again, I was relieved, and I headed to the kitchen to grab some breakfast. I knocked on Will's door on the way, but there was no answer. Amy was in the kitchen, looking a bit the worse for wear, and I asked her if she'd seen him.

'Not since last night when he came out of your room,' she replied, with a great big smirk on her face. 'Told you he fancied you.'

I was about to tell her that she'd got it all wrong, but I decided that if I denied everything, it would only lead to more questions, and I wasn't sure that I wanted Amy and my other flatmates to know about my dad's disappearance and my visit from the Police. So I smiled in a way that I hoped would make me look a bit cool and enigmatic, made myself a piece of toast and a coffee, and took it back to my room.

I tried to do some prep for my first day of lectures next day, but I couldn't concentrate. I wondered what had happened to my dad. It was so unlike him to just disappear and not be in contact. He was such a creature of habit, locked into his daily routines, it must have taken something totally out of the ordinary for him to have not come home, and not even phoned mum to say where he was. In fact, the very thought of him not being at home with mum on a Saturday night was so alien I couldn't get my head round it at all. Of course, if he was a normal person, he would have had a mobile phone so we could ring him, but he'd never seen the point in them. I'd even saved up and bought him one as a present for his 60th birthday. He'd smiled politely, thanked me very much for such a thoughtful gift, then put it back in its box and tucked it away in his desk, promising to look at it later. I never saw it again.

That was my dad all over really. Always very polite and keen to do the right thing. I'd never seen him angry, but then again, I'd never really seen him express any sort of emotion. There were times when I wondered what mum had ever seen in him. I knew he made her angry with his dryness and remoteness, but she was far too loyal and dutiful to ever say anything to me about it. But I could sense it. It would be wrong to say that growing up in Beckenham was an unhappy experience. I'd always felt cared for by both my parents, especially mum. But it had never been a particularly warm or loving home, which was one of the reasons I'd been so keen to come to Plymouth, and why I was in no particular hurry to go running back.

My phone rang.

'Jessica. It's your mother.'

She always said that, even though my phone display had already told me who was calling. I'd tried to explain this to her, but she always forgot. And she was always 'your mother.' Never 'mum.' But that's parents for you. Weird. Well, mine are at least.

'I've had a call from your father.'

'Thank God. How is he?'

'I don't know. I didn't speak to him.'

'Then how ....?'

'Sergeant Bellingham answered. He hung up before he could tell them where he was. But they've traced the call back to a small coastal town in Italy.'

I was shocked. 'Italy? But he's never been to Italy.'

'He has now, apparently.'

'But who does he know in Italy?'

'No-one, to my knowledge. But then again, I wasn't aware that he was in the habit of running from his shop with another woman. It seems there's a lot about your father that I didn't know.'

I tried not to laugh. This was a serious situation, but the thought of dad having either the courage or the inclination to have an affair was unthinkable.

'What are you saying mum? That he's run off to Italy with his girlfriend? Surely you don't think that's a possibility?'

'Honestly Jessica, I don't know what to think.'

'Do you want me to come home?'

'We went through this yesterday. You stay where you are for the time being. The Police have stationed somebody outside the house, so I won't lack company.'

'Police protection? Mum, you're scaring me.'

'I'm sure it's just a precaution. Though against what, I can't be sure. I'll be fine, really. You will tell me if your father's in touch with you, won't you?'

'Of course.'

After she hung up, I sat and tried to think it all through, but none of it made sense. What was my dad doing in Italy? Our trip to France had been a total disaster, and once we'd got back home he'd made it very clear that he would never go abroad again. And why had the Police put someone on guard outside mum's house. Was she in danger? A thought occurred to me, and I looked out of my bedroom window. It was dark, but illuminated by a street light I could just make out a police patrol car, parked outside our block. Surely the Police weren't guarding me too? Or watching to see if dad turned up? But why? What the hell had he got himself involved with?

Chapter 23.

A week went by, and there was no more news. I spoke to mum every day, but she'd heard nothing either. I didn't want to say anything to her, but I was getting increasingly worried. The Police had disappeared from outside my flat after the first couple of days, but Claire checked in with me every day to see how I was doing. She'd stopped asking me if I'd heard anything from my dad, which I thought was strange at first, until Will pointed out that they were probably screening all my calls anyway. I got very paranoid after that, and was extra careful about who I spoke to and what I said.

Actually, there was an awful lot to be said. My dad had disappeared with another woman, and left a dead Russian in his shop, which were possibly the most un-dad like two things that he could possibly have done. Either way, it didn't look good. Had he been secretly having an affair? Had he got mixed up in something illegal that had spiralled out of control? Mum said that the police had been asking questions about his finances, but as far as she was aware, he had no money problems. The shop returned a small profit, and they had no debts that she was aware of. Their joint account hadn't been touched since he had disappeared. And Italy? Italy? He might as well have phoned home from the moon. None of it made sense.

I'd been going to lectures and meeting the other people in my seminar group. I found the work a welcome distraction from my worries about dad. I still thought about Alice from time to time, but whenever I did, I found myself feeling really embarrassed. I'd obviously totally misjudged the situation there, and I dreaded bumping into her around the campus. So far, I'd managed to avoid her.

The communal kitchen hadn't got any tidier, and I'd started taking my food to my room to eat. I washed up my stuff as I used it, but I was the only one that did. Amy was the worst. She must either have been used to living in a pig sty, or else her parents did everything for her. Less than two weeks in and I was already looking forward to my second year when I could move into a communal house. I'd make sure I picked tidy flatmates. I'd just finished a baked potato with tuna, when there was a knock at the door. It was Will. He's been really sweet to me since the news about my dad, and checked in with me every evening. It was good to have someone to share stuff with. He came in and perched on the edge of my bed.

'Any more news?'

''Nothing.'

'I'm playing football this Sunday if you fancy coming to watch.'

I wasn't that bothered about football to be honest, but I thought it would pass the time and stop me worrying so much.

'Great.'

He looked at me, a concerned expression on his face.

'Are you okay?'

'Yeah.'

But clearly, I wasn't. I found the whole experience of someone being nice to me rather unsettling. I felt a big well of sadness rising inside me.

'Only, you're normally chattier than this.'

'Don't be so nice to me.'

'Why not?'

I couldn't really speak. I was worried about my dad, I missed my mum. I was living in a strange place with people I didn't really know, who didn't understand how washing up worked. I had thought I might be gay but ended up making a fool of myself with Alice. A couple of weeks ago I couldn't wait to leave home and my boring parents. Now I just wanted everything to be back like it was before. But none of that came out as words. The sadness got bigger and bigger, until all of a sudden it all came bursting out and I burst into floods of tears.

Will was great. He just put his arms around me and let me cry, until I didn't have any tears left. Then he kissed my wet eyes, which made me want to cry more, but instead I kissed him back on the lips. It felt good. Not as good as with Alice, but good enough, and right then I knew that I needed the comfort that he was offering, and that whatever he wanted to do, I would go along with, because it was better than being alone.

There was a knock on the door and we sprang apart.

'Come in.'

It was Claire.

'Sorry if I'm interrupting something,' she said knowingly as she looked at the two of us sitting on the bed. 'But I've got more news about your father.'

This was the news I'd been dreading. I was sure something terrible had happened.

'Do you want me to go?' asked Will.

'No' I said, grabbing hold of his hand. I needed a friend right now.

'Is he dead?' I asked.

'No,' said Claire, and I felt a wave of relief surge through me.

'Your father was spotted outside the British Consulate in Milan.'

'Milan?'

'Yes. From a study of the CCTV, it looks as if he was trying to gain entry, presumably to hand himself in to the authorities, or to take refuge. Unfortunately, he was intercepted by two men. He escaped with an unknown accomplice.'

'The woman from London?'

'No. A man. The Italian authorities are trying to find out who he is.'

'And the men who were chasing him? Do you know who they are?'

Claire paused before she answered.

'They are known to British Intelligence.'

'Known? Known for what?'

'They're operatives for the SVR . Russia's external intelligence agency.'

I paused to let this sink in.

'Are you seriously telling me that my dad has been captured by Russian spies.'

'No. We think he got away. But these are dangerous men. Let's hope he can get to safety before they catch him. We'll be keeping an eye on this place, so don't worry. And if he does get in touch, you will let me know, won't you?'

I promised that I would, and saw her out. Will was hovering, unsure of what to do or say. I sensed that he wouldn't have minded picking up where we left off when Claire arrived, but I really wasn't in the mood. I told him I needed to ring my mum, and he left me to it, saying we could catch up later.

I barely slept that night. Will had called back in, but I needed some time to think before I went any further with him. Sometimes I spend too much time thinking, and never get round to doing anything. Then sometimes I do things spontaneously, like kissing Alice in the middle of Plymouth Sound, and everything goes horribly wrong.

I went to lectures as normal, and was just heading home at tea time when I had a call from my mum. We'd talked the night before about the Milan thing, and she'd promised she'd ring me immediately if she had more news. And this was big news.

'Your father's been found.'

I burst into tears.

'Is he OK?'

'He's alive, yes. But he's been arrested.'

'In Milan?'

'No, France.'

'But he hates France.'

'I think he'll hate it even more now. He's been arrested for murder.'

The world reeled for a moment and I thought I was going to faint. I had to sit down on a bench.

'Jessica. Are you there?'

'Who is he supposed to have murdered?'

'I'm not sure yet, but the French police seem pretty convinced he's guilty. He's due in court tomorrow.'

'Can we go and see him?'

'I hope so. I'm trying to find out exactly where he is.'

'There must be some mistake mum.'

'That's what I said. Your father may be many things, but he's not a killer. Or an adulterer.'

She seemed less convinced about the adultery bit, but she was right about the killing. There was no way in the world that my dad would kill anyone.

'Mum, this is getting serious. I really think I should come home, even if it's just for a couple of days. We need to talk this through properly. Plan what to do.'

She didn't object this time. Things were moving so quickly, and in such unexpected directions, I needed to be at home for a bit. She offered to come and get me, but I said I'd check out the trains and come back the next day. I promised I'd take care, and that I'd let her know which train I would be getting. I hung up, took a deep breath, and headed back to my flat.

As I walked along the narrow, secluded path towards the main entrance, I noticed a man loitering on the pathway, looking at me carefully. He was middle-aged, and certainly wasn't a student. He was wearing a black coat with a hood, and carried a small blue rucksack slung over his shoulder. I looked around for the police car that had been checking in intermittently, but there was no sign of them. I suddenly felt scared. I was convinced this man wanted to hurt me. Was he a Russian Spy? A French Police Officer? An associate of my father's mysterious Milanese accomplice? He started to walk towards me and I turned and walked in the opposite direction. He followed. I broke into a run. So did he. I was scared now. Really scared.

He called my name: 'Jessica? Jessica Cavendish. It's OK. I don't want to hurt you.'

But I figured that if somebody did want to hurt you, that's exactly what they would say. They wouldn't shout 'Stop right there. I'm going to kill you.' There was no one else around. I needed to get to a place where there were other people and I ran even faster. That's when I lost my footing and fell flat on my face. Within seconds he was looming over me. He had crooked, yellow teeth and he stank of stale sweat and tobacco,

'Who are you?' I asked, terrified. 'What do you want?'

'I'm a reporter. I just wanted to ask you a few questions about your father Colin.'

'You're press?'

'Yes. Sorry if I scared you.'

He reached out a hand, helped me to my feet and produced a battered laminated identity card with a photo and his name and job title: Barry Long, News Reporter, Consolidated News Agency.

'It's an old photo' he said, apologetically. 'I've put on a few pounds and a few grey hairs since that was taken. Is there somewhere we could talk? Your flat maybe?'

There was no way I was letting him into the flat. He was a bit creepy for one thing, and I also wouldn't have put it past him to take photos of the kitchen sink and run a story about unsanitary students.

'I don't really have anything to say,' I replied.

'Really? I take it you know that your father's been arrested.'

'Yes. But I don't see what that's got to do with you.'

He took out his phone.

'I'm just going to record this. You don't mind do you?'

Actually, I did mind, and was about to tell him so, but he continued.

'It's for your own protection. Make sure I don't misquote you. As I was saying, your father has been arrested for the murder of a young man called Wayne Halliday, and connected with the death of two other foreign nationals, one of whom could have been a Russian spy. This is a matter of extreme public interest.'

'Why?'

'Halliday was gay. Did you know that?'

'I didn't even know his name until you just told me.'

'Did your father have any proclivities in that direction?'

'Proclivities?'

'Was he gay? Leading a double life perhaps?'

'What?'

'I can see this has come as a bit of a surprise. Would it be fair to say that you are shocked to discover that your father was caught up in a secret world of international gay espionage and murder?'

'Yes!'

'And I can quote you on that?'

I sensed this whole thing was running away from me. I'd barely come to terms with the fact that my dad had been arrested for murder, and now this complete stranger was trying to put words into my mouth.

'Look, I don't have anything to say to you or to anybody.'

'Are you sure? You're lucky I got to you first. I'm based locally so I've got a few hours on the London-based guys. I represent a major British tabloid newspaper. They'd be prepared to pay good money for your exclusive story. I promise you, the world's press will be beating a path to your door when this gets out. I can protect you. Look after your interests. Make sure we tell your side of the story fairly, and that you walk away with a few quid into the bargain.'

'I'll need to think about it,' I said, desperately trying to buy some time.

'Well don't take too long,' he replied, handing me a business card.

'Call me, any time. I can be here in 10 minutes.'

I took the card and headed towards the flats. He watched me walk in through the front door, and I sensed he wasn't going anywhere until he got the call he wanted. And he would soon be joined by other reporters. If I stayed here, I'd be a sitting duck – and not just for the press either. If he could track me down, so could anyone. I was in real danger. Whatever my dad had got himself involved in was getting bigger by the minute. It was too late to get a train home now. I needed somewhere to hole up - somewhere where no-one could find me. A safe house with someone I trusted. Someone who could protect me.

I headed for the back door, taking out my phone as I walked quickly down the long echoing breeze block corridor. I called Alice.

Chapter 24

Alice lived about 15 minute's walk from my flat, and she told me to come straight round. By the time I got there, I was beginning to regret having called her. As I walked down the tidy, tree-lined suburban road my steps faltered, but when I thought about Barry Long and others like him swarming around asking me questions, I realised there was no going back. It was a nice house, much nicer than your average student accommodation, and I remembered that she'd said she lived with her parents. I rang on the bell, and she came to the door almost immediately. It was great to see her, and she smiled like she was pleased to see me too.

She showed me through to the kitchen. It was the total opposite to the one at my flat: tidy, well-ordered and homely.

'Are you parents here?' I asked, not knowing quite where else to start the conversation.

'Away for a few days, visiting my nan,' she said. 'What's this about Jess?'

I told her the whole story. My dad's disappearance, the police coming to the flat, Milan, my dad's arrest, the murder charge, the spies and Barry Long. When I finished she just sat there, not saying anything for a while. Eventually, she spoke.

'Why have you come here?'

It was a good question.

'Because I needed somewhere where I'd be safe. With someone I trusted. You were so kind to me that first night in the club, when I was drunk. And then, on the boat .....'

I tailed off. This was the elephant in the room.

'Yes,' she said. 'The boat. That kiss.'

'I'm sorry,' I said. 'I haven't stopped thinking about it ever since.'

'Neither have I.'

'I was confused, that's all. About a lot of things. I shouldn't have done it, and I put you in a horrible position, and I'm probably not gay anyway, and you're probably not either, and it was obvious that you thought it was wrong ...'

She looked at me strangely. 'Obvious?'

'Yes. You couldn't wait to get away.'

'That's true.'

'There you go then.'

'Because I was scared.'

I paused for a moment to consider this. Alice had never struck me as being the sort of person who was scared about anything.

'Scared? Of me?'

She smiled.

'Of myself. I was sixteen when I first realised I preferred girls to boys. I had a few little flings. Nothing serious. I came out to mum and dad, and they were pretty good about it, to be fair. When I started at Uni I met this woman called Talia. She was the year above me. We hit it off straight away, and I fell in love with her. Big time. Head over heels. About six months ago I discovered that she'd been seeing some bloke at the same time as seeing me. Hedging her bets, she called it. He'd found out about me and told her she had to choose which one of us she carried on seeing. She chose him. I was devastated. She's moved away now, and I'll never see her again. Not that I'd want to anyway. I'm over her.'

She tailed off, a bit choked up. I wasn't entirely convinced she was entirely over Talia.

'Ever since then I've kept my head down,' she continued. 'Focused on work, keeping myself to myself. Spent the summer messing about in boats. Then I met you, and I thought you were really nice ... really nice. But I'm quite a bit older than you, and my heart's not fully recovered from being broken the last time, and I just thought it was too soon to risk getting it broken all over again.'

'I understand,' I said. 'I'm sorry. I shouldn't have come here ...'

'Yes, you should.' She said quickly. 'And I'm really glad you did. Because I've spent every minute of every day since then thinking about that kiss, and wishing you were here, and that we could do it again.'

I think I told you that my dad's a big Shakespeare fan, and I quite like some of his stuff too, even though I'd never admit it to dad. There's a few things he likes to say which have stayed with me. Whenever I was stuck with a difficult problem at school, or I wanted to give up because it meant doing something outside my comfort zone, he'd always quote Macbeth at me: 'Screw your courage to the sticking place, and we'll not fail.' I thought of my dad now, and I hoped that whatever he was going through, he was following his own advice. And although I wasn't sure what he'd have to say about me kissing a woman, I knew that this is exactly what he'd be saying to me now. So I reached across and kissed Alice tenderly. She kissed me back and wrapped her arms around me, and I felt safe and happy and in exactly the right place. Then she took me by the hand, and led me to her room.

■■

The next morning at breakfast, we talked about what to do next. I wanted to stay with Alice forever, but she insisted I stuck to my original plan and went home to see mum.

'She's going to need you, and you need to plan how you can get over to France and see your dad. You do want to see him, don't you?'

She was right, of course. There was a train to London at midday, and Alice said she'd drive me to the station. I told her I'd need to call into my flat first and pack a bag. I hoped that Barry Long wouldn't be there, and that there wouldn't be other journalists staking the place out. Alice advised me not to talk to anybody until I'd got home. We arrived at the Hall car park and she offered to come in with me, but I decided it would be best if I went on my own.

'I don't want you dragged into this,' I told her, and headed for the flat.

To my relief there was no sign of Barry Long, or any other journalists either. There was also no-one else in the flat, which was a relief. I didn't want to have to explain to them where I'd stayed last night. I thought of Will, and how things could have turned out very differently with him. I threw a few clothes in a bag and headed back to the front door. As I left, I came face to face with Claire. She had a worried look on her face.

'There's been a development,' she said.

'What's happened. Is dad alright?'

'He's fine. But somehow, he's escaped from the French Police. Two officers and his cellmate are dead.'

I could barely take in the implications of what she'd just said: 'And you're saying he did it?'

'I'm not saying anything, not until we know more. Where are you heading now?'

'To the station. I'm going home, to see my mum.'

'That's probably for the best. I'll give you a lift.'

I thought of Alice, waiting in the car park, and I couldn't bear the idea of leaving without saying goodbye.

'It's okay. A friend's waiting in the car park. But thanks anyway.'

My phone rang. I wondered if it was Alice, checking to see where I was. I looked at the number. It wasn't one I recognised.' I answered. To my total astonishment, it was the unmistakeable voice of my dad.

'Jessica. It's your father.'

I froze. I didn't know what to say. Claire looked at me. She must have noticed the look on my face.

'Everything okay?' she asked.

Again, my father's voice: 'Jessica?'

I needed to say something fast, so I did: 'How dare you call me? I don't ever want to see you again. I hate you, you bastard.'

And I hung up.

'Problem?' asked Claire, obviously intrigued. I knew I needed to think quickly.

'Not really. It was my flatmate, Will. I was with him when you came round yesterday.'

'Ah. I thought I was interrupting something.'

'You weren't. But some boys just won't take no for an answer,' I invented.

'Do we need to take an interest?'

'No, nothing like that. But he knows where he stands now.'

'Clearly. But you've got my number, just in case. Are you sure you don't want that lift?'

'No, honestly. I'm fine. I have to go. Thanks. Thanks for everything.'

I headed quickly back to the car, where Alice was waiting.

'I wondered where you'd got to,' she said. 'We need to crack on, or you'll miss your train.'

'I'm not getting the train. Not yet, anyway. Can we go back to yours?'

'If that's what you want.'

'Yes. I need to work out what to do next.'

'Has something happened?'

'Can I borrow your phone'

She handed it over, unquestioningly.

'Thanks. I'm not sure if my phone is being tapped, and I don't want this call traced.'

'Who are you calling?' she asked.

I heard the distinct dialling tone of an overseas phone.

'My dad,' I said, simply.

Chapter 25.

I looked at Turnbull's phone as it continued to ring. I didn't recognise the number on the display. What if it was one of his associates, checking in with him? If I answered, they might want to know what had happened to him. They might be able to trace me. But so what? I was going to hand myself in anyway. What was the point in continuing with my pointless mission, one which had already cost too many innocent lives? I answered the call.

'Hello.'

'It's Jessica.'

Tears sprang to my eyes. There was a kindness and a concern in her voice which I certainly had not detected in our previous call.

'Dad? Are you okay?'

'As well as can be expected, given the circumstances. How are you. And your mother?'

'We're fine. But perhaps you could tell me what the hell has been going on?'

I told her everything. The chance encounter with Anna at Victoria Station, being pursued from the shop, being drugged and dumped in a coffin, my escape from the marble quarry, being pushed from *The Madeleine,* the kindness of Mario and his family, my rescue by Wayne and the discovery of what it was I was carrying. Wayne's bravery, his death and that of Junjie, my flight from the wolves, my incarceration with Yacine and my 'rescue' by Turnbull. I glossed over how I had escaped his clutches, and focused on the fact that I was now free, but with the entire French Police on the lookout for me. I finished, and there was a long silence.

'Jessica? Are you still there?'

'Yes. I'm just trying to take it all in. Those men who died. They say you killed them.'

'I swear I had nothing to do with their deaths. My only hope is that I will be able to convince the French authorities of that fact, once I hand myself in.'

'Hand yourself in? But what about the Rostov video?'

'Too many people have died already. I have faced death myself, and have realised that it is a prospect that I do not relish. I will hand it over to the French authorities, and be done with it.'

'But you're free now. You have a car. You could get to the coast, find a way of crossing the channel. You've come this far dad. You can't give up now.'

I was touched, and indeed rather surprised by my daughter's faith in me. That had been my original plan, and now that I knew my daughter did not hate me, it seemed worth reconsidering.

'Dad, I can't bear the thought of you stuck in a French prison. Get back to England. Hand the video over to someone you trust. There's a police woman who's been looking after me called Claire. I trust her.'

There was logic in what she said, but I still wasn't sure that I had the stomach for it.

'Come on dad. What's stopping you?'

I realised I needed to be honest with her.

'There are some highly dangerous people looking for me. The next time they catch me, I fear that I will not escape alive. A lifetime in a French prison is an infinitely more favourable prospect than the thought of never seeing you or your mother again. That thought scares me more than I can possibly convey.'

'Scared? Come on dad. Remember that thing that Macbeth says? Screw your courage to the sticking post.'

I was deeply touched that she had remembered one of my favourite and often repeated aphorisms, though I felt obliged to correct her.

'It was Lady Macbeth, but the point is well made.'

'Please don't give up dad. We need to think of a plan. But in the meantime, you need to keep moving. Do you remember our holiday in France?'

At the time, my sojourn had seemed like a week spent in the bottom-most pit of hell. I now found myself reflecting back on a time of more innocent certainty with a surprising fondness.

'In Normandy? Indeed I do.'

'Make for there. There were plenty of isolated beaches, unattended boats.'

'Are you suggesting I steal a boat in order to make my escape?'

'I'm suggesting you do whatever you need to in order to get home. You get driving. I'll come up with a plan and call you back.'

There was a brief pause, and then she spoke again.

'I love you dad.'

Never have four such simple words had such a profound effect on me. My eyes filled with tears and I felt a huge sob welling up in my chest. To my eternal shame, I could not remember the last time I had said the same to her. So I did.

'I love you too.'

I disconnected the call, dried my eyes, started the engine, and set off on my long drive northwards.

++

Turnbull's car was fitted with a satellite navigation system, and after consulting the manual I was able to set a path to the small commune of La Hague, my destination on my only previous visit to France. As I have previously said, that holiday had not been a happy one, but Jessica was correct in her assertion that it would make a good departure point for a channel crossing. At this time of year the beaches would be quiet. I would deal with the problem of exactly how I made that crossing once I arrived.

I decided to stay off the beaten track wherever possible and avoid main roads, which would more likely be covered by CCTV. I reasoned that if news of the death of the police officers had reached Jessica, it would also be all over the French news media, and that a photograph of me would be in general circulation. I could only hope that Turnbull's car would not be known to the police. The journey would take about ten hours.

There were still several hurdles to negotiate, not least being able to acquire an appropriate vessel to see me safely over the channel. The more I thought about this aspect of my voyage, the further I sank into despondency. I had never sailed or piloted a boat in my life. How would I find a vessel large enough and with enough fuel to get me across the channel? And which way would I go? What if the seas were rough? As I had discovered on my last trip across the channel, I was not a good sailor. The more I thought about this aspect of the trip, the more I reasoned that it was complete madness to imagine I could possibly be successful.

The phone rang again – the same number as last time. It was Jessica.

'Dad, we have a plan.'

'We? Is your mother involved?'

'No. And I haven't told her I've been in touch with you.'

'But you must. She will be concerned.'

'Dad, she's already concerned. If we knew what we were about to do, she'd be even more concerned, so best she doesn't know. 'We' is me and my friend Alice. She's … someone I met at Uni. Do you remember that little beach we used to go to near La Hague? Baie de la Gravelette?'

I did indeed. A secluded rocky cove with a narrow path descending from the cliffs. It was the one place in France that I had felt comfortable, as it reminded me very much of Cornwall, and was usually mercifully free of any French people.

'It's ideal for what we have in mind.'

'It is indeed most secluded. But as I recall, there were no boats moored there.'

'You won't need a boat.'

'Then how on earth do you suggest that I cross the channel? Swim?'

'Don't be daft dad. We're going to come and pick you up.'

I considered this proposal for a moment. Was my eighteen year old daughter seriously proposing that she would cross the channel in order to rescue me from a French beach?

'That sounds dangerous.'

'Alice's parents have a cruiser which can get across the channel and back, providing we bring plenty of spare fuel. She's done it with them loads of times. We're going to borrow it.'

'Is Alice fully cognisant of the crimes of which I stand accused?'

I detected a little sigh from Jessica. The one she used when she felt that my language was, in her view, unnecessarily verbose.

'Yes dad, she knows. But she's up for it. She reckons that if I think you didn't do it, that's good enough for her.'

'And what about her parents?'

'They're away at the moment. We'll sort it out with them once we get back.'

'Jessica, I'm sorry, but I won't allow it. It's too risky ...'

'Dad. It's your only hope.'

My daughter has always had a way of putting things very simply, and getting to the heart of the matter. In this instance, I knew that she was right, as was so often the case.

'What time do you think you can get there?' she continued.

I glanced at the estimated time of arrival on the Satellite Navigational system. I felt I would also need to factor in some time for resting.

'Some time in the early hours of tomorrow morning.'

'Excellent. We'll cross at night and aim to arrive at first light. We're coming to get you dad!'

She hung up, and with renewed hope in my heart, I continued on my way.

The journey was initially without incident. The roads were generally quiet, and the car was mercifully easy to drive. Turnbull's phone did not ring again, Jessica and I having agreed to keep contact to a minimum in case anyone was listening in to our conversations. The fact that no-one else was telephoning, suggested that Turnbull was acting alone and that no-one was calling him to discover his whereabouts. I pondered on the fact that I had killed him, and although I regretted the loss of life, it was clear that had I not done so, I would have been the one lying dead in the undergrowth.

There had been general surprise from my parents – and indeed myself – when I had discovered an aptitude for shooting. My ex-paratrooper PE teacher, the slightly deranged Mr Proctor, had expressed what I can only describe as disdain when I turned up for his first trial session. I was twelve, and something of an aficionado of Western films, which were a frequent staple on TV screens at the time. I think it is not unreasonable to say that there was very little in my general demeanour that suggested I was anything like the rugged cowboy heroes who I admired.

Mr Proctor was clearly of the same opinion. Our initial practice was with an air rifle. He showed me how to load it, counselled me to be aware of the slight kick from the weapon as it fired, and stood back as I squinted at the small target some distance away, which consisted of ever decreasing concentric circles with a tiny dot of a bullseye at the centre.

'I'll give you sixpence if you can hit the target,' he said, disdainfully.

'The bullseye?' I asked.

'No. The whole thing, you idiotic boy. You'll never hit the bullseye. Miss it, and I want twenty press ups. If you're capable.'

I will come as no surprise to learn that at the age of 12 I had become increasingly accustomed to deprecating and scornful remarks from both my peers and many of my teachers. Then, just as now, I was most unlike my fellow pupils. The rising tide of rebellion and a spurious yearning for a not easily-defined 'freedom' had certainly not affected me. Although I may have given the impression of bearing comments such as these with a certain amount of *sang-froid,* they did cut to the quick, especially at such an impressionable age. I was determined to prove the bully wrong in the only way I knew how. I squinted carefully down the sight of the rifle, steadied my grip and my aim, and squeezed the trigger.

Proctor swaggered down the rifle rage, unpinned the paper target and looked at it carefully. He walked slowly back, and passed the target to me. With his other hand, he reached into his pocket and handed me a sixpence. I looked at the target. There was a small ragged hole, right through the centre of the bullseye.

'Every Thursday after school,' he said simply. 'You've made the team.'

And so my shooting career began. Targets initially, and then a foray into the world of clay pigeon shooting, which I never particularly enjoyed. Mr Proctor continued to be an encouraging if highly sarcastic supporter of mine, and I learned to appreciate the discipline of shooting, and the satisfaction of being good at something. There was even talk of me trying out for representative teams. Sadly, when I was 15, Mr Proctor left the school. Our progressive Head Teacher, who had long been of the opinion that guns had no place in the education system, disbanded the shooting club. I had maintained a scholarly interest in shooting ever since – hence my knowledge of the working of Turnbull's Glock. I offered a silent prayer of thanks to Mr Proctor's sixpence, which had certainly saved my life.

I still had the Glock. Although I had no intention of using it again, I kept it, just in case. A few days previously I had been excruciatingly embarrassed at having offered my seat on a train to an overweight young woman. I was moving in altogether more dangerous circles now.

Chapter 26

The first few hours of my journey passed uneventfully. The roads were quiet, and after the horrors of the last few days I was soon overtaken by an eerie sense of normality. I scanned the radio stations, wondering if I might hear my name mentioned amidst the unintelligible French babble which punctuated music of the most unimaginable dreadfulness. I was sure that there would be a concerted nationwide hunt for me, and even the French police would realise that the channel would be my most likely destination. Late in the afternoon I realised that I was hungry. Stopping to buy food was out of the question, so I pulled over to the side of the road and conducted a thorough search of the car. To my relief I discovered a fresh packet of biscuits and a bag of boiled sweets in the glove compartment, as well as an unopened bottle of water. I ate half the biscuits, savouring their buttery sweetness, and took a welcoming swig of the water. Popping a boiled sweet in my mouth, I continued northwards.

It grew dark, and although I was very tired, I determined to drive on. There were fewer cars on the long, straight roads now. I was approaching the port of Caen, and estimated I would reach my destination in approximately two hours. I could rest then, secure in the knowledge that there would be no-one at the secluded beach. I would be able to see my daughter again, and Penny. I could relieve myself of my dreadful burden, and take whatever punishment was coming my way for the death of Turnbull. I was startled from my reverie by the pinging sound of the car's warning system. I checked the fuel gauge. To my consternation I discovered that I was almost out of fuel. I would certainly not make it to Baie de la Gravelette without more petrol.

I had the euros which I had recovered from Turnbull, but there was no doubt I would be taking an enormous risk by stopping to refuel. I was certain that my photograph would have been widely circulated throughout the country. Given the lateness of the hour, my options would also be severely limited. However, I reasoned that I had no choice. I would not reach safety without more fuel. It was a chance I had to take. As I drove into Caen, the needle on the gauge was hovering on empty. I would need to stop at the first possible opportunity. It was almost midnight now. What if everything was closed?

As I approached the ferry terminal, I was delighted to see a petrol station that appeared to be open. The lights were on, and another car was just pulling away. There was no-one else about, save for a bored looking young man in the kiosk. I found a peaked cap tucked into the driver's side door compartment and pulled it low over my forehead. I checked my money supply. I had forty euros, which would buy enough fuel to see me safely to my goal. I eased myself stiffly out of the car, and started to refuel. I glanced over at the young man. He was gazing at his mobile phone, not even looking in my direction. I stopped at the forty euro mark and replaced the filler cap.

It was late, so the main shop was closed. I would need to make my payment through a hatch at the side of the building. Trying to appear as nonchalant as possible I put the notes through the window. The young man muttered his thanks, barely looking at me as he did, and with some relief I turned and headed back to the car. It seemed as if I had safely negotiated the one remaining perilous moment in my journey to safety. I started the engine and glanced in my mirror. I could see the young man looking over in my direction. There was an expression on his face – one of dawning recognition – and with absolute certainty I knew that he knew exactly who I was.

I had the Glock. There was no-one else around. I briefly considered shooting him before he could alert anyone. But as soon as the thought entered my head, I dismissed it. Too many innocent people had already died because of me. I saw him frantically dialling a number on his phone and realised I needed to escape immediately. The police would soon be after me, and I needed to do whatever I could to throw them off my trail. I swung the car back onto the main road and headed back in the direction from whence I had come, heading away from the Baie de la Gravelette.

I have always prided myself on my ability to keep a cool head in a crisis, and as I headed out of town I realised that the decisions I made now would materially affect the likeliness of my making it to the coast or not. I had to assume that the man in the garage had the number and description of my car and my direction of travel, and that by now the local police would be out looking for me. The first thing I needed to do was to get off the main road on which I was travelling – in the wrong direction - and find another route to the Baie de la Gravellette. I came to an intersection and headed in what I hoped was a westerly direction. The road was deserted, and after driving for twenty minutes or so I found myself in open country. I pulled over, and reconfigured the navigation system to avoid all major roads. The remoteness of my location was both an advantage and also my biggest chance of being apprehended. With so few cars about, the police would be bound to investigate any car found driving along remote lanes in the middle of the night.

I continued to drive, but as each moment passed, the gravity of my situation impressed itself even more deeply into my troubled mind. There seemed no doubt at all that the countryside would soon be swarming with police. It was only a matter of time before I was captured. My only hope was to drive as fast as I could to my destination where I could hide out and await Jessica's arrival. I pressed my foot hard on the accelerator and urged the car forwards through the narrow lanes.

I don't know if it was the darkness or my fatigue, but I failed to see the young woman until I was almost upon her. She was standing in the middle of the road, waving me to stop. I barely had time to register a rickety van pulled over on the verge before I slammed on the brakes and spun the steering wheel to the right in a desperate, last minute attempt to avoid hitting her. The next thing I knew the BMW had ploughed through a hedge at the side of the road before coming to rest nose down in a shallow ditch. A large air bag inflated in my face, cushioning my head as it snapped forward, and a few scant seconds after I had spun the wheel, the car came to a juddering halt.

Everything had happened so quickly. I may even have lost consciousness for a few moments. I was aware of the woman's face at the widow, her hand scrabbling at the door. She said something in a language I didn't understand, and I realised that the door was locked from the inside. My hand groped for the handle. It was dark and at first and I couldn't see it. Eventually I eased it back and she yanked the door open. I unclipped my seat belt and half climbed, half fell onto the ground outside. I staggered to my feet, dazed by the suddenness of everything. I was aware of the young woman looking at me, a worried expression on her face. On the road behind her, two small children looked anxiously on, a young boy and a slightly older girl. The younger one started to cry. The woman said something unintelligible, and the older child comforted him.

The woman looked at me.

'*Francais*?' she asked.

'English.'

'You okay?' she continued, switching effortlessly to my own language.

'I think so,' I replied, hopeful that those simple words were not the full extent of her English. I turned to look at the BMW. The front was a crumpled mess and steam rose from the bonnet. One wheel was badly twisted. Whatever else was about to transpire, there was certainly no way I was going to be driving anywhere else tonight. It looked as if my flight back to my family was at an end. I felt an enormous wave of sadness and fatigue overwhelm me. My knees buckled and my head span. The young woman saw what was happened and reached out towards me, but as she caught hold of me, I collapsed to the ground and everything went black.

■■■

I came too, to see the concerned face of the young woman looking down at me as she mopped my forehead with a damp piece of cloth.

'Welcome back,' she said.

'How long was I out for?' I enquired.

'Just a few minutes.'

'I have to get moving,' I said, struggling to get to my feet.

'I wouldn't advise it. You're concussed I think.'

'But I have to get to the coast.'

'So do I. But my van is out of petrol, and your car is going nowhere. And you're in no condition to drive anyway.'

'I am fine,' I said, certainly not feeling it.

'You British,' she said, with a smile. 'No matter what disaster comes your way, you insist you are fine. I am sorry I cannot offer you a cup of tea. I am sure that would make everything better. What is your name?'

'Colin,' I replied. I felt it unnecessary to give her my full name, but neither was I inclined to lie.

'Hello Colin,' she replied. 'I am Amira Bahar. I am a doctor, so forgive me if I do not agree with your opinion that you are fine. Ideally, you need to get to a hospital.'

'That's not possible,' I replied. 'I have to be somewhere. To meet someone. To catch a boat.'

She looked at me curiously.

'But you are heading away from Caen. There are no ferries in this direction.'

'Not a ferry. It's my daughter. She's … picking me up. Taking me home. At least she was.'

I realised that would never happen now. We were in the middle of nowhere. It was dark and the road was empty, but once dawn came someone was bound to pass by, and that would be it for me. Game over.

'And why travel so fast in the dead of night?'

I paused for a while. It was clear that she had no idea who I was, and it certainly was not in my best interests to inform her that I was a wanted killer, on the run.

'It's complicated,' I replied, simply. I studied her carefully. I guessed she was of Middle Eastern origin, judging by her skin tone, accent and the scarf wrapped around her head.

'I might ask you the same question. Why is a young lady such as yourself at loose in the middle of the French countryside with two small children?'

'It is also complicated. But I think that Allah has intervened on both our behalfs tonight.'

'What do you mean?'

'He must have done. There can be no other explanation, and I speak as a rational scientist.'

'You have lost me I'm afraid.' I replied. And she had. It may have been the concussion, but nothing she was saying made any sense at all.

'You see, I too am travelling to meet a boat, with my children. Like you, I travel under cover of darkness, because I do not wish to be found.'

'But that is an astonishing coincidence.'

'Maybe. But my religion says that there is no such thing as coincidence. There is wisdom in everything. The wisdom of God. I think he has sent us both here for a reason.'

'Madam, I wish no discourtesy to your God or your religion, but if this was His plan, I fear it has not been properly thought through.'

She smiled at me.

'I think it is you who is not thinking things through, Mr Colin. We are both heading in the same direction, for similar reasons.'

'But how can we continue? You say you are out of petrol, and my car is undriveable.'

'Indeed it is. But I assume it has petrol in the tank?'

'Yes.'

'Then our problems are solved. You strike me as being a fine English gentleman. I assume you have never siphoned petrol from a car?'

I had to confess I had not.

'Then you are about to learn a new skill. And when we have filled the tank in my van, we will continue on our way together and we can discuss our respective destinations. You do not need to tell me your reasons for your journey, but I will certainly tell you mine once we are under way. Now come. There is much to do.'

Amira worked with a calm efficiency which I could not help but admire. I was still feeling groggy, and was happy to watch her as she went about her business. From the recesses of her van she produced a thin rubber pipe and a jerry can. I had no idea why she was travelling with these items, and felt it best not to ask. She was certainly unlike any other doctor I had ever met. In a matter of minutes she had filled the can with petrol from my stricken vehicle, and replenished the tank in her own.

'I hoped we would have enough petrol to get to my destination,' she explained, as she worked. 'I'm so glad you came along when you did. I'm sorry about your car though.'

'Actually, it's not mine,' I confessed.

She gave me that quizzical look again, studying me intently with her dark brown eyes.

'I didn't have you down as a car thief.'

'I would prefer the term 'borrowed.''

'And does the person you 'borrowed' it from know that you have it?'

'No,' I answered, in all honesty. Turnbull would never know anything ever again.

She looked me dead in the eyes.

'I'm about to let you into my van with my two young kids. Can you give me one reason why that might be a bad idea?'

'On my honour, you have nothing to fear from me madam. Although, if we are apprehended by the police, you may well be guilty by association.'

'That would only be the case if I knew what you'd done. Why you 'borrowed' this car, why you're on the run from the police, and why you're travelling to the coast in the dead of night.'

'That is true.'

'So, I think it's best that you don't tell me. Now come on. We need to get going.'

Chapter 27

The van was old, and certainly not as well equipped as the BMW. There was no navigation system, but Amira did have a road map, which she gave to me so I could show her the way. Her destination, another secluded bay further up the coast, proved to be some kilometres beyond mine, but she agreed to drop me off *en route*. It was four o'clock in the morning, and her children slumbered in the rear of the van as we drove through the remote countryside. I estimated it would be light in some three hours. If we could make the Baie de La Gravelette without being stopped by the police, I could still be back in England by lunch. I thought of telephoning Jessica, but we had agreed to have no contact with each other until we were both at the rendezvous point.

'I'm from Syria,' said Amira. 'I'm trying to get to England. I was at medical school in London, and I have I have a brother living there.'

'Why did you leave Syria?'

'Because there is nothing there for me anymore. Literally nothing.'

Her voice choked as she spoke, and I sensed that she was struggling to suppress some deeply felt emotion.

'I am sorry to hear that.' Please do not feel you have to tell me more.'

'I'd like to,' she replied. 'Truth is, I *need* to.'

I fell silent, and let her speak.

'I am from Aleppo. You've heard of it?'

Of course I had. Anyone watching the television news, as Penny and I did on a regular basis, would have heard of that Syrian city and the terrible destruction that had been visited upon it.

'I returned from medical school to work at one of the hospitals there. That's where I met my husband. He was a doctor too. I took time out to have the children, but with my mother's help I was soon back at work. Aleppo was a great place to live. A multi-cultural melting pot. There were disagreements, but in the main, everybody got on. Then the war came. Pretty soon it seemed like everyone had joined in. Mujahideen, Al Nusra, Hezzbollah, the Kurdish Front, the Russian Air Force, ISIL, Al Qaeda; fundamentalist nutjobs from all over the world were having one big killing party in my city. And at the hospital, we saw the consequences every day. Dead children. Severed limbs. Shrapnel injuries. Shootings. Stabbings. Beheadings. Chemical attacks. Then one day, they bombed the hospital. I was there when it happened. Hundreds died. My husband was one of them, crushed in the rubble. I held his hand as he slipped away. I got the hell out as fast as I could. It was tough leaving my mother, but she said I should leave while I could. 'Go to your brother. You'll be safe there,' were the last words she said to me.'

'I was one of the lucky ones. We went to Turkey first. I had money, so I was able to pay a man for a passage from there to Greece. Fifty of us in a rubber dinghy, but the sea was calm and we made it okay. The same guy has contacts in France, and he said they could get us over the channel. There's a boat waiting for me when I get there. I paid him up front, so I hope he's not lying. With what little cash I had left, I bought this van. That was a week ago. I could tell you stories of things that happened from there to here, but I won't. Even with kids, a woman travelling alone is seen as fair game by some men.'

'So why help me then? You could have left me by the side of the road.'

'It's a good question. Two reasons. Firstly, you could have run me over when I was trying to flag you down. But you didn't. You drove off the road instead. So fundamentally, that tells me you are a decent man.'

'And the second reason?'

'I don't know what, or who you're running from, but I know a refugee when I see one.'

I considered this remarkable statement for a few moments.

'I certainly do not see myself in those terms. I am happily married, with a daughter, my own home and a successful business. I live a well-ordered, sequestered and entirely uneventful suburban life.'

'In that case, what are you doing scurrying around Normandy in the middle of the night in a stolen car, looking to make what sounds like an illegal trip to the UK? Hardly the actions of a suburban English gentleman.'

I had to admit that she was right.

'Would you have done the same?' she asked. 'If our roles were reversed?'

'A fortnight ago, most certainly not, if only because never in my wildest dreams could I have imagined such circumstances arising. However, these last few days have been elucidating, to say the least. My journey across Europe has not been as lengthy as yours, nor its origins so perilous, but it has certainly had its moments. I have met some remarkable people on my travels, and you, my dear lady, are yet another one. I most certainly would have done the same for you, and considered it a great honour to be able to assist you.'

'There you are then,' said Amira. 'It is the will of God.'

We drove in silence. I was very tired, but resisted the temptation to sleep. There would be plenty of time for that soon enough. My destination grew ever closer, and I even began to recognise a few landmarks from my previous visit to the area. We had not seen a single vehicle since abandoning the BMW, and it seemed as if, remarkably, I had managed to evade police pursuit by the fortunate expedient of swapping vehicles. No sooner had this thought entered my head than it proved to be premature, as in the distance, from the direction in which we had travelled, we could hear the sound of a fast-approaching siren.

'Shit,' said Amira, simply. Even I had to admit that this was a very accurate summary of our situation. We were on a long straight road, and as I craned my neck to look, I could see blue flashing lights heading towards us. Amira pressed her foot hard on the accelerator, but there was no way her rickety old van was going to outrun a police car.

'How far to where I drop you?' she asked.

'Two kilometres at the most.'

'Looks like you'll be finishing your journey on foot' she said as we approached a bend in the road.

'Soon as I get round that bend, I'll slow right down. That's when you jump out. I think it will be at least a minute before they catch me. And when they do, I'll deny ever having seen you.'

'Madam …..'

'It's your only hope. I'll take my chances with the Police, but it's obvious that it's you they're after. I've no idea what you've done, but I hope you get back to your family. Now get ready.'

Of course, she was right. I had one last chance of making it to meet Jessica, and this was it. The car skidded round the bend and she slammed the brakes on. One of the children awoke with a frightened squeal. I opened the side door as the car slowed almost to a halt.

'Thank you,' I shouted, as I jumped.

'Don't thank me. Thank God,' she replied. The door slammed shut, and she was gone, gathering speed as she did. I heard the sirens getting ever closer. There was a shallow ditch running parallel to the road, and I rolled into it, pressing myself low to the ground as a police car hurtled past in pursuit of the van. It would catch her very soon, and I needed to get as far away as I could in case they came back to check. Crossing the road, I set out across country, towards the sea, and what I hoped would be salvation.

There was a full moon that night, which afforded me just enough light to find my way across the fields which lay between me and my destination. The sirens had stopped now, and I had no way of knowing if the police had arrested Amira, or indeed if they were still looking for me. Either way, they were in the area, and perilously close to my point of departure. I wondered if they would have boats out at sea, in anticipation that I may be trying to make my escape that way. It seemed a reasonable supposition, but I was prepared to take my chance if I could only get to see my daughter again. I resisted the urge to call her. I would wait until I was in position on the beach, and was entirely certain that there was no-one else there. But why would there be? The location was remote and secluded. There would be no reason for anyone to be out and about at this hour of the night.

I scrambled across and through a series of hedges until I arrived at a path which followed the cliff's edge, descending gradually. I peered out to sea, looking for the signs of an approaching boat – a light perhaps – but there was nothing. I hoped that some misadventure had not befallen Jessica and her friend Alice. Jessica was barely out of school, and the thought of two young people crossing the world's busiest shipping channel in the dead of night was not without risk. If anything happened to her because of my stupidity I would never forgive myself.

A narrow path diverged from the one on which I was travelling. I followed it as it wound its way downwards to the beach. I could hear the gentle lapping of the waves beneath me. I reached the beach, a small strip of rocky shore some one hundred metres in length. As I had predicted, it was entirely deserted. I pulled the capsule from my pocket, and unscrewed it. I popped the tiny flash drive into the palm of my hand. It seemed remarkable that I had stumbled upon such a thing, and somewhat miraculous that I had managed to bring it this far. I was more determined than ever to hand it over to the British authorities. I still had the Glock, and decided that I would retain it until I was safely on board. There was an autumnal chill in the air, and I hoped that the boat had a cabin, and a bed. I was dog tired, and for the first time ever in my life, I felt old. I had seen such things over the last few days, this was hardly surprising.

There was a glimmer of light beginning to appear in the Eastern sky. Returning the capsule and its precious contents to my trouser pocket, I took out my telephone and called my daughter. She answered immediately.

'Dad. Are you there?'

'I am indeed.'

'And you're okay?'

I felt that a small white lie might be appropriate, given the circumstances: 'Never better.'

'We're five minutes away. Alice says there are too many rocks to get the boat to shore. We can get pretty close, but you might have to swim out. We've brought a change of clothes.'

'I am sure I can manage that. I await your arrival with keen anticipation.'

'Good.'

She hung up.

I stood at the water's edge, peering into the gloom, trying to see the approaching vessel. I heard it before I saw it, a faint spluttering sound as the boat eased itself gently towards the shore. And then I saw it, emerging from the darkness. It was a handsome looking craft, some thirty feet long, with a raised cabin at the rear and every evidence of sleeping accommodation towards the bow. Her name was emblazoned in decorative scroll across the bow. *Plymouth Princess*. A young lady who I assumed to be Alice was at the helm, and my beautiful daughter Jessica stood at her side, waving.

I was overjoyed to see her, and choked back a sob. This was no time for excessive displays of emotion. I started to wade out to sea. The water was cold, but at that moment I would have dived into the iciest Ocean if it meant getting safely onto that boat. The seabed shelved away beneath my feet and I broke into a gentle front crawl. How different this was to the last time I had been swimming. At that point I had faced what seemed like certain death. Now my salvation was a few yards away. I reached the boat, which had a conveniently placed ladder leading into the water. I clambered aboard, as Jessica ran to meet me.

She wrapped her arms around me, soaked though I was.

'I'm wet,' I said, aware as I said it that I was stating the obvious, and that neither of us cared anyway.

'I'm sorry dad,' said Jessica. 'Really sorry.'

'I don't understand.'

'She said she'd shoot Alice.'

'Who?'

'I think she means me,' came a familiar voice from the rear of the cabin. 'Nice to see you again Colin. I'm hoping you still have something that belongs to me.'

She stepped into the silvery dawn light. She was holding a gun, which was pointed straight at me. It was Anna Orlov.

Chapter 28

'Surprised to see me eh?' asked Anna, superfluously.

'Indeed. I thought you had died in the explosion.'

'I got out of the van before it went into the tunnel. Thought I'd get my car and drive round another way. Head you off at the foot of the hill. Shame about Sergei. He was a good man.'

That had hardly been my recollection of the hulking brute, but I let it pass.

'His death slowed me down a bit. I got into town just in time to see you being taken by Vasiliev's men. I was pretty sure I'd never see you again, but I thought I'd lie low for a while, just in case. It suited me if guys like him thought I was dead. Then word got out that you were still alive. Interesting and impressive trail of carnage you left behind you, by the way. Given that everyone was still after you, I figured you still had the flash drive. Who ambushed those policemen? Was it Aaron?'

I nodded.

'And you've lived to tell the tale?'

'As you can see.'

'Then I guess he's dead, because if he was still alive, you wouldn't be.'

'So how did you end up on this boat?'

'I'd been having your daughter watched in Plymouth.'

'The CIA has long tentacles.'

'I have …. contacts. In this case, a local hack called Barry Long. He let me know she'd been behaving a bit strangely. Like she was hiding something. Didn't take much to work out that the two of you were in contact. Which meant there was a very good chance she would lead me to you. I got to Plymouth just in time. It's amazing how easy it is to convince kids they should do what you say. Guns can be very persuasive. Talking of which, do you have one by any chance.'

I hesitated for a moment. She turned and held the gun to Alice's head.

'You've got five seconds. Five, four, three …'

I produced the Glock and handed it over. Jessica's eyes widened when she saw it.

'I'm so sorry dad,' she repeated.

'None of this is your fault,' I replied.

'It isn't about fault, or blame,' interjected Anna. 'It's business. Now, as you've made it this far, I'm assuming you still have the video.'

I had to think fast. I could feel the capsule burning a hole in my pocket.

'Indeed I do. It had been my intention to hand it in to the British authorities on my safe return to England.'

'Sadly, that's not going to happen. But give it to me now, and I'll let you go.'

'How do I know you are telling the truth?'

'You don't. But if you don't hand it over, I'll shoot you all anyway. So if you do it my way, at least you know you're in with a chance.'

I looked at my daughter, and Alice, to whom I had not even been formally introduced. I considered my duty and obligation to my country. I knew there was only one thing to be done.

'It seems as if I have no choice. Nothing is more important to me than the life of my daughter.'

'I knew I could rely on your sense of decency. Now hand it over.'

'Alas, that will not be possible for another thirty six hours.'

A look of exasperation came over her face. 'It must have come out by now!'

'Several times. But I simply swallowed it again. The last time was just before I swam to the boat. How else do you think I still have it in my possession?'

Anna studied me carefully, trying to work out if I was telling the truth or not. I held her gaze.

'Looks like we're back to square one then,' she said, after a few moments.

'It would seem so.'

'But just to be on the safe side, I'm sure you won't mind if I search you. It'd be a real shame to wait all that time and then discover you had it all along. Turn out your pockets.'

I stood my ground, desperately trying to buy more time, but I could see that Anna was fast running out of patience.

'For Christ's sake Colin, do we really have to do it the hard way. I've liked you pretty much from the moment we first met, and nothing you've done since then has made me like you any the less. Looks like you daughter's cut from the same cloth too. But you know I'll kill you all if I have to, and I'd really rather not. I need that video.'

'I'm sure it's worth a fortune to the CIA.'

'I'm not CIA. At least, not any more. The Agency would like to use that video as a trade off with the Russians. Turns out they have some pretty hard core stuff of their own, featuring the incompetent clown currently running the White House, but I've got my own uses for it.'

'Which are?'

'Why should I tell you?'

'When I eventually hand over the video, I would at least like to know what you intend doing with it.'

She looked at me for a moment. A seagull screeched overhead. The gloom was lifting now, as dawn broke over the Channel.

'You'll find out soon enough anyway, so I guess there's no harm. I'm not interested in keeping its contents secret. I want to expose Rostov to the world, for the hypocrite he is. I want him disgraced, humiliated and laughed out of the Kremlin. Then I'm going to find him and kill him.'

There was a clear-eyed determination in her eyes that suggested she was entirely serious.

'Why?'

'Because he killed my parents.'

'I am sorry to hear that.'

'Yeah, me too. You know Rostov was head of the KGB before he became President?'

I nodded assent.

'My dad worked with him. Alexander Spetznov. For a time they were friends, but my dad got increasingly concerned about Rostov's behaviour. Don't get me wrong, dad was no saint, but Rostov took brutality to a whole new level. People who stood in his way started to die. They fell from hotel balconies, got smashed up in car accidents, accidentally electrocuted themselves or drank tea laced with Novichok. My dad started speaking out, letting Rostov know he disapproved. I was ten years old, my dad came to my school in the middle of the day, saying he needed to take me home as my grandma was very ill. But we didn't go home. He put me in his car and drove out of the City to an airstrip. There was a private jet waiting, and he bundled me on board. I was getting worried now. I wanted to know where we were going, and where my mom was, but when the plane took off, we were the only passengers. In the air, he told me everything. My mom was dead. Officially, she'd taken an overdose, but dad knew this was Rostov's way of warning him off. He took me to the USA, did a deal with the Americans, claimed political asylum. We were given new identities and started a new life together.'

'You said Rostov killed both your parents.'

'They tracked him down eventually. I was away at University, and I got a call from a neighbour saying dad had been shot dead in a botched burglary, but I guessed what had really happened. That was fifteen years ago. I vowed I'd get revenge on Rostov, and figured that the best way of getting near him would be to join the Agency. They were very pleased to have me. I had a good back story, spoke fluent Russian. They changed my identity again, and posted me to London to see if I could infiltrate known Russian agents operating there. And so I waited, extending my range of contacts, playing the long game. No-one knew I was Alexander Spetznov's daughter, otherwise I wouldn't have lasted five minutes, especially once Rostov became president. Then we got news of the video. I knew this was my chance. I used Agency money to pay Platonov, but there's no way it's ending up back in Washington. I'm giving it to the press. I don't want it buried away and used to bail out our narcissistic Commander In Chief. And when it's done, and he's finished, I'm going to go back to Russia and put a bullet in Rostov's head.'

The seagull screeched again. Jessica stood by my side. Alice was still at the helm, off to one side, not moving a muscle. The swell was rising as the boat rocked gently from side to side. Somewhere in the distance I heard the sound of another boat. No doubt a local fisherman heading out to sea, totally oblivious to the drama being played out on the *Plymouth Princess*.

I knew then that I was going to have to give her the capsule. I also knew, with a chilling certainty, that there was a very good chance she would kill me, my daughter and Alice. Why else would she have casually divulged the name of her contact in Plymouth unless she knew the information would go no further? But at that point, I had had enough. I reached into my pocket and pulled out the capsule. She reached out for it greedily, but I withdrew my hand.

'Do I have your word that if I give you this, we will not be harmed?'

'You're hardly in a position to make demands, Colin.'

'Anna, I hope that in our brief acquaintanceship you have been sufficiently cognisant of my innate sense of decency, and the respect with which I regard members of the opposite sex. I am not making a demand, merely a humble request.'

Anna smiled and looked at Jessica.

'Does he always speak this weird shit?'

'Yes,' my daughter replied. 'Actually, I quite like it,' she added, defiantly.

'Do you '*actually*" Anna replied, scornfully. 'Well I don't. I might kill you, I might not. But if you don't hand that over now, I'm putting a bullet in your daughter's head. Practice for Rostov, if you will. So please. Give it to me now.'

She casually placed the gun against my daughter's temple. Jessica stood there, frozen with fear.

'Daddy, please.'

She hadn't called me daddy since she was seven. I saw Anna's finger tightening on the trigger, and slowly reached my arm out, the capsule glistening in the dawn light. A look of triumph flashed across Anna's face as she reached out for the capsule and took it in her hand. But the look of triumph turned to one of stunned incomprehension as she staggered forward under the fearsome blow of the fire extinguisher which Alice had just brought crashing down on her head. The gun dropped from Anna's hand, and as she fell stunned to the deck of the *Plymouth Princess*, so did the capsule. As the boat tipped in the gentle swell, it rolled across the deck before coming to rest at the very edge of a small drainage port cut into the edge of the deck.

My first thought was to retrieve Anna's gun. She did nothing to stop me, so I proceeded to recover my Glock at the same time. Anna was shaken and disorientated, and for the time being at least, incapable of movement. Alice stood there, ashen faced, astonished at what she had just done. I knew she needed her to snap out of it, and I needed her help.

'Alice,' I said. 'That was brave of you. I think you may well have just saved our lives. May I ask you if you could be so kind as to find something with which we can safely secure Miss Orlov? When she regains her senses, I fear she may not be too kindly disposed towards any of us. Pleased to meet you, by the way.'

Alice smiled back at me. 'Likewise,' she said, and headed into the depths of the boat. Meanwhile, Jessica had her eyes fixed on the capsule, which teetered at the very edge of the drainage port. A small movement in the wrong direction and it would be lost.

'I'll get it,' said Jessica.

She edged her way across the deck. Her hand reached out towards the capsule, but as she did, a small wave washed against the side of the *Plymouth Princess*. The boat yawed, and the capsule tumbled overboard. Anna had seen the whole thing. She let out a wail of protest and suddenly launched herself across the deck, her hands flailing, reaching out to grab the capsule. But she was too late. It was gone, lost in the depths of the Channel. With one last cry of rage and frustration Anna was gone too, disappearing beneath the waves with an almighty splash.

I looked around and saw a lifebelt lashed to the side of the boat, I threw it into the water, and prepared to dive in after her. Whatever my views on Anna Orlov, I was not prepared to let a concussed woman drown. But I felt Jessica's hands pulling me back.

'Are you mad?' she asked.

'I can't just leave her,' I shouted in response.

'I think you might have to,' cried Alice, as she emerged from the cabin with a coil of rope. She pointed out to sea. The sound of the other boat was louder than before, and seemed to be heading in our direction. I followed her pointing finger, fully expecting to see a police launch, or a French naval vessel. But the boat which was approaching, a few hundred yards away, was one I had last seen in the slightly warmer but equally perilous waters of the Mediterranean. It was the *Madeleine*, and at the prow stood the stocky figure of Pyotr Vasiliev. Even from that distance, I could see that he was not best pleased to see me.

As we watched, Anna rose spluttering from beneath the waves and grabbed hold of the lifebelt with her outstretched hand. To my utter astonishment, in her other hand she held the capsule. I saw the look of triumph on her face, which was quickly replaced by one of concern as she saw the *Madeleine* bearing down on her.

'Thanks Colin,' she shouted, and I swore she winked at me as she placed the capsule in her mouth and swallowed it.

'No!' cried a distraught Jessica. But now was not the time to dwell on Anna and the capsule.

'Alice,' I shouted. 'I am not sure what the top speed of this boat is, but I feel it would be an excellent idea if you were to put as much distance between us and our pursuers as possible.'

As if to reinforce the urgency of my request, Vasiliev produced a pistol from his pocket and squeezed the trigger. Almost simultaneously, a bullet embedded itself somewhere in the side of the *Plymouth Princess*. Alice jumped for the controls, and with admirable calmness and no little skill, sent the plucky craft surging through the waters, away from our pursuers.

I looked back. Anna Orlov clung to the lifebelt as the *Madeleine* closed in on her. For one moment I thought it was going to run her down, but at the last moment it came to a halt. Two crewmen reached down to drag her aboard, and making use of the precious extra moments this break afforded us, we sped away at as rapid a velocity as we could muster.

Chapter 29.

I looked back and saw Anna being bundled below deck as Vasiliev gestured to the helmsman of the *Madeleine* and pointing in our direction. The chase was on.

'Can we outrun them?' I enquired of Alice, although I was fairly certain I knew the answer to that question.

'Not a chance,' she said, glancing back over her shoulder. 'That boat is bigger, heavier, faster. Slowing down to pick Anna up has bought us some time, but I reckon we've got five minutes before they catch us.'

'Who are they dad?' asked Jessica, clinging to my arm as we skimmed across the rising surf.

'Russian Intelligence,' I replied. 'A particularly unpleasant man called Vasiliev. I was thrown off that very boat in the Mediterranean on the assumption that I would drown.'

'But why are they chasing us? Anna has the capsule!'

'Then I can only assume they don't know she has it.'

'But we can explain. I saw her swallow it.'

'I fear that we have gone beyond simple explanations Jessica. If Vasiliev catches me again, I fear that he will make absolutely certain that I am dead this time.'

I saw the look of fear flit across Jessica's face, but to my immense pride, I could see that she had not given up.

'Let's head for the shore' said Jessica. 'We can lose them on land.'

I considered her suggestion for a moment. It certainly afforded us a better option than simply being shot at sea, but deep down I knew it was futile. I was exhausted, and there was no way I could escape the pursuit of trained Russian intelligence operatives – not to mention the French police, who would still be combing the area looking for me. This time it seemed as if I had reached the end of the line. It brought to mind some lines from Titus Andronicus. Not one of Shakespeare's more popular plays, but the verses seemed apposite for my current predicament:

'For now I stand as one upon a rock, environed with a wilderness of sea …'

Jessica looked at me with an expression which veered between astonishment and contempt.

'Dad! Is this really the time to be quoting Shakespeare?'

She may have had a point, but I continued anyway.

'…Who marks the waxing tide grow wave by wave, expecting ever when some envious surge will in his brinish bowels swallow him.'

My daughter fixed me with a withering stare: 'Cheers dad. That's really helped,' she said, heavy sarcasm dripping from every syllable.

'Say that again,' interjected Alice suddenly, expressing a sudden and frankly surprising interest in the Bard's sixth opus.

I was happy to oblige. If I was about to die, I may as well do so quoting Shakespeare.

'For now I stand as one upon a rock …'

'That's it!' she cried, cutting me off in full flow.

'That's what?' asked Jessica.

Alice looked at us with fire in her eyes. I wasn't sure who this young lady was, but she certainly had courage and resourcefulness aplenty.

'This shore is peppered with reefs and submerged rocks,' she shouted, struggling to make her voice heard above the roar of the engines. 'Remember Jess, as we came close to the beach, we had to slow down and pick our way through them. We need to head back there!'

I struggled to follow the sense in what she was saying.

'But how will that help?' I asked, somewhat bewildered. 'If we hit the rocks, it will be the end for us.'

'Then I'd better not hit them, had I? I think I can remember the safe passage.'

'You think?'

'It's our best hope Mr Cavendish. If I can get us through the rocks at high speed, there's every chance that the Russians won't know they are there. Their boat sits deeper in the water than ours. With luck, we can lead them onto the rocks.'

I suddenly saw the brilliant logic of her plan.

'Like the sirens? The handmaidens of Persephone who lured unwary sailors to their death?'

She gave me a blank look. The look of someone who was sadly unaware of Greek mythology.

'If you say so,' she said.

'It is an admirable plan,' I replied. 'But what if it does not succeed? What if it is us who is shipwrecked on the rocks?'

'Then we're fucked,' she replied, simply.

It was a sign of the privations I had endured over recent days, and the steep gradient of the learning curve on which I had travelled, that not only was I not shocked to hear a young lady using such a coarse epithet, I found myself agreeing with her wholeheartedly. I looked back at the *Madeleine* which was getting ever closer. Soon it would be back in gunshot range.

'I fear you are right Alice. Well and truly fucked.'

'Dad!' exclaimed Jessica, with a look of utter astonishment.

'My apologies.'

'I don't think I've ever heard you swear before.'

'I am not sure that I have ever been in a situation such as this before.' I replied.

'Hold on tight,' yelled Alice. 'Stand by to go about!'

She span the wheel and the boat veered hard to port, heading back inland towards the cliffs. The manoeuvre clearly took the *Madeleine* by surprise, as it overshot the point at which we had turned, before executing a slower wider arc in order to continue her pursuit. But we had gained valuable distance.

'They can outrun us when we're going in a straight line,' shouted Alice. 'But we're lighter and more manoeuvrable. If we can get amongst those rocks before they catch us, we might just have a chance.'

'You will be careful, won't you?'

'I can't go too slowly, otherwise they'll smell a rat. Our best plan is to not let them realise that the rocks are there at all. Being careful might get us killed.'

'So might being too reckless.'

She looked at me with a level gaze, and my admiration for her increased even further.

'That's a chance we're going to have to take.' She said. 'Hang on!'

Alice pushed the throttle forwards as far as it would go, and the *Plymouth Princess* surged through the waves. Jessica slipped her arm through mine and held it tightly.

'It's good to see you again,' she said.

'Likewise,' I replied. 'There have been many times over the last week or so when I feared this day would never come. And I must confess, I never thought it would be quite like this. Your friend Alice is a very impressive young lady.'

'Yes,' said Jessica, looking fondly at Alice. 'She is.'

I looked back. The *Madeleine* was back on our tail now, and getting ever closer. Vasiliev stood at the prow, a loudhailer in his hands. I could just about make out his voice over the roar of the engines.

'Give it up Mr Cavendish. You know you can't escape. Just give me the video and I'll let you go.'

I seemed to remember him making a similar promise before. Since then, I had been partly responsible for the death of two of his best operatives and I felt it was extremely unlikely that he would honour his promise this time either. It also suggested that he was not aware that Anna had the capsule in her possession.

'What should we do?' said Alice. 'Will he really let us go?'

'Never' I replied. 'Keep on going.'

'Aye aye captain.'

To my consternation I saw a crew member handing Vasiliev what looked like a machine gun.

'How much further to the rocks?' I asked Alice.

'I'm not sure. A minute maybe?'

I saw Vasiliev raising the gun to the firing position.

'Jessica, please get below.'

She looked at me fiercely. 'Only if you come too,' she replied.

'Please Jessica. Get below and hold onto something.'

I produced the Glock. I checked the clip. I had two bullets remaining.

'I will try and slow them down. Now please, do as I say.'

Reluctantly, she descended into the bowels of the boat. I took the Glock and aimed at the pursuing *Madeleine*. I had no desire to be responsible for any more deaths, but I needed to hamper their pursuit in some way. The *Princess* bounced on the choppy waves, and it was difficult to hold a steady shooting arm. Fortunately, Vasiliev seemed to be having the same problem. There was a sudden moment of stillness, and I was able to loose off a shot. It was a pleasure to see the look of astonishment on Vasiliev's face as the bullet made a clean round hole in the *Madeleine's* windscreen. He ducked instinctively, and I fired again, just as the *Princess* crested another wave. My arm jerked in the air and the shot passed harmlessly over Vasiliev's head.

Vasiliev raised his gun again, and fired a volley of shots in our direction, raking the water along the side of our vessel. He had his range now. He steadied himself for another volley, and not for the first time I sensed impending death staring me in the face.

'We're there!' cried Alice. 'I'm going to try and pick a way through.'

The *Princess* swerved violently from side to side. I could see barely submerged rocks on either flank, all of which looked well capable of sinking us on the spot if we hit them at high speed. There was a scraping sound as the keel of the boat made contact with something hard. The boat juddered, but on we sped. I heard another volley of shots from behind us, but they seemed to have missed their mark. I looked back. The *Madeleine* was closing in on us now, but whoever was piloting the craft seemed oblivious to the impending danger presented by the submerged rocks. Vasiliev pointed his gun straight at me. He was less than fifty yards away, and I could see his finger tightening on the trigger as he steadied himself to gun me down.

Fortunately for me, he never got to fire those shots. The *Madeleine* suddenly hit a rock – possibly the one we had just skimmed over. But such was the velocity at which it was travelling, the rock acted as a ramp and the boat took off into mid-air. It hovered there briefly and then ploughed bow first into another rock with a horrible crumpling and grinding sound. Vasiliev was pitched headlong into the water as his precious vessel sat broken-backed on the submerged reefs.

Alice slowed the motor and steered carefully into safer waters. We looked back at the stricken *Madeleine*. There would be no further pursuit from that quarter. Alice looked at me, her face wet and shining from the spray, her cheeks glowing with excitement.

'We did it!' she shouted at the top of her voice. 'Jess! We only bloody did it!'

She was right. We had done it. We were safe. My daughter emerged cautiously from below decks, wrapped in a blanket, her face pale and drawn. I felt a strong desire to hold her close, and stepped forward. But as I did, she staggered, and the blanket slipped to the ground.

'I've been shot,' she said simply.

I saw a large red stain on the front of her jacket. Her breath was short and rasping.

'Daddy,' she said, with tears in her eyes. Her legs buckled beneath her and she collapsed onto the deck of the *Plymouth Princess*.

Chapter 30

I knelt to the ground, cradling my stricken daughter. Pulling back her shirt I could see the round red bullet hole in her chest from which blood oozed steadily. Alice was at my side in a moment, clutching a First Aid kit.

'Jess' she said, her concern plain to see. 'Jess. Can you hear me?'

Jessica's eyes flickered open She tried to say something but she was gasping for air.

'Don't speak,' I said. 'You're going to be fine,' I added, squeezing her hand, but not really believing what I was saying. She looked anything but fine.

'We need to stop the bleeding,' said Alice, producing a bandage from the bright red box and starting to unroll it. 'And then we need to get her to a hospital.'

'How long will it take us to get back to Plymouth?'

'Six, seven hours.'

I looked at my daughter, fading away in my arms.

'I don't think we have that long. Where is the closest port?'

'Cherbourg. It's along the coast. Maybe thirty kilometres?'

'Then we must go there.'

'But they'll arrest you.'

'I don't care!' I shouted, my eyes full of tears. 'We must get Jessica to a hospital before it is too late. Surely you can see that?'

'Of course,' she replied, simply. 'You make her as comfortable as you can. I'll get us there as soon as possible. The wind's getting up, and it and the tide are against us.'

We carried Jessica carefully below and laid her out on one of the bunks. A series of bullet holes had raked the side of the *Plymouth Princess*. They were above the water line, so presented no danger to the seaworthiness of the boat, but one of the bullets had clearly hit my daughter. We made her as comfortable as we could, whereupon Alice returned to the controls and turned the boat to starboard, hugging the coast as close as she dared. The sea was rising now, and the gentle swell was turning into something choppier. White horses crested the tops of the waves, which slapped rhythmically against the hull of the boat. Jessica flickered in and out of consciousness as I worked hard to stem the seeping blood. I cleaned the wound as best I could, and carefully wrapped a bandage around her. As I did, I discovered another wound in her back. It looked as if the bullet had passed clean through her body, but I had no idea what damage it may have caused. I cursed my lack of medical knowledge, and prayed that we could get her to safety before it was too late. If anything happened to my precious daughter, I would never forgive myself, and I knew that Penny would never forgive me either.

I did my best with the bandages, and to my relief, the bleeding seemed to have stopped. But loss of blood did not seem to be the problem. Jessica's breathing was increasingly laboured, and I wondered if the bullet had punctured a lung. Her eyes opened and she looked up at me, her ashen face a mixture of bewilderment and fear.

'Are we going home?' she asked.

'Yes,' I replied. 'Back to see your mother.'

'Good,' she said, and closed her eyes again. I felt a sudden pang of dread and fear. With a terrible certainty, I knew that by the time we got to Cherbourg, my daughter would be dead.

'Mr Cavendish!' shouted Alice, suddenly. 'Come quickly!'

I climbed the few short steps to where Alice stood at the helm, and followed her pointing finger. Several hundred yards ahead of us, a small rubber dinghy bobbed uncertainly in the fractious sea. Even at this distance I could see that the boat was in trouble. It sat low in the water, and what seemed to be its single occupant was waving frantically in our direction. There was a pair of binoculars sitting next to the wheel, and I picked them up, training them in the direction of the stricken dinghy.

'Thank God,' I exclaimed as I honed in on the craft as it wallowed precariously in the waves. It was Amira, the Doctor from Aleppo. The woman who might just be able to save my daughter's life.

'We must go to their aid,' I said.

'Are you sure?' asked Alice. 'It'll add time onto our journey.'

'I would not be here if it wasn't for that woman, and she appears to be in some distress. I also believe she may be able to help Jessica. She is a doctor.'

'Right,' said Alice, clearly confused by this latest turn of events. But to her credit, she accepted my instruction without further demur and pointed the *Princess* towards the dinghy. We were alongside in no time, and not a moment too soon, Sea water slopped around the flimsy craft, which was certainly not up to crossing the channel, particularly in the intensifying conditions in which we found ourselves. Amira and her children were the sole occupants, and the sight of those two youngsters, soaked, cowering and frightened in the dinghy would have been enough to soften the hardest of hearts.

'Is it really you?' cried Amira, as she saw me. 'I don't believe it.'

She passed up the frightened children and a few soaking bags of belongings, then clambered aboard herself. As she did, another wave broke over the dinghy, flipping it over completely. It had been a very narrow escape for Amira and her family. She looked at me intensely.

'Now tell me that there isn't a God,' she said.

'I may be prepared to entertain the possibility of some Divine presence,' I acknowledged.

'Particularly if you are able to save my daughter's life.'

Amira looked towards Alice.

'Is this her? She looks well to me.'

'No. This is Alice, her friend. Jessica is below. Come with me.' I took Amira and the children down below. We found blankets to wrap around the little ones, while I led Amira to my stricken daughter, who was looking paler than ever. Her breathing was coming in ever shorter gasps, as if she was having difficulty filling her lungs.

'She's been shot,' I said. 'I think I've stopped the blood, but her breathing is hampered in some way.

'What's her name?'

'Jessica.'

Amira worked quickly and expertly. She pulled back my makeshift dressing and examined the bullet wounds.

'It doesn't look as if the bullet has hit any major organs, which is a good thing,' she said. 'I think what we have here is a classic pneumothorax. The bullet has pierced her chest cavity and let air into the space between her lungs and the thorax. That space is normally a vacuum, which allows the air to expand when the lungs are inflated. Now that there is air in there, the lungs can't do their job.'

'We are heading for Cherbourg, where I am hoping there is a hospital. We should be there in an hour or so.'

Amira shook her head.

'I'm sorry Colin, but we don't have an hour. We need to get the air out of the chest cavity as soon as possible, or I'm afraid Jessica will certainly die.'

I felt as if my whole body had been momentarily frozen.

'But how can we? It's not possible.'

'Everything is possible Colin. Particularly for someone who has spent the last few years tending gunshot wounds.'

She scanned the cabin carefully until she saw what she wanted.

'It looks like a piece of pipe is coming to our rescue again,' she said, as her eyes alighted on the simple gas stove which sat at the galley end of the cabin.

'Do you see that piece of rubber tubing connecting the gas cylinder to the hob? Take it off, and wash it as best as you can.' She ordered. 'And make sure the gas is disconnected before you do' she added, superfluously.

I did so, while she reached inside one of her rucksacks and retrieved what proved to be her medical bag. The boat juddered as we ran into a wave, and I stumbled to one side as I struggled to loosen the metal clip which held the tube in place. Amira produced a scalpel and a bottle of some sort of disinfectant with which she cleaned the blade, but it was clear that she would struggle to perform what I assumed to be delicate surgery in a heavy sea.

'Alice!' I shouted through the open hatchway. 'Is there any way we can find some calmer waters?'

'We're headed against the tide,' she shouted back. 'But that's the way to Cherbourg.'

'What would happen if we turned and headed for Plymouth?'

'It would be easier going.'

'Then please do it,' I shouted back. 'Cherbourg is no longer an option. Amira needs a steady hand and we need to head for England as fast as we can.'

'Are you sure?'

To be honest, I was not sure at all, but it seemed like the best option.

'Please. It's Jessica's only hope.'

There was a brief silence, then I felt the boat beginning to turn. For a few moments we were sideways on to the running tide and the waves, and the boat pitched from side to side, eliciting squeals of terror from the children. But as we completed our turn, I could immediately feel the *Princess* being borne along by the tide and the wind, instead of labouring against it. The tone of the engine became less shrill, and our passage was suddenly much easier.

I finally managed to remove the rubber tube, and washed it as best as I could, before handing it to Amira. I held my daughter's hand as the doctor made a small incision with the scalpel. Jessica's eyes flickered with pain, and she gasped for breath, but none came. Amira widened the incision, and in an instant had taken the rubber tube and inserted it into Jessica's chest.

'I've got to go carefully,' she said. 'So I don't damage the lung. But if I've got this right ....'

Her sentence was cut short by a hissing sound emanating from the tube as the trapped air escaped. '*Mashallah*,' said Amira as she sealed the end of the pipe with some sticking plaster. 'God is on our side today. And so is science. Your daughter can breathe normally now. She is going to be fine.'

And miraculously, she was. Jessica gulped in huge, welcome breaths as she came back to life before my very eyes.

'I wish all emergency surgery was this straightforward,' said Amira to Jessica. 'My name is Doctor Bahar.'

'We met on the mainland,' I added, by way of further explanation. 'The good Doctor helped me when I feared I would not be able to make our rendezvous.'

'And you have repaid the debt ten time over by rescuing me,' replied Amira.

'What happened?' I asked her. 'I had imagined that the boat you had been promised would be somewhat more substantial.'

'So did I. But having come all that way, I wasn't going to turn back. We were doing okay until the motor failed. I thought that my time had come to an end.'

She turned to my daughter.

How are you feeling?'

'My chest hurts.'

'That is not surprising. You have been shot. I won't ask who by. And I have just sliced you open with a scalpel. I will give you something for the pain, but you must not worry. We will get you to a hospital and you are going to be okay.'

'What's happening?' shouted Alice from above. 'How is she?'

I climbed the steps to the cabin above.

'Jessica is fine,' I said. 'Why don't you go and see for yourself? I can take over for now.'

Alice disappeared immediately. I took the steering wheel in both hands and fixed my eyes firmly on the distant horizon, over which lay England and Penny. I was going home.

■■■

Some hours later I stood looking at the welcoming sight of the English coastline. Jessica was still in some discomfort, but thanks to the skill of Amira, it was clear that she was out of the woods. Amira's children, whose names, I am ashamed to say, I never learned, were asleep below. Myself, Jessica, Alice and Amira were on deck, as we pulled into Plymouth Sound. Jessica had telephoned Constable Peters, her contact in the Devon and Cornwall Constabulary, who informed us that a police launch would be on its way to see us safely into the harbour.

I had spent much of the journey looking fearfully about me, in case of pursuit from another Russian vessel, a Chinese submarine, a CIA aeroplane or the French navy. But it seemed as if I had finally evaded my captors. Of course, there was still the matter of the murders of which I stood falsely accused, as well as the death of Turnbull, to which I had decided I would confess as soon as I was in Police custody. Most importantly of all, I would be able to see Penny again.

'I am sorry that the Police will have to involved,' I said to Amira. I had told her the full story of my flight across Europe, to which she had listened with polite astonishment.

'No matter,' she replied. 'I will apply for asylum. I have family here. My children are safe. That is the main thing.'

'Indeed it is,' I said, looking fondly at Jessica. And I was not the only one. Alice had been most solicitous during the crossing, and it had become very clear to me that there was a deep affection between the two of them. In truth, I had always imagined that one day Jessica would marry and produce grandchildren, but any discomfort I may previously have felt at the notion that she had lesbian tendencies was completely overshadowed by the deep happiness that the two of them showed in each other's company. I thought of Wayne, and the rift that had arisen between him and his father because of his sexuality, and I resolved that nothing would ever stop me holding my daughter in anything other than the greatest esteem and affection.

I saw a police launch heading towards us. No doubt there would be members of the secret service aboard as well. I had a fair bit of explaining to do, but I had every confidence in the integrity of the British judicial system, and was prepared to take my chances. Whilst not exactly relishing the prospect of a spell in a British prison, I felt sure it would be infinitely preferable to its French equivalent.

Jessica reached out and took my hand.

'So glad we got you back safely,' she said.

'It has certainly been quite an adventure,' I replied.

'It's just a shame it was all for nothing.'

'What do you mean?'

'That Anna woman. She got the capsule.'

'Indeed she did. Assuming they survived the wreck of the *Madeleine* I wonder what sort of game she and Vasiliev will be playing, waiting for it to emerge. I would certainly like to be a fly on the wall of whichever room they are in. I would also give a substantial sum of money to see the look on their faces when they open the capsule and discover that it is empty.'

All three of them looked closely at me.

'Empty?' asked Jessica.

'Indeed,' I said reaching into my pocket.

'Before I swam out to the *Princess* I felt it wise to take one last precaution. My journey had been such a perilous one, marked by so many unexpected vicissitudes, that I felt it wise to remove the flash drive from the capsule and secrete it elsewhere about my person.'

My fingers found the tiny chip, nestling at the bottom of my pocket.

'And here it is,' I continued, producing the flash drive, which I hoped would expose the ruthless Rostov for the tyrannical, murderous hypocrite that I knew him to be.

The police launch was almost alongside us now.

'Alice?' I enquired. 'I wonder if you would be so good as to tell me what day of the week it is?'

'It's Wednesday,' she replied.

'Excellent. I do hope we will not be detained long. Penny will have cooked Toad In The Hole.'

THE END

About The Author

David Lloyd has written for the BBC dramas Casualty, EastEnders and Doctors. As an actor he has appeared in some of Britain's best-loved TV shows, including EastEnders, Casualty, 'Allo 'Allo, Brookside, The Bill, The Young Ones, The New Statesman and the award-winning kids series Maid Marian and her Merry Men, in which he played Graeme. He lives in North Somerset, and 'A Most Unwelcome Connection' is his first novel.

Printed in Great Britain
by Amazon